THE CHASE

RACING HEARTS SERIES

VICTORIA DENAULT

Cover: Oh So Novel Designs

Editing: Katie Kenyhercz

Copy Edits: My Notes in the Margins

Proofing: Claudia Fosca Stahl

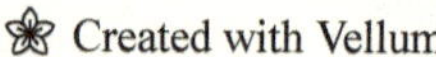 Created with Vellum

*For my husband Jack who dared to say "You should watch F1.
You'll like it, I promise."*

PROLOGUE
SOME POMPOUS PANDA

FRANKIE

Races in Monaco are the best because the parties are the best. Also, I love when my dad's team wins in Monaco, which they did tonight. His drivers are at this very party, drunk off their asses, cooing about their first and second place wins. Dad went back to the hotel about an hour ago but let me stay. Lucia had to go home though because she's only seventeen. I'm eighteen, so I pulled the 'adult' card and he allowed it. But I had to promise to be careful and come home at a reasonable hour.

I've been dancing for an hour, partying with the usual race fans and groupies – royalty, billionaire off-spring, and drivers and crews from other divisions. My bestie Jennie came to the race. Her dad is a tech mogul from Japan, and she and I met when we both went to the same boarding school at fourteen. It was my first and last year in a normal school. My mom home schooled us so we could follow my dad around the world during race season, but I begged for "normal" and they finally relented, putting me in a fancy arts-oriented boarding school. It was fun but both Lucia and I missed our parents and the racing world more than we let on.

Then mom got sick later that same year, and my dad pulled us out of school to spend as much time as possible with her. After she died, we had tutors so that we could travel again with our dad, who retired from driving the next year but started his own team. Jennie's in university now in London, but she's off for the summer and following me around.

"Tonight is perfect!" I declare as we take a break from the dance floor and make our way to the bar. I've had just enough booze that I feel tipsy. Floaty and flirty but not dizzy or nauseous. I'm careful not to cross that line. I've only done it once, last year. My dad was so pissed and worried when he found me puking my guts out at two in the morning in the bathroom that he almost took me to the hospital. I got my first grounding ever after that. Now at eighteen, he accepts I drink because it's legal in Europe, but he still worries and has a tracker on my phone he thinks I don't know about. I haven't taken it off because I'm okay with him knowing where I am. Dad loves us dearly and we are all he has left so I'm cool with letting him keep track of us. I'm not doing anything crazy anyway. I drink a little and once smoked a joint, but that's it.

"*Deux champagne s'il vous plait*," I say to the bartender as Jennie reaches for one of the cocktail napkins and proceeds to pat my forehead.

"Frankie, I wanna take a picture for social media and I don't want you shiny," she explains as I swat at her. Jennie is studying marketing and she wants to make me a thing. I wasn't even on Instagram or Facebook until she coaxed me into it last year. I'm amazed at how many friends I have already. I mean, 'friends' is an overstatement. I definitely don't know ninety-nine percent of the hundred-thousand people on my social media accounts. I guess strangers like to see the behind-the-scenes race and party stuff I post. Lately, though, there have been some assholes who say mean things about me or my dad's team. Jennie showed me how to block them.

Jennie finishes blotting me and then holds up her phone and tells me to smile. She takes a bunch of pictures until I get bored and the bartender photobombs the pic with our champagne glasses and his annoyed face.

"Merci!" I say as I turn around, reaching for the glasses.

He's also put two shots of clear liquid in front of us. "From the men over there."

I follow the bartender's bony finger as he points. There, at the end of the bar, are three guys. Three cute guys – which are my favorite kind. I smile, and so does Jennie, and they take that as an invitation to make their way over. Their names are all D names. Daniel, Dominic, and Dion. Jennie jokingly asks if they exclusively hang out with Ds only, and they laugh. We make small talk. They know who I am, which I hate. Daniel asks me a million questions about the Mirabella racing team, which I actually don't mind. I love talking about F1 and my dad's team. Dominic wants to talk about my dad's career, which I also like talking about. My dad was an amazing driver with three World Championship titles. Dion isn't chatty like his buds. He seems moody.

"You didn't take your shot," Dion finally speaks after almost a half hour.

"Right," I smile. "I don't do shots, but I appreciate the gesture."

It was Goldschlager shots that made me so sick last year.

Dion doesn't smile back. "It was a gift. Your friend accepted it."

Jennie repeats her name for him, because she hates when people don't remember it. "It was delicious. So delicious I'll do hers."

Jennie picks up the shooter from the bar as I take another sip of champagne. Dion isn't going to let this go. "It's not champagne so it's not good enough for Sebastian Castera's daughter?"

"No. I drink more than just champagne," I reply, my voice calm but hard. I hate guys like him. They meet me with pre-formed opinions. They're cocky and belligerent and gross on the inside. On the outside, Dion is buff with perfect hair and expensive clothes. It's lipstick on a pig. "I don't do shots, but I truly appreciate the gesture."

Dion huffs out a disgusted breath and mutters something but the music in the club is too loud for me to hear him. I am not about to step closer and ask him to repeat it. So I turn to Jennie, and our eyes connect, and an unspoken conversation happens. The kind bestie girls have all the time in clubs.

I want to ditch them, my eyes scream.

Just ignore the asshole, Jennie's eyes plead.

Please.

Jennie sighs, a sign she is going to give in, and she downs the shot I refused. That sets Dion into a rage. "What the fuck! That wasn't yours!"

"Whoa, chill D," Dominic advises his friend, and Daniel grabs his arm as he steps toward me aggressively.

Jennie's dark brown eyes grow wide. "Let's go."

We turn when the psycho growls. "Rich bitch! I bet you suck all the drivers' cocks, but we're not good enough to do a shot with."

I feel his hand on my shoulder. It's cold and hard, and I would yelp, but before a sound can leave my mouth, the hand is gone. I swivel back and can see nothing but shoulders. Broad shoulders and the back of a dirty blond head. "You need to back off, mate."

"Who the fuck are you?" Dion hisses.

"Someone who doesn't manhandle women who want nothing to do with me," the voice with the rich Aussie accent says. "I'll say it one last time. Back off, mate."

Dion swings. The blond head bobs and ducks and then the mystery man lifts his fist and takes his own swing. It all happens so fast it's a blur, but then suddenly the bartender is jumping over the bar, and Dion's friends are rushing toward my Aussie accented hero. A bouncer comes rushing over, and Aussie hero grabs my hand, and I grab Jennie's and we run. While the bartender is trying to hold back the triple Ds, he has left a bottle of Ruinart champagne unattended on the bar top. Hero grabs it with his free hand without slowing his pace.

He leads us to the narrow hallway where the restrooms are, and with his left foot, he kicks open the emergency exit, and we burst into the alleyway. The warm summer night air swirls around us. At the end of the alley, people bustle by, going about their night in Monaco. Jennie is the first to speak. "What the fuck just happened?"

"I saved your friend here from a super-douche," Aussie says with a smile that knocks my heart sideways.

Aussie hero is gorgeous. Thick, tousled hair, eyes like aquamarine crystals, cleft chin, two subtle dimples. He's a bucket list of physical perfection and the big, bold smile says he's not sorry about it. Neither am I. But getting a good look at him, I also realize he's Billy James.

"Thanks, I think," Jennie says.

"Definitely thanks," Billy confirms with that breathtaking grin again. Something inside me instantly hates he's unleashed it on Jennie instead of me. "Those boys were total tossers."

"Should we like keep running or something?" I ask. "In case the police get called."

"I'm always up for some cardio," Billy grabs my hand again, so I grab Jennie's again, and we run down the alley.

We run until we're all out of breath and the night air has turned salty. Larvotto beach spreads out before us. The sea is just an inky blob. Jennie rests on the small stone wall. "Holy shit, I wasn't prepared for a marathon in these damn heels."

I watch as she yanks off the high heeled sandals and Billy lifts up the champagne he's still holding. "Hydration?"

I smile at his cute choice of words, like he's offering her a Gatorade. Jennie smiles too but shakes her head. "I'm going to head back to the hotel."

"Will you stay a little longer?" Billy asks me. His smile turns soft. "I promise I didn't just save your from douchebags so I could become one."

My eyes connect with Jennie's, and we have another unspoken conversation.

I want to hang with him, my eyes say.

Hers dart up to Billy, who is starting to open the champagne with his back to me. *He seems okay. Are you sure?*

I give a small, quick nod.

Okay, her eyes say.

I turn to Billy James, the F2 driver that my father has mentioned in awe several times this season. "I'll stick around for a bit."

"Look at you, making my day." He winks.

"It's night."

"Hard to tell with you around," he retorts. "The world seems much brighter now."

"Cheesy as hell," I comment, but I'm grinning with abandon.

"I believe it's called *fromage* here." Billy winks again and pops the champagne.

He is charming with a capital C.

"Drop me a pin with your location if you move," Jennie says in my ear and she hugs me good-bye. "See you tomorrow, bestie. Bye Aussie Hero."

Billy waves at her as she leaves, and I watch her carefully as she crosses the street and walks two buildings over to our hotel. I don't turn back to Billy until I see the doorman hold the door open for her. "So, where to?"

"Beach," Billy announces. "But not this one. Police patrol it, and I don't think they'd appreciate the bottle of Ruinart. I know another one. More private."

I hesitate as he takes a couple steps. He wouldn't have rescued me just to kill me, right? Or is he the guy who does that to gain my trust so he can feed my body to the sharks after he's done with it? I hate that I have to worry about that, but I do. The joy of being a woman.

"Look, I wasn't going to say this because it makes me sound like a pompous panda, but I'm a driver," he says.

In a snap decision I decide to play dumb. "An F1 driver?"

"F2," he clarifies, and it almost sounds like an apology. "My dad drove F1 and I'm going to one day soon. I'm not going to throw away my whole future by hurting anyone, least of all a beautiful girl like you."

"That left hook probably hurt Dion."

"Okay, I let me rephrase, anyone who doesn't deserve it." He winks again.

"Also, pompous panda?" I raise an eyebrow as my lips also raise in a smile.

"Have you met a panda? They can be real dicks," Billy says with a deeply serious tone that has me bursting out laughter.

This all might be a ploy to get me to let my guard down, but the flutter in my belly falls for it hook, line, and sinker. I nod. "Take me to your private beach…"

I stop myself before I say his name because he didn't give it to me. He extends a hand, like a perfect gentleman. "You can just keep calling me Aussie Hero. I like it better than my actual name."

"I never called you that. Jennie did."

"Yeah but I was saving you, so I'm yours." He leans closer

and I feel a cannon of butterflies go off in my belly because for a second, I think he might kiss me. But he pulls back and starts walking. "Feel free to give me your name though."

I shake my head. "One day, but not right now."

He'll know who I am if I give him my name. Because he's a driver I know he knows my dad. Between his championship wins and my mom's death, which caused his retirement, and Mirabella Racing, which he named after her, my dad's name and mine has been in the news a lot. Plus, Frankie is rare for a girl and he's bright enough to make the connection. Lately, there's been rumors swirling that I might take over one day for my dad as Team Principal, because I will. He wants it, and so do I – desperately.

Luckily, Billy seems to accept my lack of answer by giving me an easy-going, uber sexy smile. "I get it. I don't want people to think they know me before they know me too."

He takes my hand as we continue to walk, and it feels intimate this time because we aren't running from anything. I think we're running toward something. And I think I like it. I'm not wrong. The beach he takes me to is a sandy alcove between mansions. We perch on a tall, flat rock, sipping champagne and spilling our life secrets. What we think of the world, the sport of racing, our families, our hopes, fears, dreams, what makes us laugh, and what makes us cry. We make each other laugh, and we don't judge each other when we both tear up. Him talking about his dad's death, which only happened six months ago during a race in Tokyo, and me talking about my mom's. We still don't exchange names, even when the night ends with the orange and pink sunrise blanketing our epic make-out session.

I leave before it goes further because as much as I want it, I also have to get home before Jennie or my sister Lucia wakes up and sees I'm not in my bed. We're all sharing the same hotel suite. Billy, my Aussie hero, begs me to see him again tomorrow night. "Meet me here again. Nine p.m.? This can't end, you and me. There's more to our story."

"Nine p.m.," I agree easily. There's no point in playing coy. He's got me. "I can't wait."

And the last thing I remember from that weekend was leaving that beach alone at ten-thirty because he never showed up. Everything after that was a blur until I woke up two days later in a hospital bed.

1

MUST HAVE A BIG D

FRANKIE (*Ten years later*)

It started out in chaos, and I guess it's going to end that way too. The good news is we have one driver *not* smack dab in the middle of the shit show. Antonio De Luca, one of the two drivers for the Mirabella Racing, was on pole for the start of the Vancouver Grand Prix. It's a city course, not his strong suit, so the fact that he somehow managed to snag the top spot in qualifying was miraculous, and I told my father on the phone last night Antonio would need another miracle to hold the position. I wasn't wrong.

On the second lap, he lost position to Sterling Samuels, the young hotshot who was world champion last year and the year before and is favored to three-peat. But then, that second miracle came early when, on the third lap, Antonio overtook Sterling. He managed to hold Sterling off until the eighteenth lap when, while gunning for an overtake, Samuels hit the DRS on a notoriously dangerous corner. Not one but *three* drivers had crashes on that corner in qualifying. Our team's other driver, Billy James, was one of them. Luckily for Billy, it was a spin-out more than a crash, and he was able to continue on. He qualified sixth overall.

"It's too tight," I tell the live feed I'm watching on my phone. "What the hell are you doing, Samuels? De Luca has position, back the fuck off!"

A second later I'm gripping my phone so hard my knuckles are white. "Antonio stop pinching him you're going to… fuck!"

De Luca's back right wheel and Samuels's front left wheel connect. De Luca goes spinning off the course into the gravel and into the barrier hard and fast – so fast that the barrier breaks into pieces flying all over the place. But there's no fire. No smoke. And when the safety team reach the car, Antonio is already pulling himself out of it. I exhale a breath I didn't realize I was holding.

There's a sharp rap on my bathroom stall door. "Frankie they're paying you to be here. And by here I mean in the club, shaking your ass to the DJ in that thousand dollar dress and holding a glass of the liquor that's sponsoring this party. Hello? Are you listening to me?"

"Yeah. Yeah. I'm coming," I call back, turning and flushing the empty toilet for effect. In that chaos caused by the over eager, testosterone fueled egos of Samuels and DeLuca, someone manages to drive their car straight through the dust and debris from Deluca's crash. He even drives straight past Samuels, who didn't spin out but slowed pace immensely as he struggled to stay on track. That driver was the current number four in the world, who started in sixth spot. Billy James. The other Mirabella Racing driver. And now, thanks to his steady driving and checked ego, my race… I mean my *father's* race team is still leading the race!

"Frankie!" My manager, and best friend, Jennie pounds the door again.

"Yes!" I begrudgingly turn off the feed and fling open the stall door. She's standing there, eyebrow arched, arms crossed.

"That time of the month," I mutter and give her remorseful smile.

"Yeah you mean that time of the race weekend," Jennie replies.

Busted. "In my defense we haven't had a driver on pole yet this season."

"It's only a few races in," Jennie says. I just nod and focus on reapplying my lipstick. No point in explaining we're actually halfway through the season and every race is important. It would be like explaining the patterns of Canadian geese migration to an octopus. She, like the octopus, would give exactly zero shits. Jennie isn't into F1, she's into me and the other influencers and brands she works with as a manager and social media strategist.

I do a once over as Jennie grabs my arm and starts tugging me out of the restroom. I look good. The dress is still pristine despite the twenty minutes I just spent sitting hunched over in a bathroom stall. It will look great, and the designer won't have any issue paying me once they see the photos splashed all over the internet. Jennie was right in advising me to wear it with my hair up because it shows off the intricate lace on the back perfectly.

Outside the restroom, the music is deafening. Nick, my bodyguard, is standing there in his usual black everything from shirt to shoes to probably undies, although I have no urge to find out. He hands me the martini glass with the rock candy stir stick he's been guarding. Both are supposed to be made with Midori, the sponsor alcohol, but mine is concocted with food coloring. I don't drink in public. Not since I was eighteen.

I plaster a smile on my face, raise the candy to my perfectly painted lips, and head back out to do my job. After forty minutes of dancing and chatting happily and posing for a billion pictures with whoever wants them, I slip into the VIP area. That's allowed, as per the contract. I stop to chat and do more pics with whoever was stupid enough to pay four hundred bucks a table for the access. The whole time, I feel my phone buzzing through my purse, which is also something I'm being paid to tote around.

Finally, I have a moment to slip into a Barcelona chair in a dark corner and check my alerts.

The first message is from my sister: *Men drive with their dicks. That was a sword fight out there between A and S.*

I smile and type back: *Luckily James doesn't get into pissing matches.*

Lucia responds a second later: *Must have a big d. Doesn't get intimidated.*

I bite my bottom lip. I have no idea, but I almost found out once. And I'd be lying if I said that 'what if' doesn't haunt me. Then I notice my dad texted me too and flip to his message.

You were right about A. Do you think B needs a miracle too?

I type back immediately, despite the fact that I can see Jennie walking towards me with a small group in tow. It will look bad to anyone who matters if I'm holed up in a corner with my face in my phone. *If the car holds, he's on the podium. Skip the second pit to maintain position. Billy can handle old tires in these conditions.*

Three seconds after I've hit send, my father replies. *You've read my mind.*

"There you are!" Jennie is smiling, but her eyes are glaring. She's great at doing that, I've discovered. Yelling at me with her eyes while smiling at me with her mouth. "This is Mike, Andrew, Amy, and Maritzia. They're from *BuzzFeed*, *Sports Illustrated*, Betsey Johnson, and Midori, respectively."

"Hi everyone. Fun night, isn't it?" I grin and lift my fake martini up toward them.

"You looked a little intense there, staring at your phone," the one Jennie said was Amy, who works with the dress company who hired me to wear this tonight, says with a lighthearted grin. But I don't miss the pointed tone.

"Me? Intense? Never," I smile back, ignoring Jennie who is screaming 'I told you so!' with her eyes.

I chat with all of them and take more pictures when asked. I understand why real celebrities hate this. Andrew from *Sports Illustrated* talks about me doing their swimsuit issue again, and I play it cool with a 'sure if the schedule allows,' but of course I'll do it. They asked me to model for the issue last year, and I was just happy to be included because it boosted my brand, but now I have goals. There's never been a social media influencer who has gotten the cover, and I want to be the first.

As I chat with them, I notice the *BuzzFeed* guy is recording me with his phone. I try not to be annoyed by that. He's just doing his job, but I prefer they tell me or ask before just hitting the video button. Then Andrew looks up from his own phone. "Your dad's race team won the Vancouver Grand Prix. Just now."

I smile and nod. "Cheers to Mirabella and Billy James."

"Ah, so you've been paying attention." Andrew looks amused. "I never said which driver won."

Oops.

"Lucky guess," I say and lick the rock candy swirl stick. His eyes go straight to my mouth. Good, hopefully it distracts him.

Unfortunately, he's a sport reporter, so he's like a dog with a bone even though I'm basically putting my blow job skills on display with this stupid candy. "You know Antonio crashed. Got too aggressive with Samuels."

"Samuels was as greedy as De Luca was aggressive. The stewards will review his track position if they haven't already. He should have given him space." I wish I could stop my mouth from talking. I lighten my tone and try to sound less knowledgeable and passionate. I'm not in the race world anymore. I abandoned it, and people who follow me don't necessarily give a shit about racing. "Anyway, accidents happen."

"That Billy James is the definition of eye candy," Amy gushes, and I fight the urge to roll my eyes. It's true, but I am so sick of women everywhere telling me this like it's news or something I need to bond with them over. Or like they are hoping I will volunteer to introduce them. I won't. I can count on one hand the amount of times I've seen Billy James in person since that fateful night on the beach.

"Only Formula One driver to hit number one on our top ten hottest athletes list," Mike notes, and his eyes, swimming in Midori, meet mine. "You know, I'm shocked you haven't dated a driver. I mean, you grew up around them, right? There's pics of you in the pit and everything as a teenager. No one got your hormones racing back then?"

I laugh at the thought. "I dodged that bullet on purpose. It wasn't luck. Drivers are needy, aggressive, and greedy as I just explained, and it doesn't stay on the track. I realized from a young age that they'd likely date me for a shot at a seat on my dad's team, not because of me. I deserve better than that."

Everyone is staring at me wide-eyed and silent now, even Jennie. I jump up, hoping to lighten the mood again. "I love this song!"

And with that, I dance my way out of the VIP area to the dance floor, Nick trailing silently behind me. Jennie is by my side moments later. "Good job back there."

"Really?" I reply, confused. I thought for sure she would be pissy about the race talk.

"You gave them something real," Jennie says. "They ate it up. And that 'I deserve better' line screams self-care and confidence, and all that shit that sells right now. So seriously, good job."

She starts to dance right along with me. I smile. Yeah, all that shit sells because people should believe it. Believe in themselves, but they don't. They just like to hear it anyway. And I'm there to peddle the image of someone who has what they want… even though I don't. Truth is, I used to fantasize about a driver. I used to want my whole life to revolve around racing forever. The reason it doesn't was because someone shattered that dream for me without my consent. And I still don't know who. But it was someone in that world. So I left my family's legacy to start a new one that I controlled completely. And I had no… well, not *a lot* of regrets.

2

———

BEFORE GHOSTING WAS A THING

BILLY

I'm twenty-seven years old. I've experienced all sorts of pleasure both physical and emotional. Nothing, *absolutely fucking nothing*, feels better than climbing out of my race car after parking it in front of the flag with the number one on it and jumping into the arms of my pit crew. Today is the first time I've done it this season, and it might be the last. You never know how a season or a life in this business is going to go. So, as always, I savor the hell out of it. The hoots, the hollers, the slaps on the back, the pats to my helmet, the roars carrying my name. All of it.

Finally, the crew settles into claps and releases me, and I pull off my helmet and make my way to the person who matters most. Team owner and Principal, Sebastian 'Bash' Castera, is standing slightly left of the rest of the Mirabella racing crew. He's got his arms crossed, but a satisfied and proud smile pulls his wide mouth upward. The wind ruffles his thick, wavy salt and pepper hair. I tuck my helmet under my arm and walk to him, leaning over the barrier. He unfolds his arms and wraps one around my shoulders. "Good job, son! Fucking great job, actually."

Right there are two things I love about Bash Castera. The way

18

he calls me son even though I'm not and the way he swears like a trucker not caring that there are cameras and mics everywhere. I chuckle and clap him on the back. "I'm glad I could get one for the team."

It's a standard, expected response. The truth is I'm fucking thrilled I got the win for *me*. There are two titles to win in an F1 season, the Constructors' Championship which is awarded to the race team with the most points and the World Championship that's awarded the individual driver with the most points. Any finish in the top ten gets points and you want your team to win the Constructors' because it's job security. It means money and sponsors and ensures the team keeps going. But as a driver you really want the World title. It's the ultimate job security because every team wants a Champion in their car.

Bash gets it because he was a driver too. One of the best in the history of the sport. I wander over to the officials to go through the post-race procedures before I move on to the media interviews. Sterling is just finishing up his interviews. He managed, despite his cocky bullshit with my teammate Antonio, to finish third.

He looks like he's still pissed, but he has no one to blame but himself. And he took Antonio right out of the race, which means Mirabella Racing doesn't get as many overall points. If Sterling and Antonio hadn't been in a cock fight, both Mirabella drivers would be in the top ten, earning points. But then I wouldn't necessarily be the one on the podium so… I have mixed feelings. Sterling storms past me with just a nod and a grunted, "Congrats, mate."

I smile, "You too. Great recovery."

He grimaces, and I go about my own interviews. Then it's podium time. I love hearing the Australian anthem as I receive my trophy. Bash is up there with me, which is odd because it's usually the chief engineer, Joaquin or track side engineering director Rocco, who accepts the team trophy unless it's the Constructors' Championship at the end of the season. Weird, but okay. Maybe Bash was just feeling it today so even though he owns my ass, I shake my bottle of champagne and spray him and the other drivers. Bash sprays back with wild abandon and then we tap bottles and take a swig of whatever is left.

As we head off the podium together, Sterling brushes past us, scowling, eager to get back to the paddock and probably lock himself away and pout. "That kid still needs to grow up a little," Bash comments to me in a whisper.

I don't react. I don't want to comment on anyone else's attitude or driving style, at least not publicly. The team surrounds us, and I let the trophy be lifted from my hands and passed around. They all helped me get here today with record fast tire changes, so they've earned it. Bash hands the team trophy to Rocco Conti and claps him on the back. "Good work, Rocco."

"Thanks. But pushing the tires and skipping the second change was all your call though. And it worked," Rocco says with a grateful nod. Rocco is brilliant at his job, which is keeping the garage and the pit crew in sync with what the engineers and Principal decide will happen in a race. Without him, we would be pulling in for tire changes and body work and everyone would be scrambling instead of ready. He's a good guy, I think. He's just… intense. I've worked with him for five years now, and I still haven't cracked him. I don't know if anyone has.

"That was actually an idea that someone whispered in my ear…" Bash smiles, and I know who he's talking about before the name even leaves his mouth. "Frankie was watching from Miami and texting me suggestions."

Rocco fights a frown and loses. His father, Dario, who is also a former driver and has a huge financial stake in Mirabella Racing and our current Sporting Director, barges up and scoops the trophy out of his son's hands. "Good job Billy the kid!"

All the love I have for Bash is matched in equality with the dislike I have for Dario. He's slimy and narcissistic. I tolerate him because I have to. I hate the nickname too. I know he does it as a put down, not because he's into the wild American west or anything. The douche is Italian, not American. He always emphasizes the word 'kid' which is why it feels like a passive aggressive put-down. "Thanks Mr. Conti."

I always call him Mr. Conti, not by his first name like I call Rocco or Bash or anyone else on this team. He's not 'one of the guys' to me, and this is how I show it. I circle back to the conversation we were having before Dario came over to molest my trophy. "Frankie told you not to pit a second time?"

Bash nods. "She told me you could manage the tire degradation. My girl has good gut instincts."

"She does." I smile as Dario scowls and Rocco just rolls his eyes. "Guess racing really is in the blood."

I like Frankie. I have since the moment I laid eyes on her at that club in Monaco when I was seventeen. I mean, visually, she's a fucking work of art, but it was more than that. There was a pull... this intangible thing I had never felt before that kept me glued to her that night. It would have kept me glued to her the second night too, but my world blew up and by the time the dust cleared, she was in rehab somewhere. When we ran into each other again six months later, she acted like she had never met me. Like, ever. I didn't challenge that, figuring it was probably for the best. I'd decided in those six months I wasn't going to commit to her or anyone until my race career was over, and it was just getting started. In the ten years since, I haven't seen all that much of her, but when she does appear at race team events, I still feel that pull. I just ignore it. The same way she ignores me.

Dario makes some weird, annoyed sound in his throat and breaks off, walking into the team trailer with the trophy. Rocco follows, giving me another approving nod before he goes. Bash stays beside me and rests an arm around my shoulders. "I know everyone still wants interviews and shit, but I need you to find me before you leave the grounds today, okay?"

"Yeah. No problem." I nod as I see Clara approaching out of the corner of my eye. Bash gives my shoulder a squeeze, and he, too, breaks off.

Then my trainer Clara is in front of me, holding out a bottle of water and a damp, cool towel. I wipe at my face and sip the water. She falls in step beside me as I walk toward yet more media. "Nice one."

I smile at her. "Just nice?"

"Yup." She nods, her thick, lush, jet black hair shimmers as the ponytail it's in shakes a little with her head movement. "You've had cleaner races. Ones you've earned out of skill not opportunity."

"Ah, but finding the opportunity and acting on it *is* a skill," I reply and give her a cocky wink. She rolls her big dark eyes, but she's smiling. "Drink your water."

"Yes ma'am," I reply and give her a side-squeeze hug. She whips my chest lightly with the wet towel I've handed back to her and steps back as I step up to the first microphone.

It's almost two hours later by the time I'm done and have made it back to my dressing room and showered off the champagne. I'm back in street clothes, a pair of black pants, black t-shirt, and Mirabella Racing jacket. Clara walks in and throws herself down on the small couch as I'm crouched by the table tying my shoes. "It's raining. Again. Every time we're in this city it rains."

"That's why the team calls it Raincouver," I remind her. "Don't worry. Our flight out is in three hours. You'll make it."

"Barely." She sighs dramatically. I smile. This is the person no one else sees. The sassy, silly, theatrical girl. The world thinks

Clara is my dutiful assistant and personal trainer. And some insinuate she's also my on-call booty since she's also a mere twenty-one and very pretty. I try not to think about that because it's fucking gross. Don't get me wrong, I have booty calls. But Clara is actually my half-sister, so gross. Of course, no one can know that, so we appear to be abnormally close to some of the overly obsessed fans and media since she started working for me last year. "Also, FYI, your mom has called your cell like five times since the win."

"I'll call her on the way to the plane," I reply. Clara pulls my phone out of the pocket of her tailored Mirabella track pants she's wearing and tosses it to me from across the room. I catch it with ease as I rise to my full six-feet. I shove it in my back pocket. "She probably just wants to complain because I wouldn't fly her out for this one."

"She does love to be here when you win," Clara remarks. "She'll be annoyed she wasn't."

"She'll live," I say and Clara grimaces ever so slightly. "No, seriously. I talked to her doc just yesterday. She will live. New meds are working well."

My mother, Sherry Buckingham, has been battling mental health issues since my dad died and left her a single mom with a teenager. The problems only got worse when, six months after he passed, we found out about Clara. The child no one knew my father had and the love affair that created her, sent my mom spiraling.

My sister pulls herself off the couch. She's tall like me, but it's one of the only features we both inherited from Tommy James. She's got her mom's dark hair and eyes and delicately exotic features whereas I've got Billy's lighter hair, blue eyes, and rougher features. She starts gathering my things for me. "Car should be waiting."

I glance at my Apple watch. "I have to see Bash."

Clara's dark eyebrows furrow. "I think he left already. I saw him getting into a car with the wife about twenty minutes ago."

"Oh. Really?" I pull my phone out of my pocket. Sure enough, I have text from him.

Adelaide is under the weather. Had to jet. Promise you're coming to the party.

I smile and text him back.

When have I ever skipped a party?

I shove my phone back in my pocket and hold open the door for Clara. As soon as we get outside, I take the trophy from her, and she tries to balance an umbrella over both of us as we dart toward the parking lot. Once in the back of the Escalade with the driver making his way through downtown Vancouver, my phone buzzes again.

Find me as soon as you get to SS. It's imperative.

I send Bash back a thumbs-up emoji, but my brow furrows, and the back of my neck tingles. Something is up. I don't know what it is, but I don't think it's good. Clara is watching me, studying me like she always does. "Something wrong?"

"I don't know." I glance over at her. "Bash is all up in my face about talking to me before his birthday party in San Sebastian."

Her dark eyes glint with excitement. "The wife is preggo!"

I fight to keep my jaw from dropping. "What? No fucking way. That would be insane."

"Why? Her reproductive system is ripe. And everyone knows men can spawn kids even as geriatrics," Clara replies.

"Thanks for that fucking visual," I mutter and then shake my head. "It wouldn't be that. I mean, if it was that, there is no need to tell me before he shares with anyone else. But he's insistent we chat privately, so it's got be team-related."

"Maybe they're dumping Antonio next season," Clara suggests. "The daughter is ready to go."

"Lucia is doing great in F2 because it's F2," I say flatly. I'm not insulting Bash's youngest daughter, but I've been in both circuits, and I know there's a difference. Lucia Castera may in fact make history and become the first female F1 driver, but it won't be after one good year in F2. It'll take a little bit more than that.

Clara gives me a long stare, her deep, dark eyes unblinking. "You of all people should realize that blood isn't just thicker than water. It's thicker than logic."

"Dario owns half the team. He's not going to let it happen if for no other reason than ego," I reply and pull up Instagram and pop in my ear pods.

Clara doesn't answer my statement, but the quirk of her eyebrow before she turns to watch soggy Vancouver blur by tells me all I need to know. She isn't sold on my opinion. Only time will tell, I guess. I turn my focus to Instagram and pretend I'm just aimlessly scrolling through the stories of the very few people I follow. But I have an aim. I am looking for one person's feed in particular. And boom. After a few seconds, there she is. Francesca 'Frankie' Castera. She's dancing on a table in the sexiest dress I have ever seen. Her thick, gorgeous brown hair is swept up. The woman has the longest, most delectably kissable neck. The video is followed quickly by another in which she is sipping a neon green drink. "Perfection," she purrs into the camera, and then she takes the stir stick made of rock candy in the same bold color and slips it between her perfect, plump pink lips, and I officially have to look away and think of my grandmother to keep from popping a tent in my pants.

Holy shit that woman is…everything I would want if I could allow myself to want.

As I'm staring at the back of our driver's head, trying to keep my dick at half-mast, a new sound fills my ears and brings my attention back to the app still playing on my phone. It's no longer Frankie's stories. It's moved on to a story from one of the sports accounts I follow. Before I can scroll past the video though, there she is again. Frankie Castera, her hazel eyes twinkling in the flashing lights of the night club. The words F1 Hot Take spin over her face and then she says, "Drivers are needy and aggressive and greedy, as I just explained, and it doesn't stay on the track. They'd date me for a shot at a seat on my dad's team, not because of me. I deserve better than that."

Fuck me. That's the most honest, unguarded thing I've heard come out of her sweet mouth since she came home from rehab ten years ago. The authenticity of it is jarring. Because she's talking about me. I think. Does she think that night we had in Monaco as kids was me faking interest to get on her father's radar? Really?

Half of me says who cares? I mean, I did ghost her before ghosting was even a thing, although not on purpose. And I made the decision to never even try and explain myself to her. To let her ignore me and act like we never had a thing... and by 'thing' I mean the strongest attraction and connection I've ever felt in my life. But for some reason, suddenly, it matters. I don't want her to think that I was trying to use her.

I close the app after watching the clip four more times, tip my head back, and close my eyes. Can I live with it?

No, jackass, you can't.

3

UNTIL REHAB

FRANKIE

I'm out of the car before Nick has even come to a complete stop.

"*Attention, Francesca!*" my bodyguard calls out in French, but I ignore him. After all, if I'm dead, my father can't ruin my life.

I storm up the steps to the front doors of Londres, the hotel my father calls home when he's visiting home. He hasn't lived in San Sebastian, Spain, since my mother died when I was fourteen, and although he still owns the family home that's within walking distance of this hotel, he doesn't set foot in it. Now in his defense, my sister Lucia and I also haven't set foot in it more than once since she died. At first, we were too young to go there on our own, and he wouldn't take us. But now… it just feels too haunted with memories we don't like to remember, like her taking her last breath in the magnificent carved wood bed in the master bedroom while the ocean breeze blew in through the open terrace doors and we all held her hands.

Dad is sitting at his usual table in the restaurant, right against the window, overlooking the ocean. His wife of six months,

27

Adelaide, is with him. Her brown eyes meet mine before his hazel ones do, and they're filled with sympathy. She gets why I'm reeling. Or she's pretending to because she's still desperate for Lucia and I to see her as more than a gold digger. Jury is still out on that.

I pull my eyes from her to my father as I skid to an abrupt halt right in front of him. "I called Doctor Sanz Amador, and he'll be here at noon."

"Why on earth did you call him?" My father's voice is soft and deep and perfectly calm.

"To have you committed," I reply. "You've lost your mind. Dario and Rocco will back me up, I'm sure. They'll hold your spot as Team Principal until you're sane again."

"Oh, the drama." He rolls his eyes. "You need to dial that back in the pit and with the press, sweetie. No one will appreciate it."

I want to punch him. That's a first. My dad has never been difficult to deal with. He's hot-headed and passionate and larger than life, but I've always appreciated every aspect of him. Until now. I ball my hands into fists, my fingers on my left hand curling tightly around the handles of the designer bag I'm holding. "You send me an email with a press release set for tomorrow telling the world I'm your replacement, effective immediately. I'm taking over your spot as Team Principal? Was that your version of a practical joke? Because the only way you haven't lost your mind is if this is a failed attempt at humor."

"Francesca," he says softly as he stands, drops his napkin on the table, and bends to kiss Adelaide on the cheek before smoothing his navy pants and reaching for my hand. "Walk with me."

I grit my teeth, but I walk. Mostly because I know he'll drag me away anyway if I resist.

"Don't forget to wish him a happy birthday!" Adelaide calls

out, and I pause to shoot her a withering stare, but she just shrugs with a sheepish smile. I glare at her, but to be fair, it's not in anger. It's more of a 'why did you let this happen?' look.

We move away from my twenty-nine-year-old step mother, from the savory smells of the hotel restaurant, to the darkly floral scent of the hotel lobby, to the light, salty scent of the ocean air outside. He leads me across the boardwalk to the white iron railing that rings the half-moon shaped beach. Only then does he let go of my arm to put his hands on the rail. He takes a deep breath and closes his eyes. The only person who loves the ocean as much as I do is my dad. My mother didn't hate it, but she didn't love it. Lucia has no interest in anything but driving.

"If Adelaide is gold-digging, someone needs to explain to her she's doing it wrong," I say flatly as I stare out at the Playa de la Concha beach. It's fairly empty right now. Less than thirty people are lying around in the sand, and about the same amount are floating in the ocean. This beach will be packed by noon. "Adelaide is supposed to make sure you keep making money, not give it up."

"First of all, *ma louloutte*," he says, using the French nickname he bestowed on when I was in my mother's womb, if the stories are true. "That's a cheap shot, and there isn't anything cheap about you, so stop it. Second of all, Adelaide wants more time with me. Being Principal of an F1 team is a twenty-four seven gig, three hundred and sixty-five days a year, and I'm pushing fifty."

"You *are* fifty. Happy birthday by the way. You're pushing fifty-one," I correct him, which makes him frown. I defend myself. "The truth isn't a cheap shot."

His glare softens a little, and he lifts one arm from the railing to run it through his thick salt-n-pepper hair. I inherited that thick, dark hair with the untamable wave. My little sister Lucia got my mother's hair, which was nearly black ringlets. We have almost identical coloring – a light, sun-kissed golden tone since both our parents had that in common. Well, maybe that's just because we tend to live in places where others vacation. Casteras didn't chase the sun, they basked in it. "Even more reason to let go of the job and enjoy the finer things while I can."

The conversation was going nowhere. "You always said creating that race team was the finest thing you ever did. And it was an homage to our mother. It's named after her for crying out loud. And now you've remarried so you're dumping it?"

His eyes always glint with mischief. The man could lose a race, crash a car – whatever – and that glint was still there. He was so damn charming that it oozed out of him whether he liked it or not. But right now, that gleam of frivolity, the twinkle of playfulness, is suddenly gone. I tense. He turns from the ocean, leaning on the railing with his left forearm while he faces me. I cross my arms in defiance. "Your mother was not replaced. That's not fair, and you're not a child anymore Francesca, so I won't tolerate a tantrum. Last warning."

"I'm sorry," I confess because I admit that was a low, uncalled for blow. He stayed a widow for almost thirteen years. And it wasn't out of some kind of need to protect his kids, or because he was too busy with his race team. He had a broken heart. I'm an asshole for insinuating otherwise. "I know you aren't replacing Mom or forgetting her. I just… I don't understand where this is coming from. I've left the racing team and my dreams around it behind. I'm doing my own thing. I figured you'd stay until Lucia retired and then give the business to her."

"Frankie you have wanted this since the day you were four and a half and toddled off from my trailer at the track." Oh my fucking Lord, we're back to *this* ancient history. He smiles, despite the seriousness in his eyes. "I was panicked. I thought you'd been kidnapped and even if you hadn't—"

"There are a thousand ways a toddler could die at a professional race track forty minutes before race time," I finish for him because he's recounted this tale in private, and public, more times than I can count. It's in magazine articles and YouTube clips and everything. "But I wasn't dead. I was in the pit. I had taken some headphones and put them on myself, and I was pretending to be the boss and telling everyone what to do."

He's grinning proudly. It's ridiculous. I was four. "And the actual Team Principal let you sit in that pit every race after that while I was on the track. He answered all your questions. He said you were voraciously passionate about the sport."

"I was," I reply breezily. "Because I was a toddler and it was my whole world. Mama, Lucia, and I used to follow you to every race."

"You were still in the pit, yacking with Principals and listening to the engineers and me bark at each other at nine years old. And at ten, eleven, twelve, thirteen, fourteen, fifteen, sixteen, seventeen, eighteen..."

"Not eighteen," I shoot back quickly. It's a warning shot.

He ignores it. "Eighteen for a while. Until rehab."

"No. Until I realized that the sport didn't interest me anymore. No offense," I reply, my words clipped. "I was around the track because I had no choice. Mom was gone, and I wasn't old enough or healthy enough to do my own thing."

Dad sighs. Hard. "Frankie when are you going to stop lying to yourself? You are still at every race, *ma louloutte.*"

I snort. It's a highly annoying, dismissive sound that I know he hates and that I haven't done since I was a teen. "I watch when I have time in between my work. Because I have my own career, Dad. And now you're trying to force me to give it up, my career and my life, for the one thing I decided I definitely don't want?"

"Taking pictures all around the globe in bikinis on boats and at clubs holding bottles of booze is not a career," he shoots back. Bash Castera is not a fan of social media. He sees it as an annoying, lowbrow thing that has infiltrated his company and his life. And his kids.

"It actually *is* a career when companies pay you to wear, drink, and use their products," I snap back because this isn't the first time we've had this conversation, and I'm sick of it. "I made a hundred grand last year from endorsement deals. I'm a brand Dad, and I've got that shoe line coming out. It's important to me."

"Well, it's your own fault that I'm giving the job to you," Dad replies with an unsympathetic shrug. "You're a brand, and you bring power and a face people want to see to our team. You bring glamor and youth, and those brands that gravitate to you will want to pay Mirabella Racing because you will be *our* brand."

"You're not making me a spokesperson. I'll be Team Principal. I'll be responsible for the safety and legality of the team's every move on and off the track. I'll be expected to soothe egos and boost them and woo sponsors and study race footage and know tracks so well I could drive them blindfolded." My voice is inching up an octave with every sentence, and I know I sound unhinged. I feel unhinged. Yeah, four-year-old me or even twelve-year-old me would be squealing with joy at this job but not twenty-eight year-old me. No. Not at all. Well, maybe a little, but I know it will be a nightmare, and I'm done living those. "I'll have to make staffing decisions and race day decisions and work with those... assholes."

Dad lets loose one of his trademark laughs. It's deep and loud. His head tilts back, and his hand clutches his heart, like always. People walking by can't help but glance over. And some recognize us. I can tell by the way their eyes flare and their mouths drop. Damnit. Attention is the last thing I want right now. I turn back toward the ocean so people can't see my face.

"Those assholes, as you call them, are very talented drivers. But if you don't want them, fire them. Find new ones. Move your sister up."

I frown and slide my eyes left to look at him. "You would disown me if I fired your golden boy Billy James. And besides, Lucia's not ready. The misogynistic sport isn't either. And they're not ready for a twenty-something female Principal either."

Dad nods but says, "Since when have you ever waited for anyone or anything to catch up? You've always just marched in and been the force you are without apology or hesitation. Just like your mother."

I smile. There is no bigger compliment to me than telling me I'm like Mirabella Castera. I feel his arm across my shoulders. It's warm, strong and safe, like it's always been. "Francesca, you are the one – the only one – who I want to succeed me in this role. I know anyone else will run this team into oblivion. It happens far too easily in this business. We need new blood. I am bowing out gracefully. Don't make me do it the other way."

He's being dramatic. Mirabella Racing has won three Constructors' Championships. Yes, the last won was seven years ago, which is a long time ago in the race world. But a driver who shall remain nameless has won the World Championship three times in a Mirabella car, the last time only four years ago. Mirabella – the team and drivers - have been middle of the pack ever since.

"If I don't name my replacement, Dario will and he'll appoint Rocco. They'll change the name. Mirabella Racing, your mother's namesake, will become Conti-Castera. He's wanted to name it that since day one." My father's words make something cold and nauseating swirl in my belly. "I named this after your mother because I wanted you to be the one running it one day, keeping her memory alive through the team. She loved racing as much as I did. And she loved that you and Lucia loved it. She would be so happy to see you replace me."

"Don't..." I whisper, my voice suddenly choked. I close my eyes and concentrate on the ocean air blowing around me, the way it caresses my cheek and plays with my hair. When I am calmer and not on the verge of tears I inhale. "That's not playing fair."

"Life isn't fair. We both learned that the hard way when we lost her," Dad says and squeezes me to him with the arm still around my shoulders. "Look, I don't have to leave, but I want to leave. And I know you're ready and you want this, even if you don't want to admit it."

"No one will approve," I mutter, and maybe that's one of the biggest problems I have with his idea. The complaints. The nasty articles and comments and passive aggressive male bullshit that will cloud my life if I take this job. Oh, and the drivers and race team members I will have to stare at every single day and work alongside—the ones I've known since I was a kid. The ones who were there when I was drugged. The suspects.

"*Louloutte*, no one needs to approve but me," he informs me with a flash of an arrogant smile. Those smiles, the cocky ones, are rare but also still charming somehow. It's the smile my mom once confessed to me, in her last year of life, that made her fall in love with him.

"Dario and Rocco—"

He drops his arm from my shoulders and puts a hand on top of mine on the railing and squeezes. "I have fifty-five percent. I bought some of Dario's shares years ago with the caveat that if I retire without appointing a successor, it defaults to Rocco and so do ten percent of my shares."

My eyes grow two sizes. "When and how did that happen?'

"Years ago Dario needed to liquidate some assets to help his brother. I only agreed to the caveat because I was sure you would take the job as Principal. So if you don't, the Contis will control everything," Dad says without hesitation. "Let me announce you as my replacement at my birthday party tonight, then Dario and Rocco won't have to like it, but they'll have to accept it."

Before he can argue further, Adelaide interrupts in her posh British accent. "Bash, my love?"

We turn and there she is, long, flowy, but lowcut dress billowing in the ocean breeze. Ankles covered, tits out. I shouldn't be such a bitch. I have a very similar dress. Hell, I have about sixty that are way more revealing. But I didn't elope with someone's dad so… Man, I wish I didn't feel bad when I had these thoughts. I wish I hated her. I don't. We actually worked together a few times on modeling jobs, which is how she met my dad. I modeled in a show with her in Paris Fashion Week and introduced them at the after party. Ugh. I sigh, and her eyes slide to me. "Frankie we both know Rocco and Dario don't deserve this. You do."

"True," I reply and give her a small smile.

"So?" Adelaide prompts.

I want to scream no at the top of my lungs, but instead I say in a resigned tone, "You're looking at the next Team Principal for Mirabella Racing."

"I'm so proud of you!" Dad pulls me into a hug as Adelaide claps like a cheerleader.

"So, birthday party. Eight. At the Maria Cristina. Key team members and investors will be there, so it's the perfect place to announce."

Dad kisses my cheek before stepping away from me and the beach to stand next to his wife, who anyone watching would think is my sister if they didn't know better. He turns with his child bride and saunters back to the hotel while I turn back to the ocean and contemplate walking into the surf and swimming away from this place and my life. It might be easier than being Team Principal at Mirabella Racing.

4

—————

MATURITY CAN BE A BITCH

BILLY

Of course she's already here even though her last Insta post was her in a tiny bikini on a yacht in Miami twenty-five minutes ago. I don't know much about social media, Clara handles mine, so I don't know how she did that. There must be a timer-thingy on Instagram or something. I would ask if I cared, but I don't. I hate social media and making a career off it seems like the seventh circle of hell to me. For Frankie, it seems to be a passion. That's not something I can understand, and it pisses me off because for twenty-four amazing hours once, I felt like I got her. On every level. In ways, to this day, I still haven't felt like I 'got' anyone else.

At the other end of the hotel bar, Frankie glosses those perfect, plump lips as a server puts a fruity looking drink down in front of her. Clara gives my elbow a little nudge with hers. "Stop being a brat."

"I haven't said a damn thing yet," I reply.

Clara smiles. "You do your best bratting with your face, Billy. You don't have to say a word."

"Excuse me?"

"Just go over and talk to her. *Civilly*," Clara orders, giving my arm another little nudge.

"I'm not here to talk to Frankie. I'm here to talk to Bash," I correct and fold my arms across my chest. "He asked me to see him before the party, remember?"

Clara lifts one of her jet black eyebrows. "You think it's smart to ignore the boss's daughter?"

She says that sentence slowly, over enunciating every word like a kindergarten teacher working with a particularly slow five-year-old. She only does that when she thinks I'm being pig-headed. Like I'm too stupid to understand her words at full speed. When we were younger, it used to annoy the hell out of me, but since she started working with me after getting her kinesiology degree, I've come to realize when she talks like this, she's usually right. Maturity can be a bitch.

I run a hand through my hair. I'm sure it's disheveled, but it tends to look like that on purpose anyway, so no big deal. I refold my hand across my designer button down which is paired with some jeans. It's as close to business attire as I like to get. Although, tonight for Bash's birthday party, I'll put on a full suit.

Frankie, at her tiny table by the window overlooking one of San Sebastian's stunning beaches, is dressed for fun. She's in a tiny, flouncy little, pale pink, backless sundress and shimmering flats with straps that wrap around her tiny, tanned ankles. Her thick, wavy hair that gets her endorsement deals with one of the biggest hair product companies in the world is swept up in the back with a few pieces left loose to frame that perfect oval face with the wide, sparkling eyes and the full mouth that makes any straight man's dick twitch.

Yeah. She's *hot*. Hotter than my tires at the end of a race. Clara gives me one more nudge. "She's looking at you, dumb ass. How can you be staring right at her and not see that?"

I blink and realize Frankie Castera is, indeed, staring at me.

The bright blue straw from her drink resting gently on her full bottom lip. I don't answer Clara because I don't think she'd appreciate the truth, which is, 'I was picturing my dick slipping between those perfect lips, so I wasn't actually focused on what my eyeballs were seeing.'

I leave Clara at the hotel bar entrance and wander over to Frankie's table. Her eyes never leave me. They never flicker with uncertainty or worry or caution. Those big, hazel eyes, shimmering with flecks of amber and moss, are stone cold. Emphasis on the cold. I've never asked this woman why she started to hate me, but I always thought it was excessive if it was just about a missed date. We were kids… right? Last night's clip has finally given me some insight, I think. I guess it's finally time to find out.

"Fancy meeting you here," she says airily.

"You think I'd miss Bash's birthday?" I say with a lazy smile.

"I guess not." She shrugs. "Well, see you there."

She smiles, but it's as cold as the look in her eyes. Frankie's been throwing me the deep freeze for a decade, and I've never tried to thaw her out. But today is the day. I pull my hands from my pockets, yank out the chair across from her, and sit down. That gets a reaction. A blink. Better than nothing. "He's been blowing up my phone all morning. Wants to see me as soon as possible. Know why?"

"Do I look like my father's personal assistant?" She's flippant and trying to blow me off, but she's also smiling. It sets the hair on the back of my neck on end. Frankie Castera doesn't smile around me. Ever. "Anyway you just missed him. He left with Adelaide."

I lean forward. My hand, flat on the table, slides closer to hers, which is next to her glass. She pulls her hand off the table like she's scared if she doesn't I might touch it. "You know something. And you want to tell me," I say and pull her glass to me. I lift it and take a sip from the straw that was between her pretty little lips a second ago. And then I almost spit. "What the fuck is this?"

"Shirley Temple."

"What are you? Six?" Okay, maybe not the right words to end this deep freeze.

She stands. "Bye Billy."

She swooshes by me, leaving a scent of something dark and delicious in her wake. I've never known what her perfume is, but I've always fucking reacted to it. In my veins. I hook her elbow before she can escape, and she spins so quickly that I know she expected it. "I saw your interview thing on Instagram."

"I didn't give an interview to Instagram."

"I don't know the exact lingo for all the crap you do, but one of the sports feeds has a video of you talking about drivers," I tell her, trying not to sound as exasperated as I am about this whole conversation. Maybe sorting this out will finally make it easy to communicate with her again, like it was that night. "The thing where you say race drivers are greedy and aggressive."

"You're man-handling me," Frankie says. "Exhibit A."

"Honey if I was man-handling you, you'd be enjoying it," I retort and I don't let go of her arm. "I also heard you say you think all drivers would only be interested in you to get to your dad. And get a spot on his team."

"You're driving for Mirabella. Have been since you began in F1," Frankie says. "Exhibit B."

Now the amber in those eyes of hers are glinting with fire and I'm sure my blue ones are gleaming with ice. "No. I swear, Frankie, that's not what *we* were about."

"There was no we," Frankie argues. "One night as a teenager does not make us a we. We never even…"

"Fucked?" I finish for her, and she yanks her arm out of my grip. Out of the corner of my eye, I see Clara start to approach.

Her steps are slow, and her eyes are narrowed. She's about to play referee. "I didn't need to use you to get to your dad, Frankie."

"Really? You want me to believe you just happened to play charming hero for his daughter? By happenstance?" Something flashes in Frankie's eyes that looks like hurt, but it disappears before I can really be sure.

"You didn't tell me your name that night," I reply. "And I believe the historically accurate term is Aussie Hero. But I'll allow charming."

My quips don't get her to relent. "You knew who I was."

"And you knew who I was."

"So you want me to believe what you are saying now?" Her left eyebrow arches. "But didn't you also say you'd meet the next night? And you didn't. That makes you a liar, James."

She turns again and continues walking out of the lobby bar. Clara reaches me as Frankie turns left, deeper into the hotel and out of my sightline. "So that went well!"

Her enthusiasm is pure sarcasm. I frown. "I'll fix it."

"Doubt it!" she calls after me, but she doesn't follow as I storm off after Frankie. I find her at the elevator. The doors have just opened and she's stepping in, alone, so I sprint and slide in beside her just as the doors slip closed.

"You again?" She rolls those big, sexy eyes. God, why can't I find her unattractive?

"You finally acknowledge that we dated and you think I'm going to let you walk out?" I ask, stand shoulder to shoulder with her instead of facing her, but my head is tipped in her direction.

"I didn't say we dated. I said the opposite. We were *never* a thing."

"You admitted we had a night together. You've never done that before."

She doesn't speak or move for a few seconds as the elevator goes upward. Then, a blink and a sigh. It's soft but carries a heaviness. And with that blink, her expression darkens. "I don't remember everything about that weekend which is apparently normal after a drug... overdose. But I unfortunately remember you, and that night. But I figured you didn't want me to remember you, since you stood me up. I was doing you a favor. And since you've never brought it up before either, I'm thinking I was right. You're welcome."

"I didn't ghost you on purpose," I tell her, the truth tumbling from my mouth before I can stop it. "I had family drama to deal with. Tommy had only been gone for six months at that point. As I told you, I was about to start racing again and my mum was still freaking out about me going back. There was a lot more going on in my world I didn't even realize, and most of it blew the fuck up about forty minutes before I was supposed to meet you for our second date."

I can tell she's almost knocked on her fine ass by my candid outburst. We've never said a kind or personal word to each other since that first night in Monaco. "I have other reasons for letting you treat me like stranger, and treating you like one," I continue, and for some reason, I take the one small step needed to bring us so close together our fingers brush. "But at that time, seventeen year old Billy James in Monaco wanted to do anything but ghost you. I swear on my life. I wanted to do everything *but* that."

Frankie turns only her head to me, so we can look each other in the eye again. She bites her bottom lip softly, somehow not disturbing the cherry red color painted on it, but definitely disturbing my dick. It twitches again, and I fight to not reach down and reposition it. "I don't know whether or not to believe you."

That damn perfect bottom lip is trapped between her pearly whites again. And then the stupid elevator pings, and the doors start to slide open, and we're on her floor. She steps out of the elevator but presses a hand to the frame so the doors don't slide closed and stares at me. "Do you know already?"

"Know what?" I blink and stare at her perfect face. She looks so conflicted and leery. Like she thinks I have ulterior motives. Bash's insistent messages that I meet him before the party tonight pop into my brain and I start to feel uneasy. "You got something to share, Frankie?"

She moves her hand from the elevator doors and turns away. I let my eyes drop down the length of her body. Since she's got her back to me, she can't see me take in her narrow shoulders, the curve of her hip, or the golden, lean and yet muscular shape of her calf. I expect her to just storm off down the hall to whatever suite is hers, but she looks over her shoulder and I'm busted. There is no way she didn't catch my eyes as they swept back up her body. But she doesn't call me out. Frankie Castera does something else entirely. She turns around to face the elevator, and I lean forward and press the open button with my thumb to keep the doors from closing. After a moment of hesitation, given away only by a quick furrow of her perfectly sculpted eyebrows, she blurts out, "Dad is retiring. I'm taking over Mirabella Racing."

And then she leaves, marching off like I'd anticipated earlier down the long hall with the lush carpet. I am left in more of a state of confusion than I would have been if she'd decked me. But I recover and manage to slide through the doors as they close without getting crushed. My pace is almost a run as she turns a corner at the end of the hall, and I manage to catch up to her just as she's pulling a key card out of her purse.

"Are you fucking with me?" My voice booms down the long hallway much louder than I'd anticipated. She shushes me.

"He's announcing tonight. I'm the new Principal." She swipes the key card and her hand reaches for the door handle, but she freezes before she can open it because I open my big, fat mouth.

"You don't even like racing."

"You're right, I don't." Frankie's hand drops off the door handle, and she turns to face me. Now we're toe-to-toe like two prize fighters in the Octagon. "I fucking love it. I've loved it my whole life. I've been in this world even longer than you."

"My dad put me in his race car when I was three months old. I have photographic proof," I counter. I mean, he literally propped me up in the seat for a magazine photoshoot, but it counts.

"My parents fucked on my dad's car after his first championship win and…" She waves a delicate hand up and down in front of her perfect body. "*Voila!*"

My jaw can do nothing but drop. "You're telling me you were conceived *on* a race car?"

"Yes." Frankie almost grins. Almost. "So I win. And I do love it, James. I just don't love most of the people involved in the sport. But the mindset, the vision, the passion, I love every single fucking second of that. So I said yes."

"What about your Instagram business? How the hell are you going to model bikinis *and* lead a race team?" I question, and I don't blame her for that fiery stare that says she wants to slap me. I want to slap me when I hear myself. But it's still the truth, so I double down like the dick that I am. "You know this sport, the fans, they're all going to laugh, smirk, make stupid comments. And if you're still peddling liquor and swimwear and charging for party appearances, they'll think less of you. They'll think less of the team. And every single fucking person associated with Mirabella Racing."

"You let me handle the tough questions, buttercup," she says sharply and with so much condescension it's almost impressive. "You concentrate on winning. And if you can't do that, or you can't handle this transition and any petty bullshit that comes with it, then feel free to shop for a new team next year."

"My contract is for two more years."

She swipes her key card again and this times opens the door

with an aggressive flick of her wrist. "I'll release you. Say the word."

She disappears without another word, just a whoosh of the door as it shuts behind her. The door beside hers opens a crack, but I ignore it and turn back toward the elevators. I know it's her bodyguard Nick. He heard us and is making sure she's okay.

Of course Frankie Castera is just fine. She's about to be my boss. She's fucking peachy. I, on the other hand, need a drink.

5

ANCHOR BABY

FRANKIE

I stare at myself in the mirror as my phone continually beeps and buzzes with messages and calls and emails I'm ignoring. Argh. How did my life turn on a dime? How do I turn it back?

You should know how easy these things happen, dumbass, my brain lectures me. *You aren't guaranteed happiness or even simplicity. Life has it out for you, bitch.*

Now the hotel suite phone rings. I ignore it like I'm ignoring my cell and stare at my reflection. I have to do this shoot. It isn't ideal. In fact, it's less than ideal. San Sebastian has temperamental weather. It turns cloudy on a dime, and don't even get me started on the wind. By the time I change into the bikini, turn on my ring light, and get my cell set up on its stand, I can barely stand on the balcony without being blown off. The only half decent shot has me clutching the railing, my wavy hair flying every which way. It's got an angry Gods, Medusa vibe to it, which I can spin. I think.

I lean forward in the bathroom mirror, touching up my lip gloss and my back instantly seizes. I gasp, my eyes slamming shut, and I take shallow, panting breaths until it passes, which is a

45

couple seconds later. Thankfully. I ignore what that means as I pull myself slowly to a proper standing position. I give myself a minute to take a couple deeper breaths and see if anything else hurts. It doesn't. I walk slowly into the main room from the bathroom. As I stare out at the sea and debate trying to do another shot in the second bikini I promised the brand I would promote, there's a loud, hard knock on the door. I know exactly who it is.

"I'm working, Nick!" I call out politely but firmly.

The door opens anyway. I tighten the tie on my bathrobe, which is wrapped over the bikini I'm wearing. Normally, I take comfort in the fact that my bodyguard always has a key to my room, but in this case, not so much. "I could have been naked!"

"Nothing I haven't seen before," Nick replies as he strides across the small entry hall into the main living space. My suitcases are open on the floor of the living room, the contents strewn about. Two of the three swimsuits I made a twenty-thousand dollar deal to promote are carefully laid out on crepe paper on the couch. "Lucia is being Lucia."

He thrusts his personal cell in my direction. My eyes focus on a series of text messages from my little sister, each of which are progressively more demanding. She's trying to get a hold of me. Each one gets more angry and laced with profanity as Nick ignored her, like I was.

"Okay. Okay," I sigh. I grab my own phone. He nods his shaved head. But instead of punching my sister's name in my contacts, I pull up the pics I took on the balcony. "I'll call her after you weigh in and tell me if any of these are useable."

He frowns. Hard. It makes him look so damn menacing. That's why my dad hired him when I was eighteen, after the incident of which we do not speak. Well, that and the fact that Nick doesn't just look dangerous. He is. He has saved my ass from bad situations more than once. Nick yanks my phone from my hand and flips through the photos. He doesn't look like he's scouring them, but he is. "Last one. It's sexy in that bad-ass dark way. Different for you. In a good way."

He shoves the phone back into my hand and glares, his dark brown eyes narrowed. "Call that hellion sister of yours."

As soon as the door clicks behind him. I punch my sister's name in my WhatsApp contacts and hit video chat. She answers before the first ring can even finish. She looks wild, like with anger or venom, but that isn't a foreign look for my sister who carries a chip on her shoulder bigger than her race car. "What the hell, bitch? Do not voicemail me ever again. Especially not in an emergency situation."

"So, you agree dad has lost his mind and it's a devastating mistake that we need to fix somehow?" I say and drop down on the chaise lounge next to the plate of chocolate-covered strawberries the hotel gave me as a welcome gift.

"What? No," Lucia barks back, annoyed. Her dark, curly hair is slicked back, like it usually is, in a low, tight pony. She's not wearing a lick of make-up, which also is pretty normal. "I mean, I didn't expect him to retire just yet, but I always knew you were his plan when he did."

"I've moved on, and I thought he knew that. I thought everyone knew that."

"You haven't moved on," Lucia replies, the expression on her face amused, which pisses me off. "It's time to stop kidding yourself. You could be anywhere in the world when the season is on, but you *always* watch."

"I watch F2 to make sure you're okay. That's it… most of the time," I fib.

"Lying causes wrinkles, Frank. Be careful or you're gonna have to partner with a Botox company," Lucia says, laughing at her own joke. "So, back to the Team Principal thing. It's crazy, but it was bound to happen. I'm just wondering why he picked now."

"Adelaide, I guess." I pick up one of the strawberries by the green leafy stem and stare at it as it dangles in front of me. "She wants more granddad dick."

"Frankie, don't. Gross." Lucia looks truly nauseous, and if I think about my words, I would be too. "What I think is… she wants a baby."

I snap up to a sitting position and wince. Fucking back. "You can't be serious. Now I'm going to puke."

"Think about it, Frankie. She's your age," Lucia replies, and there's dread dripping from her tone. Her tanned skin looks almost green. "Most normal women that age want babies from their husbands."

"Most normal women this age don't marry men older than their own dad and expect babies… do they?" I question. "Anchor baby. She's gunning for an anchor baby?"

"Isn't that when you have a baby in another country to get citizenship or something?" Lucia thinks about it for a minute. "A baby that keeps her tied to a man and his money is the same thing though I guess. So, yes. An anchor baby."

"But even if that nightmare is the truth, why would he have to quit work for that? He didn't when we were born. Hell, he only took one day off for Mom's funeral," I say and try not to think about that tidbit of family history too long.

"Yeah… I don't know, but it is a distinct possibility," Lucia replies.

"I'm taking the position." Saying it out loud actually sends a nervous shiver down my spine. I walk over to the air-conditioning and turn it down.

"Of course you are. I didn't doubt it for a second," Lucia replies, and she's walking too, down an aisle on a plane. A private one with plush leather seats. I see some F2 Mirabella people I sort of recognize in the background. I think one is her publicist and the other a marketing person. All would have signed NDAs, so I don't worry about what they might overhear. Those became mandatory in the Mirabella employment package after someone from the race group gave private info on me to the tabloids after my 'drug overdose.' "So has Douchebag or Douchebag Junior exploded yet? I mean, I didn't hear a sonic boom, but I've had my headphones on."

She's kidding, but not really. "I'm sure dad has a plan to deal with the creepy Conti family. It's not going to be pretty, I know."

"Rocco might be okay if he gets bumped to Chief engineer when Joaquin retires," Lucia surmises and her brow furrows. "Or if Dario will ever step away and let him have Sporting Director."

"Dario step away? And not get to hear his own voice on the radios every race day? Never gonna happen." I really don't want to talk about Dario and Rocco Conti. Both have been persona non-grata in my brain for a very long time. They were not only on the yacht the night I mysteriously overdosed, but Dario had been the one to charter it. I say mysterious overdose because I never willingly ingested drugs, which is something very few people know. I don't know the Contis were involved, but I don't know they weren't. I change the subject. "I've only dealt with Billy so far."

"James? He knows about this?" The amused smile tugging at her wide mouth is a copy of mine when I smile. But I am definitely *not* smiling about this. "Boy is fast on and off the track."

"Probably in the bedroom too," I snark.

That makes Lucia laugh. "Find out and report back."

"Shut up," I bark and roll my eyes. She has been making these snide little comments about Billy ever since I told her about that one stupid night in Monaco. "Billy showed up here already and I blurted it out."

When Lucia's mouth falls wide open I start trying to change the subject. "So is Billy on Team Frankie?"

"He's Team Billy," I reply tersely and try not to think about the other things he said—confessed—because I don't want my face to soften and give anything away.

"How very Billy of him." Lucia chuckles. "Did he bring his side hustle?"

"I don't think you're using that expression correctly, but the answer is yes." I walk over to the open balcony doors and stare out at the turquoise sea. The sun is shining again now, and the wind is blowing less harshly, and so the crowds have made their way to the beach again. "He doesn't go anywhere without Clara these days. Why she puts up with being his dirty little secret, I have no idea."

Lucia tugs out her pony. She gives her hair a shake and the ringlets bounce and bob around her shoulders. My sister could be a fucking super model, and instead, she wears a helmet for a living. "When the hell do you get here, by the way?" I ask her.

"I think I've got another hour before landing," Lucia says with a sigh. "I had to do a fucking endorsement thing before I left Vancouver. Mick has a car ready to go when we get there, so no delays."

Mick is her bodyguard. He prefers Michael, but we prefer calling them Mick and Nick. Annoying is kind of our thing.

"Hurry up, okay? I need you." I smile.

"You need no one, Francesca. You're enough on your own," Lucia replies. It's some of the last words of advice our mother ever told us. Whispered it to us on her death bed. *People will tell you, because you are girls, that you need others to make you feel safe or secure or whole. That's all lies. You're enough on your own.* "See you soon and stay strong. *Baci.*"

Just like mom, Lucia ends every call with the Italian word for kisses, and she even blows me an air kiss before ending the call. I bite the strawberry I've been aimlessly holding and flop down on the couch gingerly because of my back. I should probably tell Jennie about this turn of career events before she reads it in the paper. I might have to massage the egos of the brands that hired me in case they think this means I won't deliver on my deals with them. Which reminds me, I still have more bikinis to try on and photograph. And I need to follow up with the shoe company who I've signed on to do my line with. They wanted some feedback on a materials list they sent me.

"Fuck," I hiss at the coiffured ceiling in the expensive hotel suite. I hate that I hate my life right now. I know how privileged I am to have it, so I swallow down those feelings and pull myself off the velvet couch and keep working.

6

I'VE ALWAYS BEEN HIS MOTH

FRANKIE

Three hours later, which is forty minutes late, I grasp Lucia's hand in mine, and we waltz into the private event room at the Maria Cristina hotel. The room is perfectly square, smallish but ornately decorated with balconies accessed by arched French doors on three sides. There's about forty people there, and I recognize maybe ten. Most of them are Mirabella employees. My father, Joaquin Manrique the Chief engineer, Billy, who is in a dark suit that looks somehow casual and elegant at the same time. There's also Antonio, our other driver, with his wife Carlotta by his side. And of course Dario and Rocco Conti are standing on the balcony, just to my left, like gargoyles. Ugh.

"Nice of you to join us, girls," Dad says, and I know that's a sign he's slightly irked by our tardiness.

"We wanted to look pretty for your birthday, Daddy," Lucia smiles and leans in for a hug and a kiss since she hasn't seen him yet. "You clearly have no idea how long it takes to get rid of helmet hair."

People surrounding Dad chuckle, and I roll my eyes. "I have no excuse other than I like to make an entrance."

More laughter. This is what Lucia and I do whenever we're forced into Mirabella appearances. We make jokes and act like silly, playful but doting, well-intentioned daughters. I can't help but wonder now if that cutesy image will bite me in the ass as Team Principal. Adelaide steps closer and embraces Lucia like a devoted stepmom… who could have been in the same sorority as her stepdaughters, but whatever. "Lucia, sweetheart, it's so good to see you again!"

"Right back at ya, 'Laide," Lucia coos with a big smile so no one knows that it's a dig. Adelaide hates being called anything other than Adelaide, which is why Lucia shortens it every chance she gets. "Hope you've been keeping the old man happy and healthy."

"I'm fit as a fiddle and as happy as a cat trapped at a dairy farm," Dad boasts, and I try not to shudder as he wraps an arm around Adelaide, who has her cleavage on full display in a low-cut Calvin Klein number that's flowy and loose but finishes well above her knees.

As if on cue, the waiter passes, and I manage to only give Adelaide a pleasant-looking air kiss as my greeting before reaching for a champagne glass on his tray. I hand it to Lucia, but my father grabs two more and hands one to me.

I take it and brace myself. Here it comes. He clears his throat and raises his glass. "Everyone! Now that my whole heart is here…" He glances at Lucia and me and winks. She reaches for my free hand with hers as Dad turns back to the guests who have started to gather around for his speech.

"Another year in the books for me personally, and it has me reflecting," he commences, and I stand like a statue and listen to him boast about Mirabella's season so far, wax poetic about his own racing career, praise his amazing wife, and gush about Lucia and me and how we make him proud. "But the time has come to let Mirabella and the racing world shine without me. I am officially retiring. Effective at midnight."

Gasps and murmurs rush through the room like a rampant ocean breeze. Dad acts like he doesn't hear it because, in typical Bash Castera fashion, they don't matter. He's never cared how other people react to his decisions and choices. "Everyone please welcome your new Mirabella Racing Team Principal."

He turns and sweeps his arm toward me and Lucia. Lucia gives my hand one last, quick squeeze and steps back. There's more gasps and whispers that almost drown out the sound of Dad saying my name. But then, without prompting, the clapping begins and spreads until the whole room is doing it.

It makes me itch, but I plaster a confident smile on my face and then give a stupid wave like a pageant queen on a float. What the hell is wrong with me, suddenly? I can't help but catch the smirk on Billy's face when I do it, which makes it worse. Bastard and his perfect face which somehow gets hotter when it gets smug. I hate that man for everything that ever happened. And everything that didn't.

"*Ma louloutte*, say a few words will you?"

"I'm not the speech type, and I don't want to detract from my father's birthday, which is the real celebration here," I say, making sure not to flip my hair or giggle or do anything else to make that stupid smirk on Billy James' face grow an inch bigger. "I look forward to talking with all of you one on one tonight and in the days to come. And I'm looking forward to continuing my father's hard work with all of you talented people and loyal investors. So for now, cheers to Bash Castera, loving father, devoted husband, and the king of the track, even when he's not on it."

They clap again and raise their glasses with me. I put the champagne flute to my lips letting only a tiny drop dance on my tongue before I give another stupid wave – seriously, why am I doing that?! - and head directly to the bar. I plop the full champagne flute on the bar and order blood orange flavored Schweppes, on the rocks, twist of lemon. As I wait for my order I feel his presence behind me. Like, *right* behind me. I can almost feel the brush of his suit jack against my bare shoulders and instantly regret a strapless dress. Not because the thought of Billy brushing up against me repulses me, but because it doesn't. It never has.

The bartender, slides the drink toward me, and I take it and smile before turning to face Billy. He's so beyond handsome. It's not just the sandy hair and the angular jaw or the eyes the shade of aquamarine that matches the sea on its very best day. It's also the broad shoulders that are always back, never slouched. It's the powerful arms and strong hands that are tucked casually into his pockets. It's the way he walks into a room like he doesn't just own it, but he owns everyone in it too. He met a freaking princess last year, and she curtsied to him. I am not even kidding. All that confidence and swagger, it's hotter than a forest fire.

"That wave… did you learn that in Influencer school? Is there a TikTok How-To on that or did you just invent it on the fly?" His lips dance in a cocky smile as he raises his glass. It's a dark, reddish-brown liquid over ice.

"Look, don't support me. I don't care, but if you continue to make fun of me to my face, you're going to have a problem," I warn and start to walk away, but he easily falls in step right beside me.

"Sorry. I just want you to know you seem to be off your game," Billy replies. "Because this is as absurd to you as it is to everyone else. And you know it."

"Go fuck yourself, or find your trainer and have her do it," I whisper back, a smile on my lips so no one suspects the altercation taking place.

I break off from him, abruptly turning and heading toward my dad and Adelaide who are talking to the president of the soft drink company that is one of our biggest investors.

I spend the night smiling and nodding and avoiding Rocco and Dario, who are circling but not approaching, probably because Nick is less than a foot from me all night giving them his infamous hairy eyeball every time they take a step closer. Adelaide has an enormous cake brought out, and after a heartfelt ballad of "Happy Birthday," which she sings with a microphone so everyone in town can hear, my father finally stops trying to shop me to investors and canoodles with his wife. I disappear into the restroom. I'm on my fourth soda and need to pee.

When I'm done and open the door, I come face-to-face with the head of the company that makes our engines. Our contract with them is up next year. No one is talking about it yet, but I've weighed the pros and cons of re-signing. His name is Don McDougal, and he steps in front of me as I emerge into the tight hallway off the party room. The hallway is painted a gun metal gray with gold trim and a dimly lit gold chandelier. But even in the low light, I can see the unfriendly smile on his round, ruddy face.

"Frankie, sweetheart," he says, and I bristle. I fucking hate being called sweetheart by men I have no affiliation with. It's pure condescension. "Are you overwhelmed yet, darling?"

Oh, so he's double dipping on the condescending nicknames. Okay then, well, two people can play that game. I smile at him, brighter than the sun, hoping it burns him. "Not in the slightest, actually. I was born into this sport after all, so it was only a matter of time until I ended up in this position," I explain breezily, like his concern is absolutely ridiculous. To be honest, I kind of get it though I will never admit that out loud. "Despite being incredibly successful at my own brand, I've never stopped following Mirabella, giving my dad feedback, which he gladly took, and researching the sport overall. So don't worry about me, *muffin*."

I start to walk away, which is a shame because I didn't get to see his cheeks turn fully red from that, just a little pink. Luckily, he's not done, so I can turn back around and enjoy his humiliation.

"I'm not sure we're a good fit for you going forward. I mean, we'll see how you do in the next few months but… we don't want to go down in flames with this new direction. Our engines and our reputation deserve better."

I smile and sigh in mock relief. "I'm so glad you aren't dead set on re-signing with us. The repeated battery issues has meant a massive reduction in power for some of our races. Sure, you fixed it, but it cost us. Imagine what Billy James could do with a better engine. I'm just itching to find out."

I leave him in the hallway, walking straight through the party and onto one of the balconies, which is blissfully free of people. Until Billy James shows up. I don't see him, but as I lean on the railing and look out at the beautiful Basque city before me, I can smell him. That's how I know he's there. The wind is blowing from behind me and picked up his scent. Billy has been wearing the same cologne since he was seventeen, it's this mix of something zesty like bergamot and something darker like leather and something light like honeysuckle. Yes, I've spent a lot of time thinking about this. Mixed with his pheromones, which must be stronger than Thanos, my body has never stopped reacting to … that traitorous whore.

"What?" I say sharply without turning around.

"Just wanted to say thank you," Billy replies, his tone low and soft but tinged with his perpetual amusement. Billy loves playing the carefree, daredevil. The dangerous jester.

I feel like this is some set up. Like he's about to tease me again and after that altercation with Don, I am *so* not in the mood. So I turn around, ready to tell him to go to hell, but the look on his face stops the words from coming out of my mouth. He looks sincere. He steps closer. He was already close, but now we're a couple inches apart and I have to tilt my head to look him in the eye. He smiles again, and this time, that jester-vibe is gone and it's all cockiness now. "I heard what you said to McDougal. I was in the men's room, and I have to say, you owned that douchebag."

"Thanks," I say, feeling off kilter by his kindness.

"McDougal tries to blame the drivers every time his engines fail," Billy shifts his weight more to his left and tilts his head down a little, moving it closer to mine. He lowers his voice to an octave above a whisper. "It's comforting you realize that."

I take a breath. It's shaky. I hate the way he always makes me feel...not uneasy, just off-balance. I hate it because it brings me back to being that naive teenager. Billy inches closer to me, or I inch closer to him, I don't even know. He's always been my bonfire, warm, mesmerizing, and enticing, and I've always been his moth. I avoid him like the plague because of that. But now I can feel his open suit jacket brush my arms and the wind blows my hair forward, and he reaches up and pushes it back over my shoulder before I can. His fingers linger by my ear. "And it was hot as hell too."

"Frankie," Nick's voice is hard and firm and causes both Billy and me to take a step away from each other. "You okay?"

"Yes." I reply and nod because my voice feels soft and I'm scared he didn't hear it.

He looks like he doesn't believe me. "Okay, well Bash has been looking for you."

"Thanks."

Billy's tongue slips across his bottom lip. Damn that asshole and his perfect face with his perfect lips attached to his perfect body with his perfect, annoyingly sweet tenderness wrapped in sexy arrogance. I brush past him, and I swear his fingers graze my wrist on purpose. Can a heart swoon? Because judging by the flutter in my chest mine just did.

Nick holds the door open and sticks by my side, a hand on my lower back, as he guides me towards my father. It's a good thing he's doing that too, propelling me forward, because I would have stopped dead if he wasn't. Because Dad is standing next to Dario and Rocco. *F-U-C-K.*

"I got you," Nick says calmly, sensing my stress level.

He does, I remind myself. When my dad first hired him, I was fresh out of rehab and Nick was a glorified babysitter, and we both knew it. He acted like it too—terse and annoyed with me most of the time. But one night, he saw me at a club with Rocco cornering me, and he swooped in and got me out of there because he read the body language radiating off me. And I told him everything about that night I 'overdosed', all the stuff my dad didn't know and even details I hadn't told Lucia. We've been on great footing ever since. He gets me. And because of that, I can count on him, and he doesn't let me down.

"Frankie, Dario says you haven't had a chance to say hello to him yet," Dad says with a smile. I see Lucia look over from where she is talking to someone at the bar, and she begins to walk toward the group. "I told him not to take it personally. The room and the world are eager for your attention now."

I smile. It's tight and uncomfortable on my face. Dario is irked. I have to placate him, and I know it. Forty-five percent is still a big chunk of the business and he's been friends with my father longer than he's been his partner. "Dario, you know I would never give you the cold shoulder. You're like an uncle to me."

A creepy uncle with a potentially creepier son.

I lean in and hug him. Nick's hand stays on my back, which I appreciate. Rocco is standing beside his father, arms crossed and a tumbler of rye in his right hand. He doesn't say anything, but the scowl on his face speaks volumes. His dad, on the other hand, has no problem being vocal.

"Frankie, I am not going to lie, your father's announcement was a shock. And his decision was without consultation..." Dario informs me. Lucia appears at my side, and Nick steps back a foot. He knows she can handle Dario and Rocco better than anyone. She opens her pink-painted mouth to speak, but Dario keeps talking before my sister can interject. "I'm not against it, per se. But I have legitimate concerns that I'm sure the media and the fans will also note. Like will you stay focused? Will you give it one hundred percent? Can you handle the stress? You've had your fragile moments before, Frankie."

"Fragile moments?" Lucia almost snorts she's so dismissive. "Isn't there a famous picture of you passed out with your head in a trophy after you won your first Grand Prix at eighteen, Dario? I doubt your antics back then are something you expect to be judged on now, am I right?" Lucia is laughing lightly as she says it, like it isn't a biting rebuttal.

"I never over... indulged on illegal substances," Dario snaps back.

Dad's brow furrows and Rocco glares at everyone, even his dad. His green eyes narrowed and cold, like moss covered in frost. He knows exactly what his father is referencing, but he gives no hint that he knows more than the tabloid version of events the night I almost died. It was his party and his dad rented the yacht. One of them might know something even if they don't realize it. I've never been brave or strong enough to ask.

I watch my father push his shoulders back and scowl. He hates when people bring up that night. "Well, almost dying in a bathtub on a yacht actually made me stronger, not fragile. And the past is not what I judge people by, Dario. It's the present. And presently, I am a magnet for big money brands. If I am, I'll make sure Billy and Antonio are too. We'll be rolling in sponsors. Turning them away. That's what matters, right?"

He takes a moment to absorb everything I've said and thankfully stops focusing on the horrible night his son found me aspirating on my own vomit.

"That is only part of what matters, Frankie," Rocco finally decides to speak instead of glare. "But it's not everything. If all the job required was a brand magnet, we'd hire a Kardashian."

"Didn't you date one of those?" Lucia asks. I place a hand on her shoulder, and she shuts up. But the damage is done. Rocco is seething.

I continue to focus straight ahead on Dario, because like it or not, Rocco doesn't have any real power with this team. "I've also got solid ideas for the engine and some race strategies that will have Billy and Antonio on the podiums. They'll win under me."

"I guess we've got no choice but to wait and see," Dario says with a resigned sigh.

"You'll be pleasantly surprised," I guarantee. I feel like a used car salesman, and I also feel like the used car being sold. It's exhausting.

"Time for fireworks!" Adelaide's excited voice fills the room.

Suddenly everyone is moving to the balconies and a second later the skies are illuminated by a colorful display. I have to admit it's a nice touch that has dad beaming. If Adelaide is faking this relationship, she deserves an Oscar. I watch for a minute but decide this is the perfect time to make my exit, so I glance around to make sure no one is watching me. But someone is. Billy.

He's on the opposite end of the balcony, leaning against the wall, and while everyone's face is upturned, pointed at the sky, his handsome mug is pointed at me. He smiles. I turn to my father and kiss his cheek. "I'm tired. I'm going to head home."

"Okay *ma louloutte. Je t'aime.*"

"*Je t'aime*," I reply and nod curtly at Adelaide before stepping off the balcony, Nick right behind me.

Lucia is the only one in the event room now. She's at the bar.

"Want me to leave with you?" she asks as she walks over to join me.

"No. You put on heels and a dress like once a year. Enjoy it," I reply and pull her into a hug. "My back is killing me, and I just want some alone time. Find me in the morning. If you get rid of whatever hook-up you find tonight in time for breakfast."

Nick turns away at that comment. Lucia, bold and candid as always, laughs.

"I'll try my best."

I pat her shoulder and blow her a kiss as I walk away. Nick tosses my sister one last look before following me toward the exit. These two dummies think I don't know what they've been doing on and off for six months.

At the car, he hops into the driver's seat after holding one of the back doors open for me. The drive from one hotel to the other isn't long in miles, but the traffic and non-linear route we have to take due to the winding street grid makes it ten minutes longer than it would be on foot. I would have walked, but Nick can't leave the car, and I can't walk alone in case media, or worse, follows me.

"You handled all of that brilliantly, Frankie," Nick says, and I catch his eye in the mirror.

"Thanks. It was exhausting," I mutter and glance out the window. It's late, but the streets of San Sebastian are still bustling. Tourists love this place, and so do I. Or at least, I did growing up. There's a bit of a sad feeling in my chest now when I'm here since my mom died.

My parents had a summer house here because my dad grew up just across the border in Biarritz, France, and his mother's family was from here. He wanted Lucia and me to have the same sun and surf filled summers that he did. Only, we barely got a few weekends here because my mother always wanted to be with him at races. So eventually, we abandoned the winter home and life in

France and made this our full-time home. It's why Lucia and I always call ourselves mutts when people ask about our heritage. On top of our mom being Italian and our dad being French, we grew up in Spain, and although we speak Spanish, French, and Italian, English is our strongest language because it's the main language of the sport which our family revolved around.

"I don't think you can do this, Frankie," Nick says, his French accent thick. "I *know* you can, so don't let all the misogynistic politics get to you."

"It's more than that, although that does suck." I sigh and lean my head against the window. "It's all the bad things it brings up. The lies and the what-ifs about that night. Taking this job means dealing with that every damn day."

"I know you don't want to hear it, but I still think that if you would just be honest with your father about exactly what happened—"

"No," I reply, the same way I always do when Nick makes this suggestion. "First of all, I don't know what happened. There's no way to know who drugged me or with what since the hospital just assumed I was a rich party kid who took too much Molly and didn't do the right tests. And my dad... he wouldn't be able to handle the not knowing. It would just destroy his relationship with the entire racing community because every single one of those hundred people on that yacht were there because of racing."

"I know you've told me before," Nick grumbles. "If you just let him think you'd done it by mistake, you could also make it better, by letting him think you got better."

I catch his eyes in the mirror again and smile. "Those six months in rehab and counseling in Switzerland were actually really therapeutic and helpful."

He pulls to a stop behind Londres where the valet takes the keys and Nick opens the door to the hotel for me. In the lobby, we pause by the elevators after he punches the button. I impulsively hug him. I don't do that often, so he startles a bit but then wraps one of his massive arms around me and pats my back. "Thank you for believing in me."

"Frankie, I don't spew bullshit, even to my boss. So I mean it when I say you are going to crush this job," he says quietly as I let go of him and step back. He turns back to the elevator and puts a hand in the door as it opens and I step in. He follows me and punches our floor. "That thing with Billy on the balcony, you need to debrief me on that?"

"No," I say and shake my head, pushing my hair back over my shoulders. I can't wait until I can shove it all up into a topknot not worthy of public eyes.

"Because it looked intense," Nick replies, blunt as ever.

"Everything with Billy always looks intense," I mutter. "He's a lot."

"He's still on the list," Nick says, like I need reminding. I do not. Not at all. And I give him a level stare to express that.

"Sorry. It just looks like you forget that sometimes. You avoid him for a reason. You don't know where he was that night you were drugged. He might have been at that party too."

"I haven't forgotten," I reply as the elevator pings and opens on our floor. As we wander down the hall, I rub my lower back with my fingertips. I need to do my exercises, which involve a pool. Nick knows it too.

"You're going to the pool?" he asks as we stop in front of the door to my suite. I nod. "I'll make the call to Jose and meet you up there in ten."

"Make the call to Jose, but you don't have to join," I reply, and he looks confused. "Jose doesn't let anyone but us break the rules, and the pool is closed, plus it's on the roof, so unless someone is in a helicopter, no one is going to know I'm up there or be able to get up there."

If I say I go somewhere alone, I do. Nick will strongly suggest otherwise if he feels there's a threat, and I will usually listen to him because he knows what he's talking about. He nods. "My phone is on if you need anything."

I lift my arm and point between my shoulder blades. "Can you get this?"

As I slip my key card into the lock on my door, Nick unzips the back of my dress.

"See you tomorrow."

"Text me when you get back to your room so I know all is good."

"Will do," I let the door close behind me.

Fifteen minutes later, I'm staring at the luxurious, black-bottomed saltwater pool on top of the hotel. It's magical at night, with the sound of waves crashing below and the stars sparkling above. I drop my robe and towel on a lounger as Jose, my father's personal concierge at the hotel, puts the bottle of prosecco in an ice bucket on the side table next to a champagne flute then steps back into the elevator. Only then do I feel my shoulders relax. I didn't realize they were tight.

I pour a glass of the fizzy wine, take a sip, and then put the flute down and take a deep, cleansing breath of warm, salty night air. I tie my hair up into that topknot I have been dreaming about for hours and walk over to the pool, point my left foot, and dip it into the water. It's the perfect temperature. The perks of a black bottom pool is the water gets warmer faster and stays warmer longer, so it's like bath water right now, despite the sun having been gone for hours.

I glide right down the steps and into the water up to my shoulders, and swim. Laps, breast stroke, for six lengths. Then I go through all the exercises I've been doing for almost two years since I started aqua therapy for the scoliosis that's been plaguing me my whole life. And last year the doctor told me I can add degenerative disc disease to the list of issues with my spine.

Tonight, it's a battle to get through it all. I shave a couple reps off each exercise, because it's so late and I'm exhausted, and then I prop my arms up against the side of the pool. I let my body float, tip my head back against the pool's edge, and close my eyes.

Then and only then do I let myself absorb the fact that I am doing this. I am Team Principal of Mirabella Racing. My father's baby. My mother's legacy. It's mine. I'm steering the ship. That little four year old girl with the ringlet pigtails is living her dream.

I smile.

And then I smell it… *him*.

"You lied to me."

My eyes open and there he is, Billy James, standing on the edge of the pool deck looking down at me. There's a towel around his waist. It's the only thing he's wearing. "How did you get up here?"

"You think you're the only one who gets VIP treatment, Francesca?" He smiles. It's lazy and confident, and between that and his scent dancing through the air, my nipples get hard.

"Jose knows not to let anyone up here when I'm up here. No one," I say and push off the wall so I'm floating farther away from him and that damn scent.

He walks around the pool deck, one hand lazily holding the knot on his towel, to the row of loungers where my robe and towel are. He turns slowly to look at me, the pool, and the view beyond, which is the perfect horseshoe shaped *Playa de la Concha* beach. "Jose must not have told Maria you were up here. Maria's my personal concierge."

I roll my eyes because I'm annoyed by the way his incredibly hot Aussie accent makes every word sound like he's flirting with me. "Well, I'll be sure to tell Jose this Maria woman is breaking hotel policy so B-List guests can swim with their girlfriends."

My eyes dart to the elevator because Clara is stepping off. She's in leggings and a cropped tank top showing off her perfect posture and ripped abs. The dark hair is pulled up in a high, tight pony like Ariana Grande, which is typical Clara. She stutter steps in her bare feet when she spots me but only for half a second, and then she's marching with the same easy confidence her boyfriend, or whatever he is, always has. I'm annoyed by her closeness to Billy and the tall, straight way she holds her back, something that I've never been able to do. I don't slouch as badly as I used to, but my posture is visibly off. And people tend to bring it up on my social media posts. "Why so lazy?" and "stand up straight sexy girl" and "why is your hip always out? Find a new pose girlfriend" and all that crap. Anyway, Clara's healthy spine is beyond the point. It would be petty to hate her because she's never done one single out-of-line thing to me.

She drops a key card on the lounger next to my robe and looks up at Billy. "Here's your new key card. See you tomorrow. If she doesn't drown you."

Without even a glance at me, she walks back to the waiting elevator. Billy ignores her and turns back to me. "You're not going to get Maria fired. You're not that type of girl."

"Oh really? You think you know what type of *woman* I am?" I ask and swim to the other end of the pool. He walks along the edge, keeping pace with me. For some reason his constant attention makes me try harder to make my technique perfect.

"I know exactly who you are, Frankie, and it's not a bitch who gets a hard-working concierge fired for placating her high-end customers," Billy replies, and the smile is back. "Also, I'm not B-list, and I don't have a girlfriend."

"Right, I'm the bimbo trust fund baby who has more followers than brains and will tank a race team and take your career with it," I mutter.

"You could be that girl… *woman*, yeah." Billy's long fingers, the ones that wrap around the steering wheel every second Sunday and control a car with over a thousand horsepower, are still toying with the knot on that damn towel. My eyes dart there, hold a moment too long on the bulge under the front, and dart back to the pool. To be fair, it's not my fault. He's fidgeting, and he's literally got a rock hard v made of muscle on either side of the knot acting like an arrow screaming *look down and center please*! "But you aren't going to be that girl."

"You don't know me at all. We've talked more today than we have in a decade," I remind him as I fight the urge to look at his exposed torso again.

Shirtless Billy is a sight to behold. He's lean, as all drivers are since their weight impacts the car's performance, but he's also *ripped*. I lick my lips as I reach the other end of the pool and grab the edge. Remember what Nick said… Billy is part of the reason I ended up almost dying. He's the reason I was at the party – because he ditched me. And for all I know, he was at that party too. There were hundreds of people there on the three level yacht. By the time Billy rounds the side of the pool to stand in front of me again, I no longer feel drunk on his presence.

"Not for lack of trying. You refuse to say more than two words to me. But that first night we talked for five hours straight," he says. Does he really think I don't remember? "You didn't leave that beach until the sun was about to rise. You shared a lot. I know you."

"We were children."

"Yeah but some things don't change, and you aren't the girl who gets a hotel worker fired. You also aren't a bimbo social media whore that is going to fuck this up," Billy says with the same confident tone he has in pre-race interviews. Like he's won the race before the cars are even on the grid. "I heard you schooling McDougal, remember? And I saw that sexy little smirk on your lips when I walked up here. You're not only capable of doing this job, you *want* to do this job. You're not going to fail at this."

"Oh I could still fail," I say as I lift myself out of the pool. I manage to do it gracefully but Billy doesn't step back. He's right there in front of me. Close. Too close, and I can barely hold onto my balance as I right myself. He reaches around and presses a hand to my lower back, ever so gently, just enough to keep me from wobbling and falling back into the pool. My wet skin is now dripping all over his dry skin. If he notices, he doesn't show it.

I can't help but note his eyes sweep the length of my body. He isn't even trying to hide it. I'm wearing one of the bikinis I did a photoshoot in earlier today in my suite. This one is aquamarine, like the color of his eyes. It's got an iridescent shimmer, just like his eyes do with the pool water reflecting in them.

The warm air swirls around us, bringing that scent of his into my airspace again. "You can't possibly be cold out here tonight. It's still hot as hell."

"I'm not cold."

"Your nipples are," he states, and my cheeks warm. "Or they've got other reasons for being so... perfectly perky."

Kill me now.

"I should slap you for that," I reply and storm off to retrieve my towel. "Keep your eyes off my nipples."

"Can I put other things on them instead?" Billy James is officially brazen and crass. And I don't hate it as much as I'm pretending to, which is a mistake. Why do I keep letting mistakes happen around him? "Like my hands? Mouth?"

Oh my God, why do I want to say yes? The urge is so overwhelming, I can't speak for fear I'll say it. I wrap the towel around my torso slowly, my back to him and scramble mentally to find my composure. "I'm sure your bed buddy appreciates you talking to other women like this," I tell him and reach for my glass of prosecco. "You're a pig."

He smiles. "FYI, bed buddies don't give a fuck what you say

or do with other people. It's not a romantic partnership. But also, Clara is *not* my bed buddy."

I roll my eyes before tipping my head to sip my drink. He's watching me, I can feel it. "Are you going in the pool or what? I mean, why else are you up here?"

He walks back over to me. "I like to swim alone."

"So do I, but yet here you are." I finish my glass. I'm mad at myself for it because I have a mandatory two drink maximum per night, and I just guzzled that first one so quickly I didn't enjoy it. I blame Billy.

"You don't drink, so this is a plot twist."

"I do drink. I was drinking the night you met me," I remind him. How can he forget sitting on that rock, listening to the waves crash, and sharing that bottle of pricy bubbly? I thought it was the most romantic thing ever at the time. Okay, even now in retrospect. It was unpretentious and authentic despite the cost of the bottle.

"Haven't seen a glass of booze in your hand since that weekend," he says, those big strong hands still fussing with the towel. Ugh, it's torture to keep my eyes off that area of his body. "You fake it."

"What makes you think that?"

"I've seen you order seltzers and juices at parties and I accidentally drank your Shirley Temple remember? I've watched you carrying around a glass and barely sip from it," Billy informs me. "Like the champagne tonight."

"I don't drink alcohol in public," I admit and drop down onto the lounger.

"Why fake it?"

"Because alcohol beverage companies pay good money for sponsorships."

"Isn't that false advertising then?"

I shake my head. "No because I do drink the products I pitch.

Like Midori. It's delicious. I just don't drink in public. I'm working a job, I don't need to get tipsy, and also, I don't trust other people to make my drinks."

He thinks about that for what feels like an eternity but is likely only thirty seconds and then, his voice low and his left eyebrow high, he asks. "What else do you fake, Frankie?"

I ignore the truck load of innuendo he just dumped at my feet. "Look, you swim, or whatever, and let me lie here and pretend you don't exist."

"If that's the way you want it."

"Yup."

"Okay. Remember, you asked for it." He moves over one step to the lounger where Clara tossed his key card and drops his towel.

Billy James is suddenly, unabashedly, *buck naked.*

And I don't even have the slightest ability not to stare at every beautiful, sculpted inch of him. He is also half hard and it's a *very* generous half. He turns to the pool but not before I catch the beginning of the cockiest smirk that ever smirked on his face. I wait until he dives under the water to let out a long, low breath and a "*Oh mon Dieu.*"

My jaw drops. Miraculously, I manage to close it before he emerges from the water. He gives his soaking wet hair a shake, like a wet puppy, and I feel the spray all the way over at the lounger. Then he runs a hand over his face, pushing the water droplets from the five o'clock shadow on his strong jaw, and the smirk re-emerges somehow more cocky than before. And speaking of cock... "Did I forget to mention I love swimming naked? It's why I wanted privacy."

"Jesus Christ Billy, you're out of control." I drop my towel, and start to shrug into my robe, intent on getting the hell out of here. "I can't have one freaking normal moment with you."

"Clara's not my lover," he says, casually, ignoring my rant as he bobs in the water. "Everyone assumes that, and I let them because you know better than I do that fighting rumors just makes them stronger. But Clara isn't my girlfriend or fuck buddy or anything remotely like that. In fact, I wouldn't get busy with her if she was the last woman on earth, and she feels the exact same way about me."

Well that stops my feet from moving toward the elevator. I look over my shoulder at him. Thankfully for my sanity, he's submerged from mid-torso down, and I can't see what I'm not supposed to see… at least not clearly. "Why not? She's fucking gorgeous."

"So what? You think I care about what's on the outside that much?" he questions, annoyance flickering over his face. "And spoiler alert, hot women are a dime a dozen in my world."

"Whatever." I sigh and force myself not to continue this conversation. "It's not my business anyway."

"While we're at it, you should know I didn't pursue you to get your dad's attention. I was going to get that with or without your help," Billy continues. "So other men might use you for your family ties, but I didn't. Like your assumption about Clara and me, there's not a lick of truth to that either."

"So, is that why you stood me up that night? Because you realized you didn't need me to get a spot on the Mirabella team? Okay. Thanks for finally clearing that up, I guess." I turn to grab the prosecco because I'll be damned if I'll leave it for him. But then he speaks and once again, leaving is the last thing on my mind.

"Tommy James wasn't just a four time world champion and Australia's most beloved sports star. He was an opportunistic douchebag who married my mom because it served a purpose." I glance over at him and his face is hard and angry, which is such a rare expression for him, it shocks me into standing still again. "Tommy grew up in Perth dirt poor. My mother's family had money. More than they knew what to do with. Her daddy, my gramps, could bank roll Tommy's career. He wasn't as good as I was on the track when he was younger. A late bloomer, as I'm sure you've heard the racing buffs say when they refer to him. So he needed something more to get him into F1. Like money. He knew if he came with built-in funding, it would help. He wasn't wrong."

I blink and study his face as his words sink into my brain. Billy has spoken of his dad before. In the media, he usually smiles and makes some flippant remark about how he's not even trying to fill his dad's shoes but is wearing his own shoes or some such bullshit. But he mentioned him to me that fateful night we spent together, and he didn't sound like this. I knew they hadn't been close and that hurt Billy, but when he talked of his famous father he didn't sound this callous. Something has changed.

"He never loved my mom," Billy continues matter-of-factly. "And he never loved me because I was just the cost of doing business to him. She wanted a kid, so he gave her one to keep her happy and her dad's wallet open."

He dives under the surface of the water and emerges at the pool edge closest to me. His eyes are somber. I find myself walking over to him, my robe blowing behind me. "Why are you telling me this?"

"Because it's the truth, and it's all I've got," Billy explains, the pool water tossing reflections all over his face, making it even more angular, rugged, and perfect. "I wouldn't have used you like he used my mom because I lived with the consequences of a devious move like that, and it is darker and more fucked up than you can imagine."

I stare down at him. He stares up at me, his face serene and so painfully handsome. This man… he's been doing it for me since he was a boy. That admission is hard and one I rarely allow myself to make because he's off limits for so many reasons already, and today we added another. "I'm your boss now."

"Not until next weekend, technically." Billy grins and swims away from me, towards the steps in the shallow end. "I mean, the official announcement won't hit the media until dawn and you won't actually get to boss me around until the next race, so that's when it will be real."

I'm unable to do anything except watch him, even when he starts up the steps naked and glistening in the moonlight. And when he turns towards me, I don't even try to stop my eyes from sliding down his body. He walks right up to me. He's half a foot away. He reaches out and gently pushes my robe off my shoulder on the left side. The right side follows and slips down my arm. I bend my arm at the elbows to catch it before it puddles on the concrete.

"You should come in for a swim. That's why you're here, isn't it?"

"I... no."

"Well then, what else are you here for? I might be able to provide it," Billy whispers.

"No. You... this... no." Just like Cinderella's chariot, my ability to speak full sentences seems to have disappeared after midnight.

"Your lips say one thing, but your nipples say another." Billy winks and that cocky smile on those perfectly symmetrical lips is back again in full force. Then, before I can even comprehend what's happening, Billy James grabs my robe near my elbows, and in one powerful tug, he's got us both tumbling into the pool.

Under the surface I kick and flail, the weight of the soaking terry cloth robe causing it to slide off my body and sink to the bottom of the pool. I pop up, and he's bobbing there, right in front of me, and so I slap the glassy surface with my hand and a sheet of water hits him in his face. I swim toward the pool stairs, yanking the elastic out of my soaking wet hair. But his hand wraps around my ankle, and he pulls me backward. I twist in his grip and kick at him with my free foot, which he also grabs. Then his hands are on my calves, my knees, my thighs… and I'm being pulled—legs apart—closer and closer until, boom. The space between my legs is rutted up against his torso, just above his…

"What the fuck is wrong with you?" I hiss, but it's hoarse and needy. Because my body wants him so damn much. I've had dreams of him, despite everything, since I met him. Dreams that leave me panting and my panties slick.

He's not rough with me now. He's gentle but firm as he walks us both through the water until my back bumps the wall. His hands remain firmly on my thighs, holding me in place, keeping him rutted up against me. This could very easily be construed as Billy attacking me, or being aggressive, but he isn't. I still have control, and to prove it I shove him away and he steps back, letting go of my legs. Once my feet hit the bottom of the pool, I expect to feel more grounded, but I don't.

"I'd never hurt you, Frankie," he says softly.

"Again?" I ask back.

He looks confused. Authentically confused. "I was a stupid kid."

"This can't happen."

"Frankie, if it doesn't happen tonight, it never will," Billy replies and steps up into my space again. He puts his hands on either side of me, gripping the pool edge. "Just let me touch you… make you feel good. I've wanted to do that since I first laid eyes on you."

I blink and refocus so I can take in his handsome face without it blurring. Earnest and pleading, he seems so clueless. Like he really doesn't know… I watch a droplet of water fall from his hair and slide its way down his cheek, careening left toward his lips. "Why did you ghost me?"

"I had a family emergency to deal with," Billy replies, his voice low and heavy. I feel it between my legs, and it's doing nothing to stop my nipples from standing at attention.

"I need more than that," I reply, my voice way more breathy than I would like.

"I know exactly what you need," Billy counters, and his hand moves under the water's surface, moving toward my breasts. His fingertips graze the front of my bikini top but I grab his wrist and yank it away. The slight touch he managed is like a lick of flames against my skin.

His arm goes limp and would have dropped to his side if my hand wasn't still circling his wrist. "My mother was obviously a wreck after Tommy died. At that point, she didn't yet realize her marriage was a sham. She was a regular grieving widow, if there is such a thing. But then…"

I wait. He says nothing for so long my heart starts to sink. He's not going to tell me. He's not going to let me in on the truth so this isn't happening. I let go of his wrist.

He grabs mine before I can turn for the stairs.

7

YOU'RE NOT THE BOSS OF ME, YET

BILLY

Frankie's hazel eyes seem darker, like pools of decadent caramel melting on a stovetop. She also, for the first time since I met her, seems needy. Desperate. If I tell her enough of the truth, she'll let me touch her tonight, *really* touch her like I've wanted to since laying eyes on her as a stupid kid. Because she wants me as much as I want her. That realization gives me the strength I need to continue talking. "My mum snapped. The very night after we met, when I was supposed to meet you again at the beach. She was back in Australia, freaking out because I was supposed to race for the first time since he died the next weekend, which is why I was in Monaco, as you know."

"You'd just rejoined your F2 team," Frankie whispers. "My Dad was excited you'd decided to come back and were supposed to race the next one after Monaco. He followed your career closely at that point."

"Because he was already thinking of making me an offer." I nod slowly. "Anyway Mum wasn't stable and she…"

Got news that confirmed my dad never loved her and had even given his heart to someone else…

"My mum tried to kill herself that weekend. My uncle found her unconscious on the floor of my childhood house after she swallowed half the medicine cabinet and called me as I was getting ready to meet you for that second date. Mum was in the ICU so I called my Team Principal and talked to my manager, who told the world I needed more time to grieve. Then I jumped on the next flight back to Australia, where I spent the next four weeks sorting out family shit, and visiting my mum in a mental health facility."

Frankie is wide-eyed as she takes this all in. It's weird that it feels like this is the first time she's heard any of this. We'd managed to keep my mom's situation out of the media, but my delayed return to racing made news everywhere. I missed out on the Barcelona and Amsterdam races. It made sports news around the globe, poor devastated son of a racing legend can't get back behind the wheel, blah, blah, blah. I'm shocked she didn't hear about it. But then I remember, Frankie overdosed too that very weekend and was shipped immediately to a rehab facility. She was there for months. By the time she reappeared, I was racing again, and it had already been announced I would move up to F1 the following season with Mirabella.

"I'm so sorry. I didn't know..." she whispers so quietly I can barely hear it above the soft night breeze and languid slosh of the water around us. "I was... I went away."

"I know," I whisper back and stop myself from saying more. I have questions. I always have since I heard the news, because the girl I'd spent twelve hours getting to know was strong and smart and confident and not at all someone with a drug problem so intense she would overdose twenty-four hours later.

She swallows hard and looks me dead in the eyes.

"I don't regret much in life, but I do regret that," I say, my voice low but even. "I feel like if I'd been there you wouldn't have..."

"I didn't," Frankie replies in a confident, calm tone. It's so matter-of-fact it's confusing. What does she mean? How can she argue the fact that she overdosed? She was found aspirating on her own vomit in a bath tub on a party boat. "I don't want to talk about that night."

"Okay…"

"I don't want to talk at all," she says. Then she reaches out and touches the pad of her thumb to my cheek, grazing the damp stubble by my jaw until she skims over my lips. I part them and wrap them around her thumb, my teeth slowly biting down on the tiny fleshy pad. She shivers with desire. For me.

"Not your boss?" she whispers, repeating what I told her earlier.

I let go of her thumb. "Not yet."

"You went home that night instead of meeting me. You left Monaco?"

"Yes. I went to Australia." I nod. "Frankie… I can't—"

"No talking," she snaps, gentle but firm.

I smile. "Okay. Then I'm going to kiss you."

"Good."

I don't even hesitate after that. My hands emerge from the water and slip into her tangled wet hair, gripping tightly on the back of her skull as I pull her face to mine. Our lips connect and I'm instantly tumbling into a vortex of lust I've kept locked tight inside me for nearly a decade. I knew I couldn't have her, so I refused to let it out, but now… on the brink of nails being put in the box that holds these feelings, nails in the form of Frankie Castera becoming my boss, I'm being given the chance to fling it open and release all the pent-up frustration, so you bet your ass I'm not holding back.

I am shaking. I want this – *her* – that badly. Our lips crash together, and I immediately open her mouth with the pressure of my own, and my tongue slides in. This kiss is worth the decade-long hiatus. But at the same time, I am kicking myself even harder for playing it so cool back at seventeen. All we did was kiss that night, and we even waited right until dawn to do it. It had felt so right back then, so different. I was having sex already and getting it easy and fast, but Frankie had spent the night giving me something I wasn't used to, a connection. So when she only gave me a kiss, albeit a searing one that wrapped itself around the deepest parts of me, and promised me there would be more if I played my cards right, I had nodded and acted cool. Because I thought in that very moment, that we had all the time in the world. I had no idea both our lives would turn upside down within twelve hours and never be the same again. I should have begged her for sex like a desperate forty-year-old virgin.

I'm going for it now, knowing tomorrow isn't guaranteed, and even if it was, by next week she's off limits forever. So I'm kissing her with the heat and passion of every lost moment, every regret, every secret, taboo thought I've had about her. And there have been more than I can count.

"That was a long time coming," she gasps as the kiss finally ends.

"So is this," I murmur, my lips precariously close to her ear, my stubble grazing her cheek. My hands grab her thighs again and I lift her up and rut myself right between her legs again.

This time she doesn't push me away, she pulls me closer. She wraps her delicate but powerful arms around my neck and tilts her hips as she hooks her ankles behind my back, and her core, covered only with the thin glittery fabric of her tiny bikini bottom, glides right over my exposed and achingly hard cock. My groan is guttural, like an animal snared in a trap, and it brings a victorious smile to her lips.

"Don't get cocky, love," I whisper, moving my mouth to cover that smile.

I kiss her long, hard, and rough. This is not how I expected tonight to end up. Not in a million years. But it's how I wished that first night, our only night, had ended. Hell, I've wished it a hundred times over in the years that have passed. God, this was worth the wait. She feels amazing pressed between my body and the wall of the pool, every inch of her skin sliding against every inch of mine. My dick is harder than the concrete pool deck, and as I bite down on her earlobe, she tilts her pelvis and rubs herself shamelessly along my shaft.

I cup her ass and yank her off the wall, walking us as fast as the damn water will allow over to the stairs. My toes stub the last step and I lean forward dropping her perfect ass onto the wide smooth concrete step three from the bottom. She spreads her legs farther apart and I'm able to slide right between them and up her torso, gliding mine against hers. I yank at her skimpy little bikini top. "Now let me give those nipples the attention they're begging for."

"Billy, you fucking egomaniac," she says flatly but her hands are weaving into my wet hair.

"Tell me you don't want it," I reply, fingers skimming the corner of her triangular top. "You drive this, not me. I'll stop right now if you command it. Say it."

Her silence is my dream come true and I grin at her before I close my eyes, tug the fabric away, and wrap my lips around her left nipple. She sighs so loud and long it turns into a moan, and I feel it in my tight, aching balls. Her puckered skin across my tongue is heaven on earth. It's also nowhere near enough. I snake a hand down that taut tummy to her bikini bottom. She thinks I don't know her, but I do. I know if I tear them off her body, like I want to, she'll freeze up. She's not a prude, but she's got boundaries she enforces like a bouncer at an over capacity nightclub. So I hold back and simply tug on them lightly and slip my hand inside. It's surreal, feeling her wetness on my fingertips while surrounded by water, but I do feel it. And it makes my dick throb.

I gently rub her clit and equally as gently bite her left nipple and she arches her back and my name leaves her mouth in a gasp. Her left hand floats through the water, and her fingertips reach for me and manage to graze my hip. The water swirls around my cock as her fingers almost catch it, but I pull away. My lips move up the column of her neck. "No baby," I growl and capture her wrist. "This is all about you."

"Why?" Frankie whispers back. There's frustration in her tone that makes me very happy. She wants me. "This is never happening again, let me make sure you enjoy it."

It's cute she honestly thinks that this is going to start and end tonight. We have been an unfinished chapter far too long to be written to completion in one damn night. I kiss her, stopping any further questions or protests, and slide a finger through her wet folds. Her back arches again and she moves her hands to wrap around my neck. Her legs part further and I press into her body with my torso as I add another finger and pump into her slowly, teasingly. "My God, James…."

"First name," I demand because I know it's a distancing technic. "My fingers are inside your body and I'm going to make you come until you see stars, so use my first name, Frankie."

"Argh," she groans, frustrated with my words or the fact that I am going so damn slowly. Either one is valid. "Just fuck me."

"I am, love," I whisper back and kiss her again, my thumb circling her clit while my fingers curve just the slightest bit inside her, pushing into that soft, deep, unmistakable button.

"*Billy…*"

Is it egotistical or insane that my name moaned out of her perfect lips is making me fight off an orgasm? I push my tongue into her mouth and develop a rough, but perfect rhythm with my fingers. She grabs my shoulders, nails sinking in as her back arches. "I want your dick," she manages to demand into the kiss.

"You're not the boss of me, yet," I remind her, curving my

fingers again in an effort to make her break. She shudders, losing ground on that edge she's metaphorically perched on, but she doesn't fall.

"If you don't fuck me now, you'll never fuck me." I think she thinks she means that.

"Francesca, you'll get fucked when you're good and ready." She's not ready. I mean, she is physically—my wet fingers and the way her pussy pushes and pulls against them is proof—but she isn't emotionally. And if I'm honest with myself, maybe I'm not either. I need to make this less frenetic, less passionate, less everything, in order to fuck her. Because it can never be an emotional act for me. I promised myself. Not until racing is over. Then my heart can play along with my dick.

And right now, as she fights to keep her eyes open and focused on my face, as she bites the bottom lip of that mouth that tastes as delicious as I remember, as she pants out her breath because of my touch, the seventeen-year-old boy who fell madly in love in five hours is fighting to remain in control. I can't fuck her tonight, even if she's right and I never get another chance. I can't.

Clarity surfaces through the fog of lust in her eyes. In a blink, one of her hands slips from my shoulder and with a splash of water suddenly her fingers are wrapping around my cock. I open my mouth to argue but she starts stroking me, and the words become a grunt of satisfaction. "I'm ready and so are you."

She strokes again and I thrust with her fisted hand around me. Our lips brush again, and she opens for another scorching kiss, but I am too busy biting back another groan. My fingers barely moving inside her now. All I can think about is replacing them with my dick. It wouldn't have to mean anything. It might be easier to seal the deal tonight instead of prolonging it. I know I said the chapter needs longer to be finished, but would a hasty ending be the end of the world? What if we don't get another night? The universe has proven it's a fickle bitch when it comes to us.

"I want to fuck you more than I want another championship," I confess.

"So do it." She strokes me again. And again. "I don't just want to ride your dick. I need to, Billy. Please. I've been ready since I was eighteen."

Oh God… I can't.

So instead, I smile and use my free hand, the one not inside her, to wrap around her wrist and pull her grip off my cock. If it could disown me, it would. "Let me double check that you're ready."

I pull my fingers from her pussy, take a breath, and sink. Submerged under water, I grab onto her open thighs and pull my face closer, opening my mouth and covering her pussy with it. She comes immediately. I feel it as soon as my tongue slides inside her and she spasms around me. I'm blowing air hot and hard out of my nose to keep from drowning, and I know I only have seconds so I press into her and she presses back, riding my face with abandon. Her salty taste mixes on my tongue with the water, and I know I'll have to do this again. Soon. I deserve to savor her. Just one more time… right before I fuck her. And then this will be done. Our race will be complete, and we'll both have won. Tonight, only she takes the podium.

I run out of air and burst to the surface of the water. She's lying on the wide stairs, her torso exposed, nipples still pebbled, her head tipped back as she struggles to calm her breathing. The ends of her long hair float across the surface of the water, and she looks like a mermaid… after it's climaxed thanks to a pirate's tongue.

"You look…" *gorgeous, heavenly, perfect*. "Satisfied."

"I'm not," she replies but it's too weak and breathy to be completely true. "I still want you to fuck me."

"Good because I still want to." And before I can add the most important part, which is 'just not tonight, love,' there is a ding. It's the very formal, very proper, and very terrifyingly intrusive ding of the elevator reaching the roof.

She hears it too and reacts the exact same way, with panic.

She bolts from the pool, managing to get all the parts of her swim wear back in the proper place, as I swim like an Olympian to the wall of the pool closest to the doors and press my body flush against the wall so whoever is about to step onto the roof won't see I'm naked. Thank God my dick is rapidly deflating so it isn't being crushed at full mast against the wall. My forearms flatten against the side of the pool deck just as Lucia steps off the elevator.

She's removed her make-up from the party and her dress. She's in an oversized Mirabella Racing shirt and a pair of lounge pants. Her hair, darker and curlier than Frankie's, is in a topknot like her sister sported before I messed it up when I pulled her into the pool.

Lucia's eyes land on her sister and her step instantly falters. I have no idea what expression Frankie is wearing, because she's behind me and I don't dare turn around. I'm gonna guess by the way Lucia's innocent smile falls, Frankie's expression screams 'just been fucked… kinda.'

"What is going on?" Lucia asks and then her eyes scan the entire roof, and land on me. They flare. I can see the whites around the dark brown color from here.

I stare back and hope I look as casual and innocent as I think I do. Lucia's eyes fly back to her sister and then back to me and then back to her sister. Yeah, okay, I look anything but innocent.

"What are you doing here?" Frankie demands.

"What are you doing here? With *him*?" Lucia counters.

"I… swimming. I always swim. You know that." Frankie

marches over to her towel and wraps it around herself like she's bundling up for a winter storm.

Lucia cocks one eyebrow and glares at me. "With *him*?"

"Not *with* him," Frankie argues. "But apparently, he swims too. The hotel only has one pool, Lucia. What can you do?"

Frankie tries to smooth her wet, tangled hair, gives up, and reaches for the wine bottle and glass. She's leaving. She has to, I get it, so why does it bother me? Lucia walks closer to the edge of the pool where I am, so I press myself closer into the side, trying to hide my nudity without being obvious. But it's obvious, and I'm about to give up and just pull myself up and out of the pool. Fuck it.

"Are you... unclothed?" Lucia asks, suddenly prim and proper like a nun or something. I can't help but smile as Frankie grabs her sister by the arm and pulls her back toward the elevator before I can answer the question. "Is that a towel on the bottom of the pool?"

"Have a nice night ladies!"

"Was he naked? I swear I saw ass cheek!" Lucia is saying as Frankie yanks her into the elevator.

As the doors swoosh closed, Frankie's eyes lock with mine and I wink like a cocky bastard. Because why the hell not? Then I quickly get out of the pool, grab my towel, and wait for the elevator to come back and take me to my room. Because my balls are bluer than the ocean and I need to get back to my room and jerk off to the memory of her coming on my face.

8

AUSTRALIAN OUTBACK

FRANKIE

"Go back to your room, Lucia."

She yawns and stretches like a cat. Not a house cat but like a tiger or a leopard or something. Seriously the woman is tiny, shorter than me, and probably weighs less too, but yet she somehow manages to take up more than half the California king. "Nope."

I glare at her in the mirror as I look over my outfit. "Okay. Then go to Nick's room. I'm sure he's got some morning wood you can polish."

Lucia sits up. Her eyes wide, her mouth open about to spit out some words of fake disgust or denial.

"Shut up. I have known for a while you two are fuck buddies."

Her mouth closes. She rolls her eyes, which is Lucia's version of a shrug. "Whatever. He's single. He's hot. He doesn't want commitment."

"Don't hurt him because I need him," I warn.

"Don't change the subject," Lucia replies and finally drags herself out of my bed. She slept there last night, hogging the covers and the space, because I wouldn't spill the beans on what was going on with Billy on the roof. "You are trying to slut shame me so I'll leave and then you can go back to naked water sports with Billy James."

"I was not naked," I remind her.

"Not at any point?" Lucia questions, her eyebrows raising.

"Not once was I completely naked," I reply and smile because I'm damn proud of the way I manipulated the truth.

"I want details. Lots of them," Lucia demands in a whine she hasn't used since we were pre-teens. "Come on! I'm the one who has been pushing you to do something—anything—with Billy James, and now that you have clearly ventured into the Australian outback, you aren't going to tell me?"

"Lucia, I'm about to be his boss," I argue back lightly. Too lightly. It's clear I don't take the argument seriously, so it isn't going to make her take it seriously either.

"One small detail."

She's on her knees now in the center of the bed making praying hands. It's like she's twelve years old and begging me for details of my first kiss. Back then she was a timid little thing who followed me like a shadow and used to have nightmares a lot, so I would find her sleeping beside me in the morning. I used to complain until our mom died, and then I learned to live with it. Lucia has always needed me, and I definitely need her.

"We didn't have actual sex," I relent, giving her something.

Of course she wants more. "What did you have?"

"A mind-blowing orgasm courtesy of his hands and mouth," I whisper, like the room is bugged, and she squeals so loud I'm not surprised when Nick knocks on the door to my suite.

"Frankie! I'm coming in!"

The door opens a second later, and his imposing frame is filling the entryway to the bedroom. He looks stern and fierce until he catches sight of Lucia in her pajamas, hair wild from sleeping, and a flash of something softer slides over his face. Shit. She is going to ruin him.

"Sorry! My bad. I got excited over some newly acquired information. No one is being attacked or anything."

Nick frowns but nods at her and turns to me. "Frankie, you have that meeting with your dad before we head to the airport."

I nod and twirl, my skirt billowing out, and my silky camisole top lifting to show a sliver of my abdomen as I lift my arms. "Unlike Lucia, I'm ready."

"I have nowhere to be," Lucia replies and flops back down on the bed. Her curls fan out on the pillow like silky springs. Nick is forcing his eyes to stay focused on me, not her. I can tell it's a struggle. "Dad isn't giving me the keys to the kingdom. Hell, he won't even give me the keys to a race car."

"Not true," Nick counters. "You're on the F2 team."

"And if I'm not on the F1 team by next year, I'm switching teams," Lucia announces. Her words are light and casual in tone, but her eyes say she is dead serious. "I've gotten offers. I'll entertain them if I'm not moved up, Frankie."

My stomach gets queasy just thinking about it. I know she has dreams, and I fully support them as a sister. But as a Team Principal? Is she the best option next year? Billy is better than her. Antonio isn't necessarily better, but he's as good, and he's already on the team. "Cutting De Luca loose to make room for you won't look great. People will say you didn't earn it."

"Fuck people," Lucia replies flatly and pulls herself up to a sitting position, her back against the ornate headboard.

"They already think I don't deserve the position, and if I promote you right away…" I let my sentence trail and Lucia's frown deepens.

"Let me guess, turfing James is off the table now?" Lucia asks and folds her arms across her chest angrily. "Because of last night?"

"It's off the table because he's better than you, Lucia." I reply in a factual tone. "He's currently a very close second in the championship run."

"And I'm holding a strong lead in F2, which I could also do in F1 if you people would just move me up," Lucia groans. "If I have to leave Mirabella, I will."

"Okay. Okay," Nick intervenes and looks at the giant hunk of metal on his arm. Seriously, who still wears a watch let alone one that looks like it weighs as much as a Fiat? "Frankie, you'll be late if we don't head down now."

"Fine." I huff out a tense breath and try not to glare at my sister. "I love you. See you next weekend. And *suerte*."

"Yeah, yeah," Lucia mutters but then she pauses and swallows hard, regaining her composure and sticking to our promise to each other that we started after our mom died. I always wish her luck for racing in Spanish. "*Baci*."

I smile and follow Nick out the door and down the hall. It isn't until we're in the elevator that he speaks. "She isn't ready, and if you force this, it will damage your career and hers."

"I know."

"But she's serious about the offers. She *will* leave."

I nod at my bodyguard turned business consultant. "I know that too."

I sigh and wish the elevator would reach the ground floor and keep on chugging. Head right down to hell because I probably have a better chance there than I do in this new job. "My mother always told my father don't let anyone or anything force you into a decision. Be patient, and the right choice will present itself."

"I hope Lucia heard that advice too and took it to heart," Nick mutters under his breath and I don't know if he's talking about her racing threat or their fling.

The elevator doors slide open, we step into the lobby, and he walks just a little behind me as I sashay my way to the meeting.

There are people filming me on their phones. Race fans and reporters likely, although no one is technically supposed to be in here if they aren't a guest. The hotel has a hard time policing it when my dad is here, and the retirement announcement must be making it even harder.

"Frankie, a question," a dude in a ratty t-shirt and faded jeans says as he approaches me, stepping directly into my path so I have to stop. Nick steps in front of me immediately, but it doesn't stop this guy from blurting out his question. "What do you say to the comment that people who pose half naked on Instagram every five minutes maybe shouldn't try and run a race team?"

I open my mouth to answer but Nick does it for me. "What do you say about getting charged with trespassing?" He snaps his fingers. He has a way of doing it that is the loudest I've ever heard. The blonde woman at the front desk snaps her head up. She motions for the doormen to leave their post and handle this.

"Nothing?" Dude says with a sneer, ignoring Nick and baiting me.

"A general rule of thumb is not to feed the internet trolls," I reply and Nick bristles in front of me a little, which is a sure sign he thinks I shouldn't have said a thing. "Race fans are passionate and opinionated, but the real ones will be cautiously optimistic. And I won't let them down."

"What about drivers? Are you calling them internet trolls?" Dude says as the two doormen flank him and one announces this guy, and all the Randoms still filming me, must produce room key cards or leave. "Because this is a quote from Billy James."

Nick has already led me, with a gentle hold on my elbow, around this guy, and I'm almost to the restaurant doors when he calls out this tidbit of information. The sole of my shoe literally squeaks on the marble floor as my step falters. Nick's firm hand on my elbow keeps propelling me forward, inside the restaurant, before anyone can see the horror on my face. And the pain.

"He did that?" I whisper to myself more than to Nick.

"No idea. But I'll investigate while you…" his voice trails off to nothing, and as soon as I spot my father at his usual table, I know why. He's not with Adelaide, like usual. Instead the round table is crammed full of chairs holding testosterone. Rocco and Dario Conti, Antonio De Luca, and Billy James.

The mouth that was on my pussy less than eight hours ago is pulled into a smug smile. My heart tries to do a backflip but with the confusion the reporter caused, my brain is holding it firmly in place. The result is a clusterfuck of conflicting emotions that make me feel nauseous.

I force my eyes from Billy and march over to my dad. "Father," I say, indicating I'm pissed. "Is ambushing me you're new hobby in retirement?"

"Sweetheart, you're going to have to expect that every meeting will be a team meeting going forward," Dad says and stands to kiss both my cheeks. This is when I hate being European, because all the other men stand and I'm expected to double kiss every single one of them. It's custom.

I lean across the table to make the kissing rounds. One of the only things I wanted covid to change forever was this tradition, but it didn't. Billy is at the total opposite end of the table, back to the curved glass window, so I kiss Rocco who is next to my dad and Dario next to him then move to my right to do the same to Antonio and then act like the table is this Grand Canyon sized obstacle and lean over it just the slightest and blow Billy air kisses. "Gentlemen, sit. Let's chat."

"Rocco and Dario still have concerns about this change in administration," Antonio says, his Italian accent heavy. He's a good driver but lacks the confidence Billy has both behind the wheel and in life. Billy. Did he give that quote before or after he gave me the best finger fucking of my life? Either way, I'm equal parts angry and humiliated.

"And you, Antonio?"

He levels me with a point-blank stare. His brown eyes are darkened by concern. Not sure if it's concern over what to say or how I will react. Antonio clears his throat. "I have doubts, Frankie. I'm sorry. But I'll continue to try and win. As long as you are on board with that, I'm on board with you."

"I'm on board," I confirm with a nod. I turn to Rocco and Dario and wave a hand toward Antonio. "What more can I say to you two?"

"Francesca," Dario says, pausing to clear his throat. "It's been a long time since you've shown any kind of interest in this business. Whereas Rocco, he's been in the trenches his whole life. He's ready to slide over to Principal, and we always assumed he would."

"I have never left the business mentally, Dario," I counter. "Rocco is doing an excellent job with the engineering side of things. It's what he went to Oxford for if I remember correctly. But if he's looking for a new job, I think he would also make an excellent sporting director. So perhaps you should consider retiring like my Dad and giving him your job. Because he isn't getting mine."

"He has worked hard for a shot at Principal," Dario replies, voice firm and even. "And he hasn't spent years parading around the internet in lingerie or trying to design high heels."

"What a coincidence, neither have I," I snap, and I hate myself for it. I need to stay even, calm, unaffected. Because even though he just tried to demean me, if I get angry about it, then it builds his argument. Women in power don't have the luxury of showing emotions without being shamed for it. "My shoes are all flats, not heels. I walked in the Victoria Secret show, so yes, I wore underwear and it was streamed. I do believe Rocco has more than one topless workout photo on his Instagram, and it's not to promote anything other than his pectorals. And aren't you the one that insisted Billy take that *Men's Health* cover last year? The one he did bare chested with his race suit hanging off his hips?"

"That was—"

"Work. I know. And so was what I did… do. But somehow, when a woman does it, you dismiss it. I think it's time for your views to open up a little Uncle Dario." I stand. "Because the simple fact is, I am not going to be removed from this job based on your assumptions or outdated opinions. I'll leave if I fail, which, spoiler alert, I will not. Now, I'm heading to Milan to wrap up a promotion deal I have ongoing with a designer, and then I will see you all at the next race where my abilities will speak for themselves."

I lean down to kiss my father again. He cups the side of my face. His hand is warm and reassuring.

I leave without looking back, without a faltering step, and sadly without telling Billy James to go fuck himself. But in a way, I guess he did me a favor. Because now Billy James will never get his hands or anything else in my swimsuit ever again.

9

———

HELL NO

BILLY

"Was it that bad?" Clara asks me as I walk back into the hotel room. Like the perfect personal assistant she is, Clara already has my bag and hers packed and waiting at the door. She's in a charcoal gray tracksuit, her hair pulled up in another tight, high ponytail. "Your face doesn't look happy."

"She basically acted like I didn't exist," I reply and fight the scowl that wants to dominate my face. I know if I act too upset about this, Clara will ping like an Apple Alert on my watch. She was up my ass when I got back to my suite. I don't know what about my face said 'I just tasted heaven' but something did because she kept asking questions. And then I had to kick her out, and wouldn't tell her why I was doing that, so she was really annoyed. The fact is, I had to jerk off but telling her that was off the table, obviously.

"So she ignored the drivers?"

"Not the drivers. The driver. Me." I interrupt before Clara can find the right insult for Frankie's behavior. "She talked to Antonio but she couldn't even be bothered to lean across the table to greet me properly."

Clara's wide, dark eyebrows shoot up. "She ghosted you. How horrible."

Her tone is deadpan. She's mocking me. Because I treated Frankie like that, and Clara knows it. Clara knows everything. So my response is equally deadpan. "Ha. Ha. I wish I wasn't so loose lipped with you."

"But you are." She smiles. "That's what sisters are for."

I grumble and there's a knock at the door that I almost don't hear because Clara is laughing. Cackling actually. I stomp over to the door, expecting the bellhop who has come to collect our luggage. We have a flight to Barcelona in a little over an hour. But instead, I'm greeted by Bash filling the doorway. He's smiling sympathetically. "My boy! Do you have a moment?"

I nod and glance over my shoulder at Clara. She walks over and pulls up the handles on both our bags. "I'll bring these down to the lobby myself and wait for you there."

Bash gives her shoulder a squeeze as she passes him and she smiles. Then he marches past me into my suite. He walks right over to the window and stares out at the ocean view, smiling. I close the door behind Clara and wait for him to speak. After exhaling a deep breath, he turns to me. "Frankie will come around."

I try not to react. I am afraid any facial expression I give him will scream '*I had sexual relations with your daughter.*' Instead, I avert my eyes to the blue waves just beyond his shoulder and I shrug. "It is what it is."

"Look, I don't know why you two have never gotten along, but she knows you're our best driver. She's told me flat-out in the past," Bash says and crosses the distance between us. "She'll come around, and if she doesn't, I'll talk to her. Frankie is passionate and a bit outlandish at times, but when it comes to this sport, she's beyond capable and has impeccable instincts. If she could have been a driver, she'd have been better than me."

"But she didn't want to drive. She wanted to manage?" I question and Bash looks conflicted.

"It's a long story," he mutters and waves a hand in the air but says nothing else.

"Okay. Well, for the record I don't hate her or anything. I've never had an issue with her. I just…"

"You keep yourself walled off from everyone because of the secrets you're keeping for your mom," Bash nails it. "I think Frankie knows you're keeping something from her… from the world, and she's leery of you."

I shrug again. He's sort of right. I know that Frankie is mad because I ghosted her when we were kids and I haven't been completely honest about that. But I thought after last night she had enough of an answer that I wouldn't need to explain *everything* to her. "Well, Bash, respectfully, I have a right to a private life."

"Yes, but you confided in me that Clara was your sister," Bash reminds me.

"Because I knew you were watching me, looking to put me on your team, and I was going to have to skip races," I explain and try not to sound short, but I hate talking about the past. All of it but especially this part. "And I knew you'd see through bullshit, so I had to tell you my mom tried to take her own life when she found out my dad had a love child with another woman and that he wanted to leave the love child half his estate."

Bash's eyes, the same amber flecked *cafe au lait* color as his eldest daughter, grow soft. "I always hoped you'd be able to talk about it with less venom by now."

"I don't think that will ever change, Bash," I reply and hate that it feels like I'm disappointing him. He's the closest thing I've ever had to a father. He was the dad that Tommy James could never be, at least not to me. Clara has much fonder memories.

"And I don't think I can tell Frankie. At least I'm not ready to right now."

"Even if it improves your relationship?"

I just shake my head and run a guilty hand through my hair. Bash blinks and nods, accepting my answer even if he doesn't agree with it. God, I love this man. "Please don't take this as a reflection of my thoughts on your business decision because it's not. I'm sure Frankie will do great once her feet are under her. But… I'm going to miss you in the pit and you know, around."

Bash smiles deeply, causing creases by his eyes, and he yanks me into a hug. He slaps my back lovingly. "I'll always be there in the stands and you can call or text anytime. You know you're not getting rid of me."

"Good!" I grin as we break the hug.

He claps my shoulder. "You know, people are sending her flowers and gifts to wish her luck and congratulate her. Maybe a small token from you will smooth things over a bit?"

I thought the orgasm I gave her did that, but okay. "I'll try and send her a little something."

"Good. Well, whether you decide to tell Frankie or not, I know you two will sort it out. I have faith in you both."

He leaves me alone in my suite, and I watch from the doorway as he marches confidently down the hall. Adelaide is waiting with the bodyguards by the elevators. She's perched on a settee wearing one of her typical vintage dresses. She stands as soon as Bash approaches and she kisses his cheek. I can't help but notice, as they step into the elevator, that his hand moves to cup her midriff. And she tips her head to lean it on his shoulder where he kisses the top of it again.

I know people think these two are some sort of stereotypical delusional old perky man and gold digger, but I've honestly never seen anything that backs that up. They seem to have a genuine affection for each other that I hope to have with… someone. One day. I mean not now, but later in life. Hopefully before I'm Bash's age though.

Clara is standing by the front doors, waiting for me. She tilts her head and lowers her sunnies on the bridge of her narrow nose. "What are you thinking about?"

"Frankie Castera." An idea hits me and I grin. "Do you know where I can get a stuffed panda?"

Clara doesn't follow as I breeze by her, scooping my bag from her hand and wheeling it along beside me. I would take hers too, but Clara hates when dudes do chivalrous things for her. "What the hell does a stuffed panda have to do with Frankie?"

"Long story. I guess I could get one on Amazon."

"Don't get distracted by your dick or some such nonsense," Clara warns. "Make sure your head is in the game, Billy. You've got a championship to win."

AND LESS THAN seven days later, I definitely have my head in the game as I get out of the car Mirabella Racing supplies for me at each venue and make my way to the paddock. Of course, there's a handful of photographers snapping away as I walk, Clara just a smidge behind me. She hates being in photographs, which is ironic because she's the better looking of Tommy James' two kids. Clara has my dad's sharp cheekbones and hazel eyes but she has her mother's delicate nose and tanned skin and raven colored hair. She's got Tommy's height though. She's only two inches shorter than my six feet.

"Billy, how confident are you in your new Principal?"

I smile. It's large and easy but it's my only response. I know these guys too well, and some of the more rabid fans can twist any comment into something it's not. We reach the gate, and I sign autographs for almost fifteen minutes until everyone who wants something signed has it. I don't deny my fans anything. Their support is a vital part of my career, and I don't pretend otherwise. Antonio blows them off occasionally, and I keep warning him it will bite him in the ass one day. Neither one of us can deny that Lucia is gunning for one of our seats, and the fans always loved the Casteras. Getting one of them back in the driver's seat of an F1 car is the stuff of most fans' wet dreams. And the fact that it's a smoking hot female adds to that. Sure, some are Neanderthals with cave men 'women shouldn't be driving' mentalities, but most, if they live in the modern world, at least think it would be cool.

So I work the crowds wherever I can to keep me in their hearts so that when one of us has to go to make way for Lucia Castera, I'm not the one they volunteer as tribute on social media and news posts. I'm luckily having a better year than Antonio too, which doesn't hurt. I usually do. To be honest, when Mirabella signed him a few months before me, I was shocked. And the fact that he's remained with them this long is also a head-scratcher to a lot of people, including me. Antonio isn't consistent in his performance, and it took him a long time to really find his groove at this level. A lot of teams wouldn't have given him that kind of time. Bash has insinuated more than once over the years that the loyalty to Antonio is Dario's, not his.

Clara is carrying a bag full of my essentials as we clear the fans and press and make our way between the rows of trailers emboldened with the various logos of the teams and painted in their team colors. Red for Ferrari, Green for Mercedes, Mango for McLaren, and Ocean Blue for Mirabella. We're positioned dead center, across from Red Bull and in between Mercedes and McLaren.

Antonio, speak of the devil, is standing in front of the main doors to enter our two-story paddock, which is made up of five adapted storage containers stacked on top of each other, and include a conference room, private rooms for me and Antonio, a crew lounge, and a cafeteria. It's a beast. Our European set-up always is. "Hey," Antonio grunts at me. "Are you ready for this shit show?"

"I'm always ready for anything on race weekends," I reply calmly. He is anything but calm. His face is creased with worry and stress. The one piece of advice good old cheating Tommy James ever gave me that I've bothered to hold onto is 'Don't sweat the small stuff. And it's all small stuff.'

Antonio's got these really strong features: roman nose, wide-set eyes, jet black hair. And it makes his frowns look like scowls. He folds his arms across his chest, which is clad in a Mirabella Racing T-shirt. He looks so annoyed. "Word of advice," I tell him as I reach for the door. "Frankie is amazing at picking up on the energy around her. Yours is negative and impossible to miss. I'd change that if I were you."

"She's definitely going to turf one of us when this season ends." Antonio follows me inside, not bothering to wait for Clara to enter before him. I get it, he doesn't know she's my sister, but she's still a woman, and letting her enter first is just simple politeness. Clara rolls her eyes but says nothing. "She and Lucia are best friends, not just sisters. She'll give her whatever she wants. One of us is screwed."

"We'll see," I mutter as I reach my dressing room door. I pause and allow Clara to enter first.

"Hopefully, when we start losing races, Dario or Bash has the common sense to pull the plug on this nonsense and send her back to modeling bikinis," Antonio says as he reaches the door to his own room.

He disappears inside before I can say anything, which is fine. I don't have much to say to him. Insecure asshole is the only thing that comes to mind, and that's not going to help anything. I sigh and go inside. Clara is already setting up her stuff beside the couch.

I grab my race suit out of the closet and head into the bathroom to change. When I'm done, Clara and I run through a few stretches and exercises, mostly for my neck, and we head down to the garage. Practice session starts in less than ten minutes, so everyone is bustling. My eyes fly straight to the monitors. There's a row of five seats in front of them and they're all occupied. It's the middle seat that holds my gaze. The one containing the only female. Frankie is perched on the seat, leaning forward, and Dario is talking beside her. They're both gesturing wildly, her at the screen, which appears to be showing some kind of previous race footage, and Dario at Frankie.

I walk right over. As soon as our eyes connect over Dario's shoulder, Frankie stops speaking. She just stares. What I don't see in her eyes is even a flicker of acknowledgement of what transpired between us a week ago. It was good for her, not just for me. I know it. I felt it around my fingers and on my tongue. But clearly not good enough if she can pretend it didn't happen this easily. I'll have to work harder next time. And there's also no glimmer of a smile over the gift I sent her, which was a genius idea if you ask me.

"Dario, Rocco." I nod at them as they turn to Frankie and I say, "Hi boss."

That softens her a fraction. "James. The team's probably ready for you."

She tilts her head toward the car parked a few feet away with my number 87 on the front and about ten people gathered around it, tweaking and fussing with various parts. I nod and am about to shelve my need to talk to her, to touch her, to wear down that Teflon resolve of hers, but then Dario speaks. "Before you jump in the driver's seat, Billy, maybe you can help us solve a debate."

"Always willing to help."

"There's a forty percent chance of rain on race day, at the moment," Dario explains. "We're debating tires."

"So intermediates are a must," I reply without even thinking about it. "But at forty percent I'd also personally like the blues on hand."

"But forty percent is low," Rocco says, although he's barely opening his mouth. His jaw is clenched, so I'm thinking he is not the one that is on my side of the debate.

"Yeah, but Barcelona has a history of moderate showers turning into unexpected downpours, so I mean, it is a bit of a gamble, but do we want to be stuck out there without blues if we have standing water?" I ask innocently. "We may be down a set if it doesn't rain, but I can go the distance on intermediates in dry conditions."

I finish speaking and Frankie's beautiful, fuckable mouth spreads slowly into a grin that is equal parts proud and smug. Rocco then stands abruptly, his stool scraping against the concrete, and he marches away from the garage, muttering something about water. But there's a mostly full bottle beside the seat he just vacated.

Dario rolls his eyes and stalks off.

Frankie looks at me again and smiles. It's brief, but I take it as a win. I wasn't trying to purposely side with her. I just voiced my honest opinion, but it's reassuring she thinks like I do. We might end up making a good team on the track, not just in a pool after midnight.

I take this opportunity to get a good look at her outfit. All race team employees wear their team's clothing on race weekends. Frankie somehow, in a week, had a custom jumpsuit designed. It's a nice, pristine white with the Mirabella ocean blue trim. It's form-fitting, clearly custom made to hug every curve, and it's lowcut. Her perfect cleavage on display. She wears turquoise earrings that match our logo. She looks… like she should be pinned up on my childhood bedroom wall.

"I see you managed to find some race gear," I say under my breath so no one overhears. "I bet you're the only Team Principal fans jerk-off to."

"Does that bother you?" she mutters back out of the corner of her mouth, keeping her eyes focused straight ahead as she sits back down in her seat at the pit wall.

"I don't care who jerks off to thoughts of you," I whisper back and lean my ass on the table in front of her so we can face each other. "As long as I'm the only one you think of when you masturbate."

Her cheeks pink. "Billy, not here. It's my first day."

"I know. I sent you a welcome gift and an apology." I lean back on my elbows.

"Yes. The pompous panda." Her smile is so subtle but fucking sexy. "Nice gesture, but do you even know what you're apologizing for?"

"Billy!" Joaquin, our Chief engineer calls my name and waves me over to where he's standing at my car.

"Duty calls," I say begrudgingly and leave her.

We go through all our pre-practice checks and discussions, and then I head back to my room to get into the rest of my gear. Clara follows me back out to the garage. I'm not sure what happens next, I realize.

Bash and Dario always spent the fifteen minutes before a practice giving Antonio and me directions on how to handle the track. Bash always made sure to let me speak my mind too, but generally, they have a good feel for what I should and shouldn't be doing. Both are former drivers, so I heed their advice even if their time in a car was decades ago. They also do ample homework, studying the track every year before the race. Of course, so do I, including simulation races.

Frankie walks over, and I fight like hell not to let my eyes slip to her perfect tits. "We're gonna let you do what you want here."

"What?"

"You've run a simulation or two already?" she asks, and I nod. "And I'm sure you remember how things went last year, and they've made no modifications to the track since then. So we're going to let you take this practice and run with it. Do whatever you think feels right, and then we'll meet after and break it down."

"Okay…" I sound hesitant but I'm not, so I nod and add, "New strategy and I respect it. Thanks."

"You're welcome," Frankie says with a brief, restrained smile. When she turns away, she adds something I know she knows I can hear. "At least someone appreciates it."

I assume she means Antonio is pissed about it, which after the practice, I find is an understatement. After I get out of my gear, get a bottle of perfectly chilled water from Clara, and change into a pair of team track pants and a Mirabella T-shirt, I head to the conference room on the second floor. Antonio is already there. He had a shitty practice and spun out on turn three.

"It's hard with the Chicane right before it," Rocco is saying. "You have to really manage the brakes, Antonio."

"This is where it differs from simulation," he barks and glares at Frankie for a moment before turning back to Rocco. "This is why Bash and Dario's advice is pivotal."

"Any damage?" I ask to announce my arrival. Everyone turns to face me.

"Car is fine," Rocco pipes up. He's the only person actually sitting at the conference table. Dario and Frankie are standing in front of it, chairs behind them, like they had been sitting at one point. Antonio is pacing back and forth by the sliding glass doors that lead to the deck on the front of the building that is shared with the cafeteria and lounge across the hall.

"It's just Antonio's ego that got dented," Frankie says, and Dario frowns at her as Antonio blows up.

"With all due respect, I'm not going to be patronized by you."

"Oh come on, Billy did fine," Frankie argues, and I stare at her, begging her to meet my eye before she makes this worse. Luckily, she must feel my eyes boring into her because she does glance over, and when I give my head the slightest little shake, the kind I hope no one else notices, she blinks. Then when she speaks again, her whole tone has changed and it's less dismissive. "If you're more comfortable with a little guidance from Dario pre-practice then we can continue that hand-holding. You can even call my Dad if you want."

"Great," Antonio mutters and finally sits across from me at the table.

We go through the rest of everyone's thoughts on the practice session and our ideas on strategy going forward and I have to say, Frankie knows what she's talking about. And I appreciate that we were allowed to make our own decisions out there to start, and she's open to my ideas now. Antonio isn't me. He's always craved Dario and Bash's decision like an orphan in need of a father. I'm not that guy. This is going to work out well for me, I think.

After an hour and a half, we wrap up. Frankie thanks Antonio and me, and without so much as a smile, she leaves and everyone else does too. I head to my dressing room where Clara is blaring Eminem and eating a rice cake. I wrinkle my nose. "You should gnaw on the drywall. Probably tastes better."

"If you ate more rice cakes, maybe you wouldn't have to worry about your weigh-in at the beginning of every season," she snarks.

"My weigh-in issues are because I'm such a fucking stud. All muscle and almost too tall for this damn sport," I remind her. I love weight-lifting, which isn't a great hobby for this sport, and I'm six feet tall, which means a couple more inches and I wouldn't be able to fit in the car. Clara herself is almost five ten, just like Tommy was.

I throw on some street clothes and mull over what to do tonight. Tomorrow is another practice day, so I can have a little fun tonight. Just a little. Clara drives us back to the hotel. By the time she hands the keys to the valet, she's totally read my energy. "So, club or restaurant?"

"Club," I say.

"I'll change and then meet you in the hotel bar in fifteen," Clara says.

Two hours later, I'm buzzing on some beers and a couple shots of tequila as I sit in a smooth leather booth and look through the glass partition that separates the VIP area from the dance floor. Clara is down there shaking her money-maker, and my urge to scowl has never been stronger, but I fight it with another shot of tequila. I've scowled at my sister's dance moves before, and people have caught it on their camera phones and labeled me a jealous boyfriend. And then I want to hurl, so I'm more careful about my facial expressions now. I scowl because she's my sister, and watching her bump and grind is gross.

"Worried?" a voice says, and my head swivels, and I find Frankie standing in front of me. She looks like a walking wet dream in a clingy, shimmery deep purple dress. Her hair is loose and wavy, and her lips are painted a dark, sexy red.

"About the race? No," I reply. "Join me."

"I'm not joining you," she responds without even thinking about it. "You're busy making sure no one macks on your girl, and I wouldn't want to distract you."

"That's not what I'm doing at all," I reply and clarify. "I'm making sure whoever hits on her isn't a fucking predator because she's my friend, and I care about my friends."

"Uh-huh. Sure." She says it like she doesn't believe me, but something softens in her expression.

I pat the plush leather seat beside me. "Join me."

"No."

She turns to leave. "Okay then, join me at the hotel pool later."

"Hell, no." She retreats back to the table she's sitting at with Lucia and Jennie, who has her face buried in her phone.

She was firm in that hell no response, but I decide to go to the pool anyway when we get back to the hotel. The Four Seasons has basically the entire F1 staying in their two towers, east and west, that are joined in the middle at the fourth floor by the amenities. An indoor pool, a gym, a spa, and a few conference rooms.

Clara, despite the fact that her room is in the east tower and she usually takes her own elevator, walks to the west tower and waits for the elevator with me. When it arrives, she steps inside when I do, and I raise both my eyebrows. "This have anything to do with your disappearance?"

She had disappeared for about an hour off the dance floor when I went to the bar to order another beer and got locked into a conversation with a guy from our pit crew. Clara stares straight ahead, arms crossed over her chest. "Mind your business, bro."

I open my mouth but force it to close before I can say anything. She's right. Her sex life is not my business, and although I worry about her, I also trust her to know what she's doing. Also, Clara has a black belt in Tae Kwon Do. I know because after my dad died, I made sure the estate kept paying for her needs, educational and otherwise. She doesn't get off the elevator at the fourth floor, which would be the last way she could make it back to her tower and her room. I get off on my floor, which is the second from the top, but she hasn't hit a button or gotten off. I step out and block the door from closing. "Have a safe, fun night."

"Thanks. You have a fun night too, but don't do anything

stupid," Clara adds as I move my hand from the doors and they start to close. "Like your boss."

"My boss is not stupid!" I protest but the doors are closed.

Fucking hell. She knows me too well. And she isn't wrong. Although Frankie is far from stupid, meeting her at the pool is a very dumb idea. Nothing good can come of it. Well, I mean the sex that will come from it will be good. But that's about it. The rest… it could be disastrous. But damn if I don't want it anyway.

I quickly change out of my club clothes, throw a robe over my bare body, shove my feet into some slippers, and head to the elevators again. I had planned ahead, and my personal concierge Pamela had granted my key card after-hours access to the amenities when I checked in. It's no rooftop ocean view pool, but it's decent. The walls are frosted glass to keep peeping eyes from nearby apartments and offices from glancing in. At night, the window frames glow a pale pink thanks to led lighting. The pool is a simple, saltwater thing. Rectangular with a shimmery pearl tile. Tucked into the corner of the area, almost unnoticeable, is a cave-like room. It has walls made of mineral rock, heated marble floors, and double-wide plush loungers spaced evenly against the back wall that also has a waterfall. Pamela must have turned it on, anticipating I would be using it.

At least, that's my first narcissistic thought, but then I see two tiny, high-arched feet on the tip of the farthest lounger. The delicate toes covered in perfect glittering seafoam green polish. I walk toward those delicate feet, trying not to smile in victory. Frankie will hate the smugness of that. My dick, on the other hand, is already celebrating, straining excitedly against the soft terry cloth of my robe. My eyes slide up her smooth, sculpted, bare calves and my mouth actually waters when my gaze reaches the apex of her thighs, which is covered in a simple, tiny, pure white bikini bottom.

Frankie Castera came. And now she's going to come.

10

YOU OWE ME NOTHING, LOVE

FRANKIE

I wait as his eyes wander their way up from my ankles. I can almost feel them like a touch, sliding their way over my skin. When his pale aqua eyes finally make it up to my face, I'm working my butt off to make sure that I don't look the least bit turned on even though my bikini bottom is wet from more than the pool I was in ten minutes ago. I guess I don't do a good job because he smiles as he leans against the half-wall that sections off the meditation area I'm in. "Who you pretending for, love? We both know you want to be here more than anywhere else in the world right now. Or else you wouldn't be here."

"Whether I want it or not doesn't mean it's right."

"Nothing that tastes as good as your pussy can be wrong." He says it so casually and somehow that makes it so much hotter. I know my cheeks are turning the same pink as the mood lighting in this place.

Billy isn't fucking around tonight. He stalks right over to the lounger I'm splayed out on, not even attempting to hide his excitement as he unties his robe, exposing his perfect physique and his long, hard dick. His hands dent the cushion on either side of my head, and he hovers above me like he's about to start doing push-ups.

"I'm your boss now." Am I reminding him, or myself? I have no clue. It doesn't matter. Neither of us are going to listen.

"You haven't even run a race yet. We've got time," he whispers, dipping his head down so his warm breath tickles the column of my neck. Every nerve ending in my body is tingling with anticipation. I want him to touch me with his lips, with his fingers, with his tongue, with everything. I am struggling to stay rational. I feel my limbs extend, my hands above my head, legs long and toes pointed, like I'm stretching. It's either that or I reach up and grab him and pull him over me like a blanket.

"Is there even an official rule about this?" Billy questions. "Does Mirabella care? Do the race stewards? I mean, we can't be the first people working for the same team to fuck."

"We haven't fucked," I whisper.

"See? We aren't even breaking imaginary rules." He grins. "Yet."

"Do you really want to fuck a woman who is only good at posing half naked on Instagram every five minutes?" I ask pointedly.

Disappointment flickers across his ruggedly handsome face. Because he thinks I'm shutting him down. And I am... right? I can't let this go on. Even if, after some investigation, I realized the comment Billy made was actually said in jest about Rocco at a press conference a few weeks ago when an Instagram picture Rocco posted in his gym shorts went viral last year.

"That reporter-slash-douchebag misrepresented my quote to try and make drama for Mirabella." Billy tells me what I already know. "So basically, if you don't let me give you another orgasm right now, you're letting the haters win."

"Nice logic, James." I smile. "But even the pompous panda you sent me knows there's much more to it than that."

There's so many cons and very little pros. I mean sure, orgasms and fulfilled teenage fantasies are a pro, but heartache and work complications and the fact that I'm still not one hundred percent sure I can trust him are huge cons. The cons you can't ignore… even with his perfect dick pressed against my thigh and that talented mouth gently pressed to the shell of my ear.

"Why did you come here then?" he asks me, his tone pure challenge. He's daring me to lie because he knows the truth. He can read my body like a book, and right now it's screaming 'bodice ripper!'

"I owe you," I whisper, his lips brushing by mine so lightly I almost think I'm dreaming it. "For the other night."

"You owe me?" Billy pulls back a little. "For what?"

"What happened in San Sebastian."

I can feel tension replace desire in his muscular body. Billy's sandy eyebrows furrow. "You think you owe me for pleasuring you? Like I did it as a favor? Like there was nothing in it for me?"

"No. Not… I mean I know…" I'm the most articulate person I know. I make my living off speaking about things, at least I *did*. But this thing with Billy James has me out of my element. I feel like a timid teenager. So instead of talking, I crane my neck so our lips connect.

Billy is no longer concerned with my need for a score sheet. He devours my mouth like it's a decadent dessert. I do the same because kissing him is the most incredible thing in the world. He's so dominant and reckless in the way his tongue moves and his lips nip at me and I can't get enough.

Our bodies move closer. He's draped on top of me now, full contact. My tiny bikini suddenly feels as big as a snow suit. It covers all the parts I wish were bare. His long, hard cock rubs shamelessly against me, pushing against the thin fabric of the bikini bottom between my legs. His lips drop to my neck and he sucks gently right above my collarbone and I arch even further into him. His skin is supple and hard and warm. Between him and the heated lounger, I'm on the verge of burning up.

"You owe me nothing, love," Billy tells me, lips against the column of my neck.

But he's wrong. I have to even this score, so we can both walk away satisfied. "Did you leave that night and jerk off? Thinking of it? Of what we did?"

"I did. With the taste of you still on my lips," he admits, and I want to moan at the vision it puts in my head.

I run a hand into his permanently tousled sandy hair and curl my fingers, tugging him roughly down to my mouth again. We kiss and grind against each other for long, blissful minutes until we're both panting and my lips are swollen, my chin red from his scruff. I push him off me, despite the throbbing ache between my legs that I know only he can cure. Well, him or my hand later. And I promised myself it would be my hand. I can't… even if a crazy, unbridled part of me wants to, desperately. I can't fuck Billy James.

He's kneeling between my legs, halfway down the wide, double lounger. The robe is hanging off his bare shoulders and his perfect body is on display. All of him, and he is anything but shy about it. His hand wraps around his cock and he smiles. Oh that smile. It's like having the sun caress your skin on a warm, deserted, white sand beach. "You want to pretend you're in control tonight? That's cool."

"I am in control," I reply sternly. His grin deepens. "I'm not going to fuck you."

Before he can argue with me, I kiss him again, pushing the robe off his shoulders and then moving my mouth down, over his exposed skin. From his mouth, to his neck, to his chest, his perfectly rippled stomach. And then, before he can even really comprehend what I'm about to do, I grab his cock and slide my mouth over it. I feel his body relax right into me—melt. That's really the word for it, and his left hand drops to the back of my head and slides over my hair.

"Baby… Jesus fuck."

I start to bob and wrap a hand around his shaft, squeezing slightly. But just when my pace finds its groove, he pulls me off him. Tangling both hands in my hair, he pulls me to my knees so we're face-to-face and he kisses me. Long and hard. "I want more."

"I can't give you more," I reply. My voice is firm, my willpower isn't though. I want to give him everything. I want to take it all from him too—all the lust his blue eyes are reflecting back at me, all the sweet, sexy banter he wants to whisper, all the cocky charisma he wants to ooze. I want it all.

"I won't," I say out loud because it looks like there's a debate happening here, and there isn't. I can't, won't, let this go on or go further. Tonight, I even the score, and we move on as boss and driver. Because this isn't a love story. It's a kinky, smutty novella at best and it ends tonight.

But then Billy does something unexpected. And annoying. He gets up off the lounger, grabs his robe, and holds it in front of the masterpiece that is his nude body. He looks at me but not for long before he turns away. "Then this isn't happening at all."

He walks off toward the pool, and I watch, stunned, for fifteen minutes while he does laps. Butterfly of all strokes, the one that looks the sexiest of course. My God this man… what am I going to do with him?

My brain thinks back to that night when I was younger and how he swooped in out of nowhere. My Aussie hero. How different would this all be now if his mom hadn't had a crisis that next night? In all honesty, we would both be exactly where we are now, boss and driver. Just hopefully with far less secrets to hide. I wouldn't be hiding from him and most of the world that I was drugged. Billy wouldn't be hiding whatever he's hiding. Because I know, even after his confession about his mom's mental health crisis, that there is more to the story he's not sharing.

Billy looks up at me now as he casually swims to the side of the pool where the stairs are and smiles. "You enjoying the view, love?"

"I'm waiting for you to stop stalling, so I can pay you back."

The smile I lust after disappears. "I don't play that way, Frankie. You owe me nothing. If you want me, you can have me, but not in some kind of act of debt repayment."

He emerges from the pool, and somehow the pool water knows exactly what good parts of his naked body to cling to. Then again, there aren't any bad parts. He doesn't walk towards me, he veers slightly left to one of the giant marble walk-in shower stalls that creates the division between the loungers and meditation area and the pool. The showers are open to the pool but blocked from the entrance and other areas.

I glance around the pool deck area. No cameras anywhere. I step onto the pool deck and over to the stall. His head is tipped back, and his eyes are closed as the shower water rains down over him. It's probably the most perfect thing I've ever seen, in part because he's still half hard, which means he still wants me. Knowing his rejection isn't concrete gives me confidence, and I step into the cavernous stall with him.

He opens his eyes and levels those baby blues right at me. And I stare straight back and start stripping. It only takes one simple tug and the top of my bathing suit drops to the marble floor. I bite my lip and my hands move to the tiny string tie on the side of my bottoms. "Francesca if you take that off…"

"If you can walk around naked, why can't I?" I ask in my best innocent voice. I am thinking far from innocent thoughts, so it's not easy pulling it off. Especially because I'm also currently wrapping my hand around his cock. His eyelids flutter, but he manages to keep them open as I give him a long, slow tug.

And then, with my other hand, I undo the string on my bikini bottom and it drops. His eyes slide down immediately to stare at my pussy and then his hand roughly cups the back of my neck, and before the bikini bottom even hits my ankles, he's claimed my mouth in a hard, needy kiss.

I give into his mouth, his tongue, but never let go of his cock. I rub it slow and firm until he has to break the kiss to groan. And then I take advantage of the situation by dropping to my knees. My lips are a fraction of an inch from his tip, which is already glistening with pre-come, when he grabs my hair and yanks me back gently. "Don't."

"You don't want to fuck my mouth, feel my tongue slide over you as I take you down my throat?"

"Holy fuck," he gasps and his grip on my hair loosens.

"Tell me to suck you off, Billy," I beg. "Please. I want to so badly."

"Suck me off, love," he rasps.

And I do. I give the best fucking blow job of my life, and I love every single second of it because it's Billy James. The longest crush of my life. The sexiest man I've ever known. My Aussie hero. And before I know it, that hero is warning me he's ready, and I suck harder and longer and take him as deep as I can, slipping a hand from his balls to his taint and…

He comes with a long, loud, deep groan that I swear has my clit tingling. Oh God, I need to go home and touch myself until I'm panting his name. I'll be lucky to last a full sixty seconds. I'm that turned on. It would be way more enjoyable if I could just let him take care of me like I know he still wants to. What kind of masochist turns down Billy James?

The kind that doesn't trust him or any man, my brain reminds me sternly. That reality is the only reason I start to quickly put my bikini back on. He's still panting, eyes barely open, leaning against the shower wall for support. "Where do you think you're going?"

"To my room," I reply, lifting my arms to tie my triangle top behind my head. "To play with myself while I think about this."

His eyes are wide open now and no longer satiated. They're filled with desire again. He reaches for me but I manage to escape. I march back to the lounger where my bathrobe is, and he follows, not bothering with a robe or anything. "I'm not done with you, Frankie."

"But I'm done." I toss him one of the towels rolled up decoratively on the shelving between the loungers because if he doesn't put something on soon, my willpower will melt like a chocolate bar left on an Arizona sidewalk in July.

He begrudgingly wraps the towel around his waist. But before I can finish tying my robe, he's got his arms wrapped around my waist. Our bodies are touching everywhere, and his lips are by my ear. "It doesn't have to be like this, Frankie."

I pull away just enough to look him in his eyes, which are earnest and soft. "How else can it be?" I sound needy, like I'm begging him for something. I'm not... am I? I mean, he can't change the reality of our situation. And I don't even want to. Do I?

His lips dance across mine. "Come up to my room."

There's a distinctive clack of metal. Someone is pushing open the door to the pool area. Billy and I both realize it at the same time, and I tie my robe, and he finally wraps that damn towel around his waist, but *not* before Nick appears a few feet away. I swear he got a partial glimpse of Billy's bare ass. His face is made of stone though as he clears his throat. "Frankie, you said if you weren't back in your room in an hour, I should come get you."

"Right. Thanks Nick."

Billy raises his sandy eyebrows. "You made your bodyguard into a chaperone?"

"I have a conference call with a brand partner in a different time zone," I say, and he smirks because he knows it's a lie. Billy James is too smart for his own good. "See you tomorrow, James."

"Uh-huh."

Nick doesn't speak again until we are safely inside the elevator, and then he lets me have it. "You're playing with fire and breaking all your own rules."

"No. I'm not. I was evening the score," I reply, and that makes the shock on his rugged face deepen.

"I am too scared to ask what score involves James' naked ass," Nick says, and like always when he's agitated, his French accent gets thicker.

"It doesn't matter. It's done," I say, and I know I sound melancholy, because I am. I want more of Billy James. There, I said it. But as usual, Nick is there to be the voice of reason.

"Leopard's don't change their spots, Francesca," he reminds me. "That man, for whatever reason, stood you up. That night led to the worst night of your life. I'm not saying that what happened next, the drugging and you almost dying, is his fault, but if he'd kept his promise to meet you, it wouldn't have happened."

"I know that, but do you honestly believe…" I pause and try to come to terms with the fact that I'm about to defend him. Billy James, who broke my young, naive heart. "You think if Billy knew what was going to happen to me that night, he would have still left me on that beach alone? He didn't know. I can't hold him responsible for the chain of events after his mistake. And he's explained that."

Nick doesn't say anything as the elevator keeps chugging along. It isn't until it opens on our floor and I'm about to enter my suite that he speaks.

Nick sighs. His brown furrows. "If you were one of my guy friends, I'd tell you you're thinking with your dick."

Before I can even begin to figure out how to respond to that, Nick says goodnight and disappears into his room. I blink and struggle to push open the door to my room. Is this door heavier than I remember or is it just the weight of the truth bomb Nick just dropped on me?

11

I'LL RACE IN ONE OF THEIR BIKINIS

BILLY

"I gotta hand it to the girl," Clara says as I storm my way toward the paddock. "She's got some balls on her and quite the sturdy backbone."

I look at my sister. Her eyes are on Frankie, who is standing in the second-floor balcony area of the Mirabella paddock. She's got a bottle of water in her hand, a team radio on her hip, and is gesturing wildly to Rocco. They're both smiling, and I can't hear a whisper of what they're talking about. They want people to think it's just normal engineer-Principal race day chatter, but I can tell by her abrupt gesturing hands and the way his shoulders are so high they're almost pinned to his ears that it most definitely is not. Plus, the way the last four races have gone, I know it's not pleasantries being exchanged.

Today will be the fifth race since Frankie took over as Team Principal, and to say it's not going well would be an understatement. We haven't podiumed, let alone won, since she took over. In Barcelona, I had engine trouble and dropped out in the twenty-seventh lap. Antonio was in third until the sky opened up and rain came down in sheets. Despite a pit for those wet tires Frankie smartly kept on the roster, De Luca finished sixth, and the media blamed her for some reason. Then there was Amsterdam, where I managed fourth and Antonio fifth. France, where Samuels collided with me and the car was damaged beyond repair. Samuels was hit with a time penalty, but that didn't earn me any points. Antonio, despite having no apparent race issues, slipped from third to ninth. The media and the asshole demographic of our fans were blaming Frankie for everything, and a sponsor even pulled out. Not a big one, but still.

"A sturdy backbone? Because she's standing up to Rocco?" I ask quietly as we walk. My eyes dart around behind my sunglasses to make sure none of the ever-present media has a microphone close enough to hear me.

"No," Clara smiles, deviously. "Because she's not bowing to any of the damn pressure. Except for the outfit, she's holding strong to her beliefs and running the show the way she wants."

The outfits, right. Frankie's fun and flirty versions of Mirabella gear with the low V-necks and body hugging bottoms have disappeared since internet trolls started making memes out of pictures of her calling her outfits "distracting" and "inappropriate." One even labeled her outfits Mirabella stripper wear, and another went so far as to say 'I guess if she can't win races, the least she can do is give us some T and A.' She's worn lose, androgynous styled shirts and pants ever since. Even her cute, sparkly trainers have been switched up for boring, white, sparkleless shoes.

"And avoiding distractions, AKA, you." Clara smirks.

I frown. "We talked after practice yesterday. For like an hour."

"With Antonio, Rocco, Bash and Dario, and ten other people," Clara reminds me. "And then she acted like she didn't hear you when you asked to have a word after the meeting. And I heard she moved hotels. No longer stays where the Mirabella team stays."

"She did," I admit and try not to frown any harder. I found

that out when I ran into Lucia, while I was wandering like a lost puppy through the lobby earlier this week, hoping to run into Frankie. She told me her sister had decided the Ritz across town was more her jam.

That's utter bullshit. She was avoiding me. I had to take several hours to talk myself out of moving hotels as well. What the hell was wrong with me? I never let women get to me like this. Not a single one. Not since... well not since Frankie got to me back when I was a kid.

"In case you haven't bothered to notice, I don't care."

"Yeah you do," Clara replied airily.

"Shut up."

She smiles.

"If you were anyone else, I would fire you right now."

"If I was anyone else, I'd take your money and keep my mouth shut and let you continue to put all your energy into fooling yourself instead of into your driving," Clara replies as she holds open the door to the paddock for me. I refuse to walk in and instead take the door from her so she can walk in. I may be annoyed with her, and she may technically be my employee, but I'm still not that dude who let's women serve them. Unless it's Frankie Castera serving my cock. I would gladly let that happen again.

I think back to how she looked a few weeks ago, on her knees, water slipping and sliding down her naked, perfect body, and those lips... I have dreamed about having those lips around my cock since the very first time she smiled at me. Frankie Castera looks like an angel hiding all the devil's secrets. It's such a fucking turn on. I'm far from over her, Clara is right.

I suddenly realize Clara has stopped talking and walking. I stare at her. "What?"

She closes her mouth and swallows, eyes glued to something

down the main hall of the paddock. I turn my head slowly and Clara says the name as my eyes find her. "Sherry."

"Mum!" I say and walk slowly toward her. "Why are you here?"

"Well, that's hardly a greeting, now, is it?" my mother, Sherry Buckingham, says with a careless little chuckle, as if her little boy did something silly on the playground. "Come give me a hug."

I do what she asks as Clara stands stiff and quiet beside me. I feel her tension like it's my own. Clara's hard feelings for my mom have been earned, unfortunately. My mother opens her arms and pulls me to her. She's rail thin, like always, and her glossy blonde hair doesn't have a strand out of place. She's wearing jeans and a cranberry-colored, clingy sweater, which you bet your ass are designer. My mom knows there'll be cameras here, so she's ready for her close-up, even if it's just because she's standing next to me.

"You look well, Mum. But I didn't know you were coming. We hadn't discussed a visit," I say, trying to sound casual. In all honesty, I wish she wasn't here. She's never easy to be around. I hate the guilt that fills my gut because of that, but it's the truth.

"Australia is freezing right now, honey," she explains. Australia, at least our part, is never freezing. The woman acts like it's Fargo, Minnesota, in January. "I needed some sun and some culture. And to see my baby."

She cups my face in her hands. She looks happy. She looks… balanced. I know that sounds weird, but she gets this look in her eyes when she is off her meds that I've learned to identify. Thankfully, she doesn't have it now. But this surprise visit is a red flag. "Why not come to my dressing room? I have to get ready. We can catch up."

"I'll meet you at the garage. Text if you need anything," Clara says to me, eyes purposely vacant of emotion. And then she turns so fast her sneaker makes a little squeak sound on the concrete floor.

"Clara, you…" *don't have to leave* is what never makes it out of my mouth. Because there's no point. She won't lock herself in my tiny dressing room with my mother, and it's probably better this way. Even though I hate it. I turn to my mom. "Let's go. I don't have much time before qualifying."

Mom smiles brightly, drapes an arm on my shoulders, and marches down the hall with me. She rattles on as I get dressed in my race suit. She's got a million questions about Frankie's new position and why my last few races were less than great. "They can't all be winners, Mom," I mutter to that last question.

"They need to be, Billy," she replies, with the stern tone of a parent looking at a subpar report card. A normal parent, not mine. Both my mom and dad have always cared more about my track results than my school grades. "You've left yourself with very little wiggle room."

"I am far from being at the bottom of the pack," I say as I zip up my suit and step into the main room from the bathroom. "I'm two wins away from taking the lead in the Championship standings and there's more than two races left."

Mum is sitting on the couch, rummaging around the fruit bowl they always leave on the coffee table. She plucks off a grape and examines it. "You're currently fourth overall. Middle of the pack might as well be bottom. There's no title for anything other than first."

"Thanks for the pep talk, mummy dearest," I mutter.

She glares for a second but not for long because she doesn't want to get wrinkles one day. Her words, when asked last year by a reporter why she always looks like she's in a good mood. "You want to beat that man's record, don't you? I'm just thinking of you."

That man, as she constantly refers to him, is my father.

Tommy won four world championships by the time he was thirty. I'm twenty-seven, and I've won three. The door is closing, and the only person who wants me to beat my father's record more than me is Sherry Buckingham. Formerly Sherry Buckingham James, but Mum dropped the James as soon as she found out dear old Dad had been having a nine-year affair with a woman from Montreal, Canada.

"I don't need the reminder. It's all I think about lately." Well, that and my Team Principal's BJ skills. Oh, and how her pussy felt against my tongue.

"Billy..?" I snap out of the sex fog and find my mother staring at me with a tilted head. "What's wrong with you? Is it because Bash abandoned the team and gave his job to his daughter? Is she causing this drama with you?"

I shake my head. "She's really not. Sure, it's a bit of an adjustment, but it's fine. It will be fine."

"Antonio doesn't think so," Mum replies. "I ran into him in the cafeteria as I was looking for you when I arrived. He said this girl will tank the entire team if someone doesn't remove her soon."

"He's just mad he's underperforming more than usual this season," I open the door to my room and motion for her to leave. As we walk, I twist my neck from left to right. "I'm going to need to do some drills with Clara and get her to work on my neck, so I don't know if you want to stick around here or head up to the lounge and watch qualifying from there."

"Honestly? I'd love to watch from the garage, but until you fire that girl, I'll be upstairs," she says bluntly and with zero remorse for her harshness.

"Then you'll likely never see the garage again," I reply, equally blunt. But then I kiss her cheek to soften the blow. "That, by the way, will be the last time you reference Clara while you're here. Love you, Mum."

I turn and stride down the hall and out the doors. I hate how much Mum hates my step-sister. It's not her fault that our dad was a cheating ass. She didn't ask to be born the way she was, and Clara is a great person. The best sibling I could have asked for. I wish Mum could see that. It's been ten years for fuck's sake. It's time to try and accept Clara or at least be civil to her.

I'm agitated by all of this when I walk into the garage, like I need anything else to screw with my confidence. I need to qualify high, and this track has never been strong for me. Clara makes eye contact and looks instantly contrite as she approaches. "How are the shoulders and I'm sorry for the extra drama."

"You have nothing to apologize for," I remind her like I always do when she tries to take on the responsibility of my mother's behavior. "As for the shoulders, tense to say the least. The left one is worse."

Clara yanks a wand massager off the tool belt type thing she carries on her during race weekends and gently tugs at the Under Armor shirt I wear under my race suit, which is hanging from my hips, only half-on. She's standing behind me and she presses the massager just behind my collarbone and turns it on. There's instant relief. I sigh. "We have to work on reflexes next," I mumble and my eyes close as my neck sags a little.

"I'm NOT putting that on MY suit," Antonio's angry roar fills my ears, and my eyes fly back open.

"They're a new sponsor. It's not a request, it's an order," I hear Frankie reply. Her voice even but low. The kind of growl only a woman is capable of that is calm but yet terrifying anyway.

"They make bikinis," Antonio barks at her, and he's standing way too close to her. Looming over her, finger pointed at her. "Do I look like I wear a fucking bikini?"

"They make sundry items, including bikinis, sunglasses, and men's swim shorts," Frankie corrects, and then she seems to grow an inch as she pushes back her shoulders and tilts her head up to look him square in the eye. Her delicate jaw is clenched for a moment, and her hand gives the slightest of shakes, the kind you wouldn't notice if you didn't know her well, as she places it on her hip. "And you wouldn't talk to my father like that, so I suggest you don't talk to me like that either. I am your boss, and they are a sponsor, and that logo will be on your race suit by morning."

"Your father and Dario have earned my respect by helping me win," Antonio shoots back as Frankie moves to sit down. "You haven't."

I'm walking and am standing between the two of them before I even realize I've done it. I turn to Antonio, and in my most casual voice, I say with a smile, "I think you need to go and get ready now, don't you? Get your trainer to work on whatever you've got all twisted in knots."

Antonio glares at me and tosses the logo patch he was holding onto the ground at my feet before he storms over to his car. It's as far away as he can get while still being in the garage. Frankie sits on her stool and stares at the bank of monitors in front of her, but I know she's not really looking at them. She's trying to rein in her emotions. I pick the patch off the ground and look at it.

It's a bit much. A teal, glittery palm tree with the name in cursive font underneath. The company is mostly known for making very skimpy, very expensive bikinis, but they have recently branched out into men's beach wear and sunglasses, she isn't lying. I glance at my own race suit, it's got logos all over it —a tire company, motor oil, the car company that makes our engines, a cellphone provider. Sure, this logo might be more flashy than the others, but who gives a fuck if they're helping us on the track?

"You gonna bitch about a little fucking scrap of fabric too?" Frankie asks, her eyes still glued to the blank screens.

Today her hair is swept up in a high ponytail, and she's

wearing a loose fitting Mirabella T-shirt. It's slightly longer in the back to cover that perfect ass of hers, and she's paired it with black leggings and a pair of simple, black trainers. She's subdued make-up and no jewelry. Still the prettiest woman I've ever seen, but not her trademark flare. "Hell, I'll race in one of their bikinis if they pay me enough."

Even Rocco beside her chuckles at that as he stands and leaves the monitors to go check on something. Now, it's just Frankie and me in the tight space, and she caves and cracks a small smile at that. So I double down. "You think they make that little shimmery white number you had on in Barcelona in my size?"

The smile grows, and her eyes dart to mine, but it's too brief. "I think it might be hard to find a bottom that fits. Especially if we're talking the size you were that night. That was pretty big."

She didn't. Oh man...

"Pretty big? I think you mean big and pretty."

A soft, almost soundless chuckle escapes her lips, and she covers her mouth with a hand to hide it. I notice her nails are plain white polish. For the last several races she's had the Mirabella logo on her nails. The taming of her personal style because of judgmental assholes hiding behind keyboards contin-ues, and I'm saddened by it. Bash always wore a crazy, colorful, and sometimes downright gaudy, pocket square in the navy blazer he used to wear every race day. No one ever slammed him on the internet for it. She glances around to make sure we're still as private as possible before she responds. "The only thing bigger than your ego is your dick."

"I love how you only give backhanded compliments. Like you think I can't see right through them." I grin, step closer, and lower my voice. "You loved having your lips on my cock as much as I loved it."

"Work, Billy," she says, growing serious and moving the

conversation back on track. "So you're fine with the new sponsor?"

"Of course. But their patch *is* ugly." I can't help but be honest and I can see the resignation in her eyes.

"It's not ideal, but the eighty grand they're giving us, per season, to wear it is." Frankie sighs and folds her arms across her ample chest. "Antonio is also pissed off that we've decided to replace his engine this race, which means he takes a grid penalty. It was going to have to be done eventually, and he had a lot of trouble last race, and Rocco told me the sooner the better. I picked this race because, historically, he performs better than you here so he has a better chance at bouncing back."

"I'll talk to him."

"Thanks." Frankie gives me another small smile. "His attitude is getting old."

"I know." I want to give her shoulder a squeeze, or her hand, but it wouldn't be deemed appropriate, I don't think. I don't know why. I mean, I've hugged Bash and Dario a ton in front of the crew. But for some reason touching Frankie in public feels… off. "I've got to get ready. Try and focus."

She gives me a little nod and turns back to the monitors, fixing an ear piece into her ear. I can't deny Frankie's logic, and I wonder why Antonio is. It makes sense that the engine get replaced on this track. I vow to talk to him after qualifying, but for now, I need to get myself ready. I find Clara in the corner of the garage, behind my car, holding two tennis balls. "Ready for some reflex tests?"

I stretch. "Let's do this."

An hour later, I'm slipping into the driver's seat as engineers and mechanics and the rest of my team buzz around the car. I do my initial laps, and it goes well. Better than well. I finish round one of qualifying in second. Round two, I manage fourth.

"How you feeling?" Rocco says as he leans over the car as

I'm adjusting my helmet, getting ready to head out for the final round of qualifying, fighting for that pole position with the nine others who made it this far.

"Good. All good. What happened with Antonio? New engine having problems?" I have to sound casual and chill because we have mics in our headsets, and we're often recorded, and it's used on TV. Antonio didn't make it to round three, which he needed because of the pending engine penalty. Putting in a new engine means an automatic five place grid penalty, which isn't so bad if you make it to round three of qualifying and finish in the top ten. But he didn't make it to round three. So now he'll start seventeenth tomorrow with the penalty.

"Not engine. Just bad luck."

Rocco's mossy eyes are narrowed, and there's a crease between his eyebrows that says luck had nothing to do with it. Antonio fucked something up. I nod back and concentrate on my own final qualifying lap. I push all the emotional garbage out of my head and focus as I pull out of the pit lane. I fly through the course, which is tricky with a lot of banking turns and a chicane. But I do incredibly well and manage a second place finish. Not first but it still feels fucking great.

I go through the flurry of media, high-fiving every team member I can find with Clara nearby giving me water, holding my helmet, doing whatever I need as always. Then I strut back toward the Mirabella paddock, and that's where Clara leaves my side. "She's in the lounge?"

I nod.

"I'll be in your dressing room. Or maybe the car. The car feels safer," Clara muses, genuine concern on her face.

I hug her. "I am not letting you wait in the car like a Golden Retriever. Take the car and head back without me. I'll text you when I'm back at the hotel."

Clara is shocked. "But how will you get home?"

"Sherry. Or someone. I'll figure it out." I wink at her. "Even if I have to hitchhike."

She laughs but her shoulders relax, and I know it's because she has been given permission to escape her step-monster. I watch her go for a minute and then I head to the lounge. Mum is sitting on the balcony. She's added a wide brim hat to her wardrobe to shield her from the sun, and she's giggling at something Bash has said. She drops one of her manicured hands on top of his on the table. I don't hate that she flirts a lot with almost any man that walks by her. But her habit of flirting with *married* men like Bash really annoys me. I pick up my pace as Bash subtly moves his hand away from my mom.

He sees me first and stands, extending his arms. "My boy! Great job today."

"I am planning on taking over the lead by the third lap," I assure him as I hug him back.

"Billy, baby, don't get cocky," Mom advises as she stands to also hug me, but sadly, hers isn't as warm or heartfelt as Bash's.

"Confident and cocky aren't the same thing," I reply, trying to sound less annoyed than I am. Then I see Frankie walk into the room, and my annoyance evaporates. She's smiling and looks truly happy, and I know it's because of me, my race results, and I realize in that moment that I love making her smile, even if the reason doesn't involve nudity.

Her eyes scan the room and find mine. I grin at her, and her smile deepens, and she makes her way over. "Great job!"

She gives me a congratulatory punch on the arm. For real. Like, what the actual fuck? I almost laugh out loud. Bash actually does. "Frankie, you can hug your drivers. Especially the ones that are poised to bring you Constructors' points. I always did."

"You are a male in a patriarchal sport. You can do whatever you wish, Dad." Frankie tilts her head back toward me. "Anyway, great job out there, James. Did it feel as good as it looked?"

She is fighting a blush because she knows as well as I do her words are a lot of double entendres that only she and I understand, like a private joke. "I'm sure it looked incredible. But I can assure you it felt even better than you could imagine."

"Okay then." Frankie smiles. "I expect nothing less than a podium tomorrow."

She slugs me merrily on the arm again and gives my mum a friendly nod and says, "Nice to see you again, Ms. Buckingham," before walking away.

Adelaide walks in and waves at Bash, who leaves me to be with his wife. He calls a quick good-bye over his shoulder at me and my mother, who is frowning. Bash definitely didn't notice. His eyes are on Adelaide, and no one else in the crowded lounge.

"Are you staying here to find someone else to flirt with or are you leaving? Because I need a lift back to the hotel. I let Clara go ahead without me."

Mum frowns again. This is becoming a habit. "That woman… must be nice to just seize your car whenever the whim hits her."

"She isn't seizing anything." I level her with a warning glare. "She's my sister, and siblings share."

"William Thomas James!" She hisses my entire name so I know how very angry she is in this second. And it is only a second. She relaxes moments later and smiles tightly as her eyes bounce around the room to make sure no one heard me spill the family secret. "You shared a sperm donor. And no one ever needs to know that. I understand we're saving your father the embarrassment, and he doesn't deserve it. But I do. I would be devastated and humiliated beyond comprehension if the world knew that I was used and swindled by that man."

Her blue eyes well up like they always do when she is forced to confront the reality of her marriage. Man, it's been years and as much as she hates Tommy James, she is also still so wounded by his actions. "I can't… Haven't I been through enough?"

In the decade since Tommy was killed racing in the French Grand Prix, Clara's mother Shiloh was about the only woman not to go public with her extra-marital involvement with him. Four other women have sold their sordid stories to tabloids. All claiming the affairs happened in the first five years he was married to Mum. This is the only reason she hasn't crumbled emotionally under the whispers and sneers. Because the media spins it like Tommy married too young and therefore had some indiscretion, but in the end, he stayed with and devoted himself to Sherry Buckingham and their little boy Billy. The truth is he stopped cheating when he met Shiloh and had Clara. It was her he was being faithful to in his later years, not my mum. God knows what she will do if the world finds out the truth.

"Okay, Mum. Okay." I lean in and wrap my arm around her shoulder. "Where are you staying?"

"The Ritz."

Frankie's hotel. I smile. This is perfect. "Let's go have dinner at your hotel okay? Just the two of us?"

She sniffs discreetly and nods. We walk out of the lounge and start down the stairs to the main level. Mum seems to perk up a little. "Bash's girls are just so cute, aren't they?"

"Frankie and Lucia?' I ask for some reason because who the hell else would she be talking about. "Do you mean cute, looks-wise? Because that would be an understatement."

"Well, I mean of course they're stunning. Mirabella was just gorgeous and Bash is… well he's as handsome as they get," Sherry says as we hit the landing. "But I mean they're cute as in adorable. The way she punched your arm all sweet and cute. I think she might have a little crush."

"Mum… that's conjecture," I mutter, but inside I'm like a grade school boy clinging to the idea with blind hope. God, does Frankie have a crush? Does she like me for more than just my sexual compatibility with her? I shouldn't want her to, but I do.

"I'm just saying… there are worse girls whose garage you could be parking your car in," Mum replies airily, and I cringe.

"That is the worst pun ever," I tell her flatly. "And also, I do not want you thinking about where I park my car."

Mum laughs. "Billy honey, you can't be single forever. And I would rather you strategically pick a mate than be trapped with one because you accidentally knock someone up. Like how Bash is trapped."

She says the last four words under her breath in a stage whisper so only I hear. I swivel my head so fast I almost pull a muscle. "What the hell are you talking about? Bash is far from trapped. He was the one who pursued Adelaide. And they're very happy together."

"Uh-huh. She's pregnant, so whether they're happy or not, he's now trapped," Sherry whispers back.

I stop walking as soon as we reach the main level hallway. "What the hell are you talking about?"

"Oh. It's not public yet? I thought when she told me…" Mum shrugged. "Oopsie."

"Adelaide Castera told you she was pregnant?" I am in utter disbelief, but then my mind flashes to how she has been wearing more than her average amount of loose cotton hippie dresses and the way Bash cradled her stomach that day in the elevator in San Sebastian… why didn't I figure that out? "Why is she telling you and not anyone else?"

"I found her puking in the bathroom off the lounge during the qualifying," Mum explains. "She's having a hard first trimester. I think that's karma for forcing Bash into a baby at his age."

"Shh!" I demand. I feel like if this was public news, Frankie would have mentioned it. Or Bash. Someone. And I do not want the racing world to find out from my mother.

"Okay, take a chill pill Billy." Mum laughs at her own antiquated expression. "We can go back to talking about how cute the Castera girls are."

I groan, and that just makes her laugh again as we walk toward the back of the building where my dressing room is. "It's like you're a twelve-year-old boy again, and I'm bugging you about that crush you had on Sofia Muldoon," she says. My mother loves to tease me. About everything. All the time. "You wouldn't ask her to dance. You were so shy. I hope you ask girls to dance now, Billy. I need a grandbaby one day. And that Frankie Castera looks like a good dancer. I follow her on the 'Gram."

"Of course you do, Mum." I roll my eyes. The conference room has Antonio and his agent in there. Antonio is pacing. I have no idea what's going on, and normally, I would check in on him, but with my mum here, I just want to get the hell out. So I ignore my teammate and keep walking.

Mum plays on her phone while I do some light stretching before I change out of my race gear. I head into my bathroom and put on my street clothes, a pair of tailored canvas joggers and a fitted, cashmere shirt. She really won't let this thing go about dating one of the Castera women. "Listen to me, Billy. I swear I know what I'm talking about. Both of those women are lovely, inside and out."

"They are," I agree, trying to sound disinterested.

"You marrying one of them would be this sport's version of a royal wedding."

"Mum, a wedding? Seriously, get a grip," I bark out. I realize that's harsh and try to explain away the sting to my words. "I'm not dating anyone, let alone marrying them, if my daily job..."

Oh fuck, I think as I hear her sharp intake of breath. Finishing that sentence with the truth – that I won't get attached to someone when I might die every weekend from this career – would be sticking my foot in my mouth like a boss. So I quickly rephrase the rest of that sentence. "When I'm traipsing all around the world isn't an option. You hated being left alone while dad worked, remember."

"Yeah. I remember," she mutters but then she smiles sheepishly. "Okay, okay, well can you muster up some flirting? That could help you."

Mum's tone grows a little bit more serious. "If you were to start a little something with one of them, it will help your chances at keeping your spot. Frankie is the better bet, since she's the Principal now, but flirting with Lucia wouldn't hurt either. She's not going to steal her crush's spot."

I just stand there, staring at her, dumbfounded. She blinks, realizing the source of my astonishment and shakes her head. "No it's not the same thing. At all. You're not trying to steal some spot on a race team, or some funding to get on one or anything like that. You're just ensuring you stay exactly where you belong. You've already earned your spot, but we both know that isn't always enough. An emotional attachment as a wee bit of job security is all."

I open my mouth to argue. But suddenly there's a lot of loud voices in the hallway outside my room. Loud and angry. I dart to the door and swing it open in time to see Frankie stumble and bump into the wall awkwardly. Antonio is standing in front of her, looming aggressively, and something in my brain short circuits. I leap to the absolute worst case scenario. I get right in between them and right up into Antonio's face, grabbing him roughly by the front of his race suit which he is still in for some reason. "Did you fucking touch her? I will fucking—"

"He didn't!" Frankie says. "Let him go, Billy."

Before I can honor her command, Antonio pushes my hand away and gives me a shove. "What the fuck is wrong with you? We're supposed to be a team, you and I. You haven't had my back since Bash gave his job to this…"

"Watch your fucking words, De Luca," I warn in a low snarl.

"And my loyalty is to Mirabella, not you. Yours should be the same, so get your fucking head out of your egotistical ass and grow the fuck up."

"Your loyalty is to Mirabella?" Antonio levels me with a cold, hard smirk. "You fucking liar. Oh and FYI, she was eavesdropping on you when I walked out here. I caught her, and she tried to deny it, and that's what we were fighting about."

"I was about to knock on his door. I wasn't standing there with a glass to it for god's sake!" Frankie replies and rolls her big hazel eyes.

Antonio turns to me. "Probably should have just filmed her and loaded it to Instagram since that's her version of reality."

He storms off adding a "fuck this!" I want to chase after him and punch him in the face, but I can't because that would be like pouring gasoline on a fire. Instead, I turn back to Frankie. She's righting herself, her hands on her lower back as she winces.

"Are you okay?"

"No, but he didn't push me or hit me or anything," Frankie replies and rubs her lower back with the tips of her fingers. "He just got in my face and I… I stumbled when I took a step back. I shouldn't have cowered. Now he thinks I'm a weak little girl."

She sighs, annoyed with herself. I step a little closer. "He shouldn't have gotten in your personal space. That's weak, douchebag behavior, Frankie. You're not the one who has to worry about looking bad. Antonio is out of control. I think you need to tell Dario and Bash. This should be escalated."

"He's pissy because I replaced his engine and because he finished in the shitter," Frankie replies and then my mum pops her head out of my room. Perfect timing as always.

"Frankie, sweetheart. Everything okay?"

She clearly couldn't be bothered to get off the couch and come see what was happening a minute ago. Frankie blinks and it's like she's just remembering something important. And awful.

She clears her throat and pushes her shoulders back. "I'm fine, Sherry. Enjoy your stay this weekend. Bye."

She starts down the hall, and I notice she's favoring her left leg just a little bit. So no, she is not fine. I follow her. When I reach for her arm, she stops walking but pulls her arm out of my gentle grip.

"I don't need you. Also, I don't want you." She pauses. "To sacrifice alone-time with your mum. She came all this way to spend time with you and give you *business* advice."

She keeps storming away.

Fuck. Frankie heard my mom trying to coax me into pretending to like one of the Castera sisters. God damnit.

12

MAKE ME YOUR BITCH

BILLY

I have an early dinner with Mum at her hotel, which is also Frankie's hotel. That's a fact that doesn't leave my head the entire time I'm there, in the hotel's rooftop restaurant, enjoying my steak tartare while Mum picks at a chef's salad but concentrates more on polishing off the bottle of Malbec. Claiming to be wiped from her long day, she leaves me with the bill and a kiss on the cheek and heads off to her room, where I have no doubt she'll order another bottle of wine for herself. I pay and head down to the lobby bar, where I decide to have a sparkling water and sit before heading back to my hotel.

From the end of the bar, I can see the front doors and the elevators. Frankie has to walk through the lobby at some point, right? She doesn't, but just as I'm about to give up and go home, I spot Nick striding across the lobby carrying a take-out bag from a fancy sushi place I know and love. I intercept him just before the elevators. He stops and glares. "Princess Castera has a craving for sashimi tonight?"

"Rolls actually."

"Cool. So can you do me a favor and—"

"No." For a big, bulky guy, he sure as shit moves like a cat. He's around me and punching the elevator button before I even have a chance to blink.

Luckily, the elevator is on a different floor, and he has to wait. "Look, I am not a bad guy."

"When it comes to Frankie, you're all bad guys until we can prove otherwise," Nick grumbles.

I have no idea what that means. I don't have time to ask. The elevator will be here any moment, and Nick will walk through me if he has to—and he can—so I have to stay on point.

"I'm a good guy. I want the best for Frankie, and I know I'm not it… right now. So don't worry about that."

Nick lifts one of his eyebrows but keeps his eyes straight ahead, not bothering to look at me. "That's exactly why I'm worried about it. I know she's finally given in, to some extent, to her inexplicable soft spot for you and so if you know you're not right for her, why are you here. Why are you *always* here?"

"She basically runs my career now, you get that right?" I say, annoyed. "Anyway, even if I didn't need to be civil with her, I would want to be. She's a good person. I like her. I just can't be, like, a partner or anything. Not that she wants that. Anyway, I look out for her too, you know? I saved her once as kids and I was there for her today when you weren't. Where were you, anyway?"

That gets his attention. He finally turns his head to me and ignores the elevator as it arrives and the doors slide open. "She sent me home early. I let her do that when I think she's somewhere safe. What happened? She's said nothing."

"She and Antonio got into it."

"Physically?" Nick somehow stands straighter and looks even bigger. I know there's some Hulk shit about to happen.

"No. I mean she said no. But when I opened my door, she was kind of hunched over and leaning against the wall and rubbing her back," I explain. Something I said seems to turn off the impending Hulk-mode.

"Thanks for telling me," Nick says. "I won't leave her alone at the track again."

"You're welcome. Now, can you do me a solid?"

"My entire job is to protect her, and you think I'm gonna tell you her room number?" Nick huffs out a sarcastic breath.

"How about you let me deliver the food, you can come with me, and if she tells you to get rid of me, than you can haul my ass out of there. Use as much force as you want," I lift my arms in the air. "Make me your bitch."

Nick is still frowning, but he's also not moving. Not laughing in my face, not trying to get into the elevator without me. Instead, he takes a deep breath and gives me the smallest nod I've ever seen. I would punch both fists into the air like I do when I win a race, but then he might change his mind, so I simply follow him when he gets into the elevator. He hits the top floor, and we chug upward in silence.

I have so many questions for Nick because I know he knows her best. Maybe even better than Lucia. Nick knows why she limped today and why she doesn't drink alcohol in public and why she hates racecar drivers. But I know he's not all that thrilled with himself for giving into me on this, so I don't want to push my luck. I stay silent until he hands me the bag of sushi outside Frankie's hotel suite door, and then I thank him and knock.

"That better be food, I'm starving!" I hear her bellow through the closed door, and when it swings open, she has a smile on her face, which immediately evaporates at the sight of me. "What the fuck."

"Hey love," I smile. "We need to talk."

Her eyes fly up behind me to her bodyguard. "If you wanted to be fired, you should have just asked."

"Why bother firing a bodyguard you don't actually use

anyway?" Nick fires back. I am amazed at their brother-sister-like relationship. Also, relieved. The dude is big, rugged, good-looking in an 'I will fuck you up' sort of way, and the first time I saw him in photos, lurking around her, I thought she was doing him. Honestly, I've always wondered if there was hanky panky because it's not unheard of in this world. People end up shagging whoever is closest and cutest out of convenience. It's why people think I'm banging Clara.

Frankie's beautiful face scrunches up in confusion. "What the hell are you talking about?"

"Antonio accosting you. You don't think I should know about that?" Nick asks and now she's glaring at me with the fire of a thousand exploding racecar engines. Great.

"We both know that he's not actually going to hurt me, physically, in the paddock," Frankie replies coldly. "Thanks for sharing, James. Asshole."

"Someone hurt you, and he's on that list, Frankie," Nick says, and it's like a lead bowling ball being hurled at my chest.

"What? When?" I ask but Nick and Frankie are in some silent fighting match, glaring at each other. "Hello. What the hell is he talking about, Frankie?"

She snatches the bag of sushi out of my hands. "Thanks. Bye."

She starts to try and close the door. I jam my foot in it, and Nick's massive, strong hand clamps down on my shoulder. Frankie's pretty eyes widen, and she re-opens the door. "A big part of me wants to watch you two fight like school girls in this hallway right now. And I don't even know who I want to win at this point."

She sighs and runs a hand through her hair, which is loose and messy around the shoulders of the hotel bathrobe she's wearing. "You can come inside for ten minutes. No more. Do you understand?"

"Perfectly." I also understand that she is going to break that time limit willingly.

Nick makes a growling noise but doesn't object, and he stomps over to his room next door.

There's a big, long hallway with a powder room at the end, and then it banks left and opens up into a huge living room with a bar and floor to ceiling windows. Frankie has left the curtains open so the city below twinkles and glimmers spectacularly in front of us. She pushes past me and walks over and puts the sushi down on the mirrored glass coffee table next to the pink velvet couch before making a point of closing the double doors that lead to the bedroom. I smirk. "Not sure what that is supposed to stop. We haven't needed a bed yet."

She blushes but remains cold. "What do you want, Billy?"

"To make it clear, again, that I would never date you to secure my spot on this team," I tell her, and she strides past me and sits on the couch.

She starts to cross her legs, but it makes the robe slip at the bottom, exposing her smooth tanned legs to halfway up her thigh. So she uncrosses them and tugs the robe closed again. I almost groan like a child who just had their candy taken away.

"You keep saying that. I keep finding reasons not to believe you," she counters. "And if what you told me in San Sebastian about your mom is true, then why would she even suggest such a thing?"

"Because she's heavily medicated and mixes it with booze," I blurt out before I even realize what I'm admitting. "She has bad judgement and a heightened ability to avoid reality. She doesn't talk about what my father did or admit it in public. No one but Clara and me know the full extent of the secrets."

"Clara, huh?" Frankie leans forward and starts to open the bag of sushi. "There's another thing. You keep denying you're close to her, but now you're telling me she knows your family's deepest, darkest secrets. You trust her with that, but you aren't into her? Hard sell."

"I never said I wasn't close to her. We're very, very close, emotionally. I said I wasn't sexually involved with her, and that's the God's honest truth. I would never touch her," I reply as she pulls out the sushi.

"I can't imagine why you wouldn't be banging her."

"Because I didn't tell her my family secrets." I can't believe I'm about to share this but yet, I am. "She is one. The biggest one."

That's got her attention. She's stopped fussing with her dinner and is staring up at me with an intense, unwavering stare. I swallow. "Clara is my sister."

"What?"

"Tommy is also Clara's dad," I go on. "Her mom worked in Montreal, she was part of the local company that worked the races there. Shiloh Ravenhart was a marketing minion, according to Clara. Very low position, but somehow she was assigned to escort Billy to press conferences while he was there, and he flirted with her. Shiloh was enamored. She willingly had a fling with him. Well, she thought it was a fling, but he kept in contact. Even had secret little trips to see her and flew her to wherever he was when she could get time off, and my mum was distracted in Australia with me. He demanded she be his only handler the next race in Montreal the following year. They were madly in love by then, and that's when Clara was conceived."

"Oh my God. Are you serious?" Frankie is blinking rapidly and her perfect mouth is hanging open.

I rake a hand into my hair and close my eyes. "This would be a bit much to make up, wouldn't it?"

"Yes. Of course. I didn't mean…" Frankie pauses, and when I open my eyes, she's standing in front of me. "I'm sorry."

"Sorry that my father was a two-timing manwhore?" I chuckle because she looks horrified by my bluntness. "I'm not really all that sorry Tommy did it, to be honest. Clara is great. The sibling I never knew I wanted. But I do want her in my life. She's been amazing. My mum, on the other hand, refuses to acknowledge her place in the family. Won't let us talk about it publicly. Threatens to try and off herself again if we tell people."

"Billy… that's horrible."

I nod and avert my eyes from her sympathetic gaze. I appreciate it, but I also hate it. I stare out at the twinkling cityscape in front of me. "The first time she tried it was when we found out about Clara. Her mother, Shiloh, had climbed her way up through the PR firm that managed the Montreal circuit. In part, it was because of my dad. People did what Tommy James wanted, but she was also skilled and good at her job. Of course, people liked to focus on the other stuff. When Clara was born, no one had proof she was Tommy's, but people judged Shiloh harshly anyway. And when Tommy died, she was fired within a week. That and his death cut off all her financial avenues."

"Tommy had been providing for them?" Frankie asks, slightly incredulous.

"Oh yeah he was dad of the year for Clara and partner of the year for Shiloh," I explain and move to the window. "He bought them a house Shiloh couldn't afford to keep without his help and her job. Had Clara in a fancy private school Shiloh couldn't afford to pay for without him. And no one in the sport wanted to hire Tommy James' side tail."

"Fuck."

"So, Shiloh contacted the lawyers. She wanted financial help. Give her child support or she would go to all the tabloids. Sure enough, when I found out about all this and dug deeper while Mum was in the psychiatric hospital, I did find emails from

Tommy to his lawyer talking about putting Clara in his will. He wanted everything split equally between Clara and me, but it just didn't get written up before the crash, so it wasn't legally binding," I explain and sigh. "I made sure it happened anyway. Mum is still not happy about it."

I can see her reflection in the glass of the window I'm standing in front of. She's like an apparition of an angel, hovering behind me. Beautiful, lovely, perfect. "I'm trusting you with this information."

"I won't tell anyone. Not Lucia or Nick or anyone."

I turn to face her. "Now, will you trust me?"

"With what?" She whispers and she looks scared. Terrified actually.

"What is going on with you? What happened to you?"

"That's too vague a question," she gives me a small, sad, self-conscious smile. I'm blown away by how little ego this woman really has. Under all the Instagram selfies and boisterous posts, she's just as self-doubting as the rest of us.

"Let's start with why wasn't Nick concerned when I told him I saw you limping?"

"Because he knows I have scoliosis and degenerative disc disease." Frankie says it without hesitation. My brain scrambles to remember what the hell scoliosis is. She explains before I have to ask. "Scoliosis is a curved spine, essentially. I've had it since birth. It's not going to kill me, but it makes life uncomfortable. Degenerative disc disease is being managed by cortisone shots and exercise. But all of this is why I never wear heels. It's why I use the pools in hotels for exercise. It's why I get so many massages and why I'm not a driver like Lucia. Like you."

"You wanted to drive?"

"More than anything," Frankie smiles, but it's dark and sad. "But my doctors explained without a shadow of a doubt, early on, that would never happen. But Dad made sure I knew I could still love racing and be a part of it. He encouraged my interest in the other side of Formula One. He never let me feel like I was giving anything up."

"Look at us with the verbal trust falls," I say and give her a wink. I'm being lighthearted because everything feels heavy right now, and I don't like it. I don't do heavy, not with women. Not in this way. But right now, Frankie Castera is like an emotional weighted blanket I want to bury myself under.

Frankie smiles. It's soft and sexy, and I try to tell myself the thickness of the mood in the room is just pure lust. Nothing more. Because *that* I can deal with. I step closer to her and dare to reach out and cup the side of her face. I am honestly not sure how she will react, but she doesn't slap my hand away. She leans her delicate jaw and high cheekbone into my palm, almost nuzzling me like a kitten. She inches closer. We're half a foot apart now and my free hand goes to the tie on her robe.

"This isn't a good idea."

"It's not an idea," I whisper back. "It's an unavoidable reality. And it's definitely going to be good."

"You make it sound so easy."

"Not easy, but worth it." I lean in and capture her mouth with mine. She kisses me back, without the hesitation I was expecting.

My hand tugs her robe open as my tongue pushes her lips apart and her arms curl around my neck. She is gloriously and completely naked under the robe, which my hands find out as they begin to explore. I am not stopping now. I'm not going slow. She's giving every sign that she's ready for it all now.

I let her start to pull my pants open enough to slide her hand inside and she cups my hard cock. I push myself into her and kiss my way across her neck. "I want to fuck you tonight."

"That's another trust fall for me, Billy," Frankie whispers her confession against my cheek.

"I know, love," I whisper back and cup her bare, beautiful ass. "I'll catch you. I'm your Aussie hero after all."

I scoop her up, and she lets out a squeak of surprise and repositions her arms around my neck again as I walk her past the long forgotten sushi, into the bedroom. I toss her onto the bed, and she lands with another squeal. Her robe is open, barely clinging to her shoulders. Her hair is fanned out across her pillows, her plump lips parted in a smile. This moment is absolutely fucking perfect.

I pull my shirt up over my head and drop it at the foot of the bed, where I also toe out of my shoes and tug off my pants, but not before grabbing the condom I shoved in the pocket earlier, hoping against hope. I crawl onto the bed, kissing and licking my way up her smooth legs. Her skin smells like lavender and vanilla. It's lovely. She's lovely.

I reach the apex of her thighs and give her a long, slow lick. She arches her back and curls her fingers into my hair, so of course I do it again. And a third time just for luck. She's wet and ready, and I am beyond impatient. I kiss her belly, and her breasts, swirling my tongue across her nipples, which are like rocks.

"Billy…" My name is caught between a moan and a demand.

I find her lips. "Tell me you want it."

She kisses me back, hard, her tongue sweeping over mine. With her left hand she plucks the condom from my hand and tears the package open without breaking the kiss. Then she pushes me so I'm on my back, and I gladly enjoy the show while I watch her take the condom and roll it on my cock, but not before giving it a sweet caress and a couple of euphoric tugs first.

But when she moves to climb on top of me, I flip her. I do it as gently as possible because of what she told me about her back. I know less than squat about scoliosis, but I intend to research the hell out of it. Later. "I said *I* wanted to fuck *you*."

I crawl over her and settle my hips between her long legs. Her hazel eyes are glassy like she's been drinking, but I know it's not alcohol. It's desire. I must look the same way. This has been such a long time coming. Still, I refuse to rush. "You didn't tell me you want it."

"I want you Billy. I've always wanted you, even when it felt masochistic," she confesses.

"Because I ghosted you?"

"Because I…" That sentence never gets finished. She stops herself, and I want to challenge her on that, but she's kissing me again, and I lose focus on anything but that. When she breaks the kiss she says, "I want to ride you."

"Next time," I promise and I can't believe I'm turning her down. Normally there is nothing I love more than a woman bouncing on my cock while I play with her tits, but tonight… I want her under me. I'm not some domineering twat. I just don't think I'll last long enough if I let Frankie take control.

I reach down and grab my cock, sliding it slowly across her opening. She arches her back a little and whimpers. "There isn't going to be a next time, Billy. We both know there can't be."

I wish she was wrong. "Later, then?"

"I've never come missionary," she warns me softly as I still play at her entrance. "I have to come with you. I need it."

"Sweetheart, I promise," I promise and push just the tip in. Oh fuck that's heaven. "I'll take you to that finish line."

She opens her mouth to argue, but instead I slide into her even more, and any words she might have spoken are gone. It's a blessing, really, because I wouldn't be able to form a response to anything she said anyway. I am too wrapped up in the feeling of her slick, warm heat hugging every inch of my dick. I feel my stomach drop, my balls tighten.

She says my name. "Billy."

It's breathy but firm. And our eyes connect as I slide in completely. This is it. Teenage fantasies come to fruition at long last. She's this race I didn't realize I've been competing in for a decade. And now, the checkered flag is flying high and this… this is the victory lap I am going to remember for the rest of my life. I slide out, almost completely, and back in. "Your pussy was meant for me."

Her answer is a long moan. I find a rhythm. It's not perfect because I have to slow down every now and then to keep from coming too soon. She's writhing under me, shifting her hips and chasing that elusive missionary orgasm. I reach up behind her head and grab one of the pillows. "Put your feet on the bed and lift that sweet ass."

A flicker of skepticism passes through those amber eyes but she does what I ask and I slip the pillow under her lower back. Our eyes meet, and I kiss her and then ask softly, "That okay?"

"I think so…" I slide into her farther and the 'o' in that last word slips into a moan.

"Wrap those gorgeous legs around my thighs, love," I whisper against her neck and she follows orders without a flicker of hesitation this time. I push higher into her. And holy shit. I am seeing stars. She must be too because that breathy moan of hers has climbed an octave. The base of my cock is buried against her clit and I barely have to move my hips to more pleasure than I've ever felt in my life. She feels it too and reaches up for me as I roll and grind so deep inside her, so in-fucking-credibly deep… All it takes is a few long, slow, aching strokes and then I feel the world start to slip away.

"Oh my God… oh God… Billy…" She whimpers and comes, like a warm tsunami, that rushes in and takes my own orgasm with it as it rushes out a few moments later.

My arms quiver and give up, and I drop down on top of her. Her legs are Jell-O slipping off the back of my thighs and she takes a slow, shuddering gulp of air. I smile against her silky hair fanned out under my cheek on the pillow. "Can't say you never came from missionary now, can you?"

"You really are a hero." She sighs and we both start laughing.

I must have drifted off after I pulled out of her and dropped the condom into a waste bin, because suddenly, I'm waking up. I don't think it's been too long, but Frankie isn't in bed with me. I sit up and spot her crossed bare feet on the ottoman in the living room. I untangle myself from the sheets, pull on my underwear, and join her. Frankie is stretched out on the sofa. She's wearing the shirt I walked in here wearing and a pair of silk boxer bottoms and is popping sushi into her mouth. Next to her on the couch is the tiny little crocheted panda I ordered off of Etsy for her back when she got the job. I'm thrilled she kept it and has obviously been toting it around. That's why I picked the smaller one on the site, so she could travel with him, if she wanted to. "I'm starving."

I smile and lean on the door frame. "I can see that."

"Sorry not sorry if I look like a pig."

"You look like a sexy, incredible woman," I explain and push myself off the wall to walk toward her. "A ravenous one, but still sexy and incredible."

I lean in and reach for a piece of sushi for myself. She narrows her eyes and I grin. "You wore me out too, love. If there's going to be a round two, I'll need sustenance."

She lifts an eyebrow, but she's also fighting a smile as she tries to say in a serious tone, "Who said anything about another round?"

"Tell me if I walk over there and stick my hand in those cute little boxers I won't find the perfect little pussy wet and eagerly awaiting round two," I challenge, and my words make her blush just the slightest.

"Eat your sushi," she commands without answering my question, which is answer enough. She glances at the crocheted stuffie beside her and back at me. "I don't need two pompous pandas in here."

I pop a piece of dynamite roll into my mouth and walk over and drop down on the sofa beside her. As I swallow and lift her legs onto my lap instead of the ottoman, she grabs a spicy salmon roll expertly with some chop sticks and holds it in front of me. I open my mouth, and she drops it in. When I'm done eating, I wink at her. "For the record, I'm leaving room for dessert."

My eyes boldly slide to those boxers I mentioned earlier, and she puts down the chop sticks and the tray of sushi.

"No one said you had to wait until the meal is over to eat dessert."

"You're fucking incredible, you know that?" I yank on her legs, dragging her closer to me on the sofa and lay her out on her back.

She's giggling joyfully as I slide my hands up her thighs and tug off the boxers.

Round two is just as mind-blowing as round one. I let the post-orgasm haze blanket over the dark thoughts that lurk in the back of my mind. Thoughts about how I'm going to live the rest of my life without a round three, or four, or four hundred and fifty-four.

As she lays half asleep and spent on the couch, I walk into the bedroom, grab a blanket and come back in. I sit down beside her and cover her with it. She curls up next to me, and I reach for the sushi tray again. I pop one into her mouth after dipping it in soy.

"How do you know I don't want wasabi or ginger?"

"Because it was one of the many things you mentioned that night while we talked until dawn," I remind her and grab a piece of ginger and drop it on top of an avocado roll and pop that into my mouth. "You only ever put soy sauce on sushi."

"You remember that little detail?" I nod and she smiles. "I'm touched. I wish I remembered more of that night but the whole weekend is foggy thanks to the drug thing."

I reach down and grab the complimentary bottle of sparkling

water the hotel must have put in a champagne bucket for her. I open it and drink straight from it, instead of bothering with glasses. She takes it from my hand when I'm done, and as she takes her own sip I ask, "I had no idea you had a drug problem when I met you. You hid it well."

"I hid nothing. I didn't have a drug problem," she replies quietly and swiftly. "I know that sounds like denial, but it was a one-time incident."

"But you went to rehab."

"Because my dad needed me to," Frankie replies and snuggles closer as she grabs another roll. She's not bothered by discussing this, and I see it as a good sign but also a warning. She is vulnerable with me. This is new and a sign we're getting closer, which we shouldn't because, as she herself has pointed out, we can't go anywhere with this. "He was terrified, and it brought up all this repressed guilt he had over my mom and how he parented without her. He blamed himself, and he needed me to go for his peace of mind more than my own. So I went."

I absorb that information and wrap an arm around her as her cheek presses to my chest. "But you didn't need to go?"

"No. I didn't take… drugs before that night. I'd smoked weed once in boarding school at fourteen. That was literally it," Frankie says, and the hesitation in her voice, the way her sentence stuttered for a second makes me think there's something she's not telling me. Why? "Anyway, it wasn't a bad idea. Recovery centers are good for more than just addiction issues. I needed the calm, the solitude, and the therapists for other things."

She falls silent and doesn't elaborate on that. I want her to, but at the same time that little bit of emotional distance she is keeping between us is for the best. For both of us. So I change the subject. "Bash is a great dad."

"He is."

Which reminds me… "I think Adelaide is pregnant."

The mood, the warmth of the bond we were beginning to form, is blown right out of the hotel room like someone just turned on an industrial fan. She stiffens under my arm and then sits bolt upright. "What?"

I explain what I saw but avoid telling her Adelaide confessed openly to Mum. I don't want to start bad blood between Adelaide and Mum or anyone else. Judging by the look in Frankie's eyes, she believes it without that information anyway. "Shit. Lucia and I joke about that all the time. It can't be real. Holy shit, did she really go for the anchor baby?"

"I don't know if it's that so much as, you know, actual love and a ticking biological clock," I reply cautiously.

Frankie frowns at me like I just said the stupidest thing ever and springs off the couch, in search of her phone. She grabs it from the chair by the windows, and I know she's immediately texting Lucia. Which means our time is done because there is no way her sister isn't going to beeline it right over here as soon as she gets the news. So I stand and try to take the phone out of her hand. There's a small, silly little struggle which I win by distracting her with a searing kiss. But it's too late. A text has been sent.

"No round three now," I reply sadly.

She looks as sad as I feel but she says, "It's probably for the best. One more time and this might become…"

"A habit."

"An addiction," she replies.

"I thought you didn't have those."

"I think you might be the exception," Frankie whispers and walks right up to me and cups my package through my boxer briefs as she presses the full, perfect mouth to the space just above my collarbone. I push my dick into her hand and grab her hair and tug her head back so I can claim her mouth.

And then the expected fist is pounding on the hotel room door.

We break apart… our hands clinging together as long as possible until she's one step too close to the door and I'm one step too close to the bedroom, and our fingers can no longer touch. I push the bedroom door closed and dress quickly. Lucia has burst into the suite, talking a mile a minute about Adelaide, using words like gold-digger and social climber and expressing concern her dad is possibly senile.

When I hear Lucia say, "Where did you get that shirt? It's way too big to be yours," I open the door and step out and all talk stops entirely. Lucia's big brown eyes widen to the point where I worry they might fall out of her head.

"Lucia," I say and smile. I hand Frankie her silky tank that matches her boxers. "I'm gonna need that shirt back, love."

"Love?" Lucia repeats, eyes still the size of tires.

"Relax," Frankie warns her sister as she turns her back to us, pulls off my shirt and tosses it in my general direction, and starts to put on her tank. Lucia turns her back to her sister and glares at me, which I ignore.

"The glass is acting like a mirror, love. Not that I mind," I explain to Frankie as I take in the jiggle of her full, bare breasts as she changes.

She turns back to me as I pull on my own shirt. "Get some sleep. I need you to perform tomorrow."

"More than he's already performed tonight?" Lucia mutters, and I grin and lean toward the younger Castera.

"I've got enough in the tank," I promise. Lucia wrinkles her nose and turns away from me with a gagging noise.

I walk over and kiss Frankie. I mean it to be chaste, but I'm suddenly filled with melancholy at the realization this is probably our last kiss, so I deepen it. And only pull away when Lucia bellows. "Enough!"

I break the kiss and smile at Frankie but it's soft and probably a little sad, because that's how I feel. "See you tomorrow, boss."

"Tomorrow," she murmurs, and I leave. Closing the door to her suite is way harder than I want it to be, and I barely sleep all night because of the dull ache in my chest at the idea that tonight will never happen again.

13

MY HEART BEGS TO DIFFER

FRANKIE

Dad is smiling so big and so proud it's impossible to yell at him, which is all I actually want to do. But that smile... he's so happy. And Adelaide looks positively joyful and glowing, which I'm surprised I missed before.

"We didn't not tell you on purpose," Adelaide says as we all sit on the private terrace off their hotel suite. There's fruit and croissants and carafes of coffee and herbal tea in front of us, but I'm not touching any of it. Neither is Lucia. "Your dad thought it best you both focus on the season, because there's so much at stake for you both."

"You can frame it however you want, Adelaide. But this is a family matter, a big one that affects our entire lives, and keeping it from us for any reason is just a lame excuse," Lucia replies and turns to our dad. "Is this why you retired?"

"Partly, yes," Dad says and stirs a heaping spoonful of sugar into his coffee. "I didn't get to spend as much time with you girls as I wished I had, and I didn't want to make the same mistake with this one."

Adelaide smiles and gently places a hand on the back of his

157

neck. Holy shit… she might actually love him. I feel like I'm spinning through the Twilight Zone because I've never let myself think that this was truly real. I thought I knew her too well because after all, I used to model with Adelaide. She never, in all our time together, acted like she wanted anything more than a glass of fine champagne and someone else to pay for it. Love? Kids? Thoughts on those things were never expressed by her.

"To be fair, Louie, we also wanted to make sure this one stuck around before we announced," Dad says, using the nickname he bestowed Lucia when she was a little girl. His eyes grow dark, as does the expression on Adelaide's pretty features, and my heart clenches.

"We had a miscarriage before this," Adelaide confesses. "So we're tentative."

"I'm sorry," I blurt out and I mean it. She gives me a soft smile. I blink, trying to wade my way through all of the information and emotions that are swirling through my brain. "I love you Dad, but… you're—"

"Old," he finishes for me. "Honey, fifty is not old and I intend to remind you of the hassle you keep giving me when you turn it. Anyway, Adelaide is young, and healthy and full of love. If this baby may one day have to be raised by just her, so what? You two were raised by a single parent and you both turned out spectacular."

"And, in case the concern is for more than his health, the baby gets nothing of Mirabella Racing when your father passes. That's solely for you two to do with as you wish," Adelaide explains. There's no venom in her voice, or annoyance.

Lucia voices my thoughts, loud and clear. "You actually fucking love him?"

"Oh for God's sake, Lucia, you really didn't believe that until now?" Dad barks, and he's uncharacteristically angry. It's proba-bly, rightfully, fueled by hurt. "You have such little respect for me that you think I wouldn't see through her if there was anything less than love between us?"

"No, Dad, that's not what I thought." Lucia stands up. "Men just as strong and brilliant as you have lost their common sense due to loneliness and a tight piece of ass."

"Lucia!"

"It's fine. She called my ass tight," Adelaide tries to joke, but the fury in my dad's eyes will not be easily quelled.

"I'm sorry Adelaide, but you were a party girl model with a bankrupt family," Lucia doubles down, and the rage brewing in my father reddens his cheeks. "He's about to be a senior citizen with a bank account and legacy worth millions. You have to know how that looked. How this baby will look."

"I do know. I just don't care," Adelaide counters and still, there's no malice in her voice. "I think you would be a better driver too, Lucia, if you stopped caring how everything looked and just went for it. You stress and worry about the weight of being the first female driver about to crack F1. Fuck the haters who think you're only there because your daddy owns the team. Screw the way it looks."

"I do not need racing advice from you," Lucia seethes and stands up.

Dad stands up too. "What you need is a lesson in manners and respect."

"Then I guess you didn't do such a good job raising me after all, huh?" Lucia snaps back and I feel my stomach drop.

"Lucia. Enough," I warn, but I don't know if she hears me, because she's halfway out of the suite.

Dad storms out after her. I want to chase them both and play referee, a job I've had my whole life, especially since my mom passed. But as I stand up, Adelaide reaches across the table and puts a hand on mine, freezing me in my tracks. "Let them work this out on their own. You have enough on your plate."

"I appreciate the idea, but honestly Ade, I don't need your input here," I pull my hand away but what she says next stops me in my tracks.

"I'm part of this family now too, Frankie," she announces, firmly. "I've been quiet and bowed out of most discussions that involved you, your sister, and your father, but that was a grace period. I was giving you time to adapt. Now I'll be speaking up for me and for this bambino."

"Since we're being honest, I don't agree with the blunt force my sister uses when she speaks, but I don't disagree with her opinions," I tell her. "I knew you Adelaide. You were not interested in a long-term anything."

"I wanted love," Adelaide replies. "I had a pretty face and not much else. Lucia isn't wrong, my dad notoriously gambled away my family's money. I couldn't even afford the shared flat in London that I was living in when you met me if I hadn't been giving the landlord blow jobs a couple times a week."

I cringe but she doesn't. "Your dad knows about it. He knows it all. And he loves me anyway. Did I expect to fall in love with your dad? No. When I met him I just saw a charming, handsome dad of a friend. Someone who might bank roll a few rounds of drinks or a vacation if I stayed close to you. But then he asked me out, and I said yes because of the way you had always talked about him. You made him out to be this perfect man, and guess what? You were right. Even I wasn't stupid enough to pass that up."

I stare at her. My heart is hammering in my chest. I want to hate this… her… but as always, I don't. And now, I also don't feel angst about that. She really does love my father and as her hands rub her tiny belly, I let my thoughts jump to the idea that I'm going to be a big sister again. It's not an unpleasant thought. "It's going well this time?"

"Splendid. We find out the sex soon. Your dad doesn't want to know, but I do," Adelaide replies. "I'm all over the place with names and knowing will help me focus."

"Charles if it's a boy. It's what my dad would have called Lucia or me if we'd been one," I tell her. "It was his dad's name."

She shakes her head, then brushes back a strand of hair that's fallen from the side of the French braid. "He said that was for him and Mirabella. He doesn't want to use it now, with me. I respect that."

I take a shaky breath at the mention of my mother. "He'll be a great dad."

"He already is."

I nod. "And you'll do a bang up job too."

She smiles. "Thanks."

My dad barges back onto the terrace. He sits down and we finish breakfast in a heavy silence. Then he scoops the blazer with the Mirabella crest off the back of the chair he was in and slips it on. "We're going to be late if we don't leave now."

He doesn't mention Lucia, and so I don't either. He holds Adelaide's hand all the way down to the lobby, where he climbs into his car after her, and I climb into my car alone. Nick puts the car in gear and pulls into traffic. "I saw Lucia storm out, so that went well."

"Dad knocked…" I pause and realize I don't want to refer to my impending sibling that way. "Adelaide and Dad are having a baby."

I watch his eyes widen in surprise through the rearview mirror. "That's… well, I mean… congrats."

"Yeah. I know. It's a dramatic shift to say the least."

"And you and Lucia are still questioning Adelaide's motives, so I can see where a fight might have happened," Nick replies. I nod.

"I don't think I'm questioning Ade's motives anymore," I reply as I watch the world whiz by outside. "I really do just want him to be happy. And I don't hate the idea of a sibling. I hope it's a boy."

Nick smiles. I can tell by the way his eyes crinkle in the corners in the rearview. "There's nothing a male child could give Bash that he doesn't get from the two of you."

I smile back at him through the mirror with gratitude.

"So… I take it you're also not questioning Billy James' motives anymore?" Nick asks quietly as he pulls to a stop at a red light. "Judging by the way he didn't leave your room after ten minutes last night."

I purposely look out the window to avoid him reading anything I'm not willing to say on my face. "I have new information that has changed my perspective on him and our past. He wasn't using me to get to my dad."

"And now?" Nick pushes. "Is he using you now?"

"No. I mean…" I bite my bottom lip. "Well, maybe, but in the same way I'm using him."

I glance in the mirror and see Nick's eyes cloud with confusion. "Sex," I clarify. "We were using each other for sex."

"TMI Frankie."

"Yeah, because you don't know anything about bed buddy life, do ya Nick?"

His eyes slide away from the mirror, away from me. "This isn't about me," he replies, ignoring my reference to him and my sister. "And I noticed you used the word were. You *were* using each other."

"Because it's over. It's run its course," I say airily like I'm talking about why I'm donating clothes that have gone out of style. Oh, if only it was that simple. My heart begs to differ. "I'm his boss, technically, and under way more scrutiny than any other Team Principal may be in the history of this sport. So I need to not be caught naked with my driver."

"Since when have you bowed to the patriarchy?" Nick asks as

he flashes his credentials at the gates to the track, and we pull into the VIP lot. "Didn't Bash raise you two to give the patriarchy the middle finger instead of worrying about what box they want to put you in?"

"Mom taught us that. Dad backed her up," I clarify and fuss with my hair. It sounds stupid, but I worry about how I wear it. I hate wearing it back or up because it is so thick and heavy it makes my head hurt and I'm always fussing with loose ends, but I wore it down to the first few races and the press—and assholes on the Mirabella Racing Instagram—made comments. Nasty shit like 'Oh, princess got a new blowout for the occasion' and 'Well if you're going to tank a race team, you might as well look good doing it.' So now I've been trying to look more business, which I've equated with less feminine. Which suddenly angers me.

I get out of the car, not waiting for Nick to walk around and open my door like I usually do. I open it myself and push my shoulders all the way back, which makes my shirt feel tight. So, I unbutton the top button, which I'd stopped doing. I've been shamed by trolls on social media, and I've been letting them win. Nick is right. I can be a woman, whatever version of woman I want, and not have it alter my qualifications or abilities. And anyone who thinks otherwise can go fuck themselves.

I walk with Nick toward the paddock. Lucia's race should have already started. I hope she got her head clear enough that she can do well. I don't begin to understand Lucia's brain. She is an athlete through-and-through, so she is nothing but adrenaline, focus, and passion. She's so hyper-focused in racing it's bled through to everyday life. Everything is black and white to Lucia. Right or wrong. Yes or no. And change… and things like unexpected siblings, are a harder adjustment for her than me. I know my dad will realize that when he calms down.

The look of determination she gets in her dark eyes when she is about to climb into that car, I've never seen on anyone else.

And yeah, I guess Billy and Antonio and the other drivers get that too, but even they don't reach the level of intensity Lucia does, and that's because they don't have to. They're men.

"Someone is getting her mojo back," Nick murmurs and I give him side eye, which leads to a cheeky grin on his ruggedly handsome face. "You should let your hair down too."

"I see why my sister likes you," I reply casually because the photographers that are here are kept behind a rope so no one can hear us with my voice so low. I yank the elastic out of my hair and give it a subtle fluff with my hands.

"Lucia doesn't like me. She likes fucking me. There's a big difference," Nick replies. "Believe me, she's explained it. Ad nauseum."

I wrinkle my nose for a millisecond, hopefully not long enough to get the expression caught by the photogs. "Lucia is a turtle. She has a hard shell she hides in as long and as much as possible. But sometimes she surprises you. On her terms of course, in her own time."

"Frankie!" I hear my name as we walk through paddock row as I call it, toward the Mirabella paddock. They've put petunias around each patio here in a dark, rich gold color. And just beyond them is Rocco, standing with Antonio and Billy.

As soon as Billy's eyes meet mine, my body has a visceral reaction. My blood warms, my heart beat picks up, and the corners of my mouth want to turn up into a smile, but I fight it. I fight all of it. I can*not* look like a lovesick fool because I'm not one. I just have oxytocin still bouncing around my system. It's science, nothing more.

"We're calling an early meeting," Rocco says.

I glance at my phone. Our first strategy meeting of the day shouldn't have been for another forty-five minutes. Billy and Antonio should be in their respective rooms with the respective trainers doing pre-race exercises. Plus, our strategy was basically worked out yesterday after qualifying. This meeting that I clearly walked up on is way more intense than should be necessary looking at their stern faces.

"Okay. Let me get a coffee and meet you in the conference room," I say easily.

"Can we skip your fancy latte, or can you have your assistant get it?" Rocco replies and I bristle. "This can't wait."

Nick stiffens because that assistant comment is being hurled at him.

"Okay then," I say and the easy tone is gone. "I'll skip the caffeine, and Nick is not my assistant. He's my bodyguard. If you'd like to know what the difference is, I'm sure Nick can show you exactly what he does."

"Would be my pleasure," Nick growls.

"Oh good, now she's threatening us," Antonio barks.

"Tony, relax, mate," Billy replies, and when Antonio turns to him ready to complain further, Billy's expression darkens immediately. "I'm not kidding around."

"We need to move inside," Rocco says quietly, his eyes darting around to make sure we don't have an audience.

Everyone swivels to the door, but Nick steps forward and blocks the men so I can enter first. I pretend like it's not a big deal, but I know it makes Antonio rage even harder. I knew Dad giving me this position would be a hard sell for everyone, but I can't for the life of me figure out why Antonio is making this as difficult as he is. Even Rocco has moments of professionalism, and he basically lost the job he has wanted his whole life. So why is it Antonio losing it every five minutes? Is it just the threat of Lucia moving up on the team? Because that's always been there too, with or without me.

We enter the conference room, and I motion for Nick to stay outside. I know he doesn't like the idea by the grimace on his face as he nods, but if I want to shift people's perspective, I need my bodyguard to distance himself at least a little. Otherwise, I'm still the little girl who needs watching. People don't think he's protecting me from others, they think he's protecting me from myself.

"Antonio doesn't like the strategy. The Plan A," Rocco explains.

I fold my arms over my chest. "Okay. Why?"

"Because I'm only seven points off Billy," Antonio says. "And you're basically ensuring his win. Telling me to back down at all costs."

"Yep," I reply calmly. "Billy is second on the grid. He has the best shot. If… when you start higher than him again, you'll be Batman, he'll be Robin. I promise. Does that make you feel better?"

"No," he growls. "It should be a fight no matter who is where on the grid. I have a shot at the Championship right now as much as Billy."

"This is nothing new, Tony. We did this all the time when Bash was in charge," Billy tries to reason with him.

"Yeah, and it gained you a championship but never me, and I'm in it this year for my life, just like you," Antonio barks back and stands so abruptly his chair topples. He glances over his shoulder at the television in the corner.

Someone before us had turned it on to the live stream of the F2 race. Lucia is in the lead. All our eyes go there, and I sigh. "My promotion doesn't automatically mandate that she will get one of your spots next year. It's no different than when Bash was in charge."

"Yeah, well, she is having a hell of a season so far, and I'm not an idiot, Frankie. If she wins F2 she needs to move up," Antonio replies. "So let me do my thing and secure *my* spot. Unless you've already made your decision."

"I haven't," I say and my frustration shows in my tone. "I

won't keep placating you. You're a big boy, Antonio. Be an adult, which includes following a strategy set forth by your team to garner the best results for Mirabella. Not for you or Billy. *Mirabella*."

"You want no rules, mate. I'm up for it," Billy says suddenly. He turns to me. "I'm sorry. I'm not trying to undermine you or your strategy, but seriously, Frankie, I'm getting as sick of this as you are. If Tony thinks he can take me, let him try. If he gets himself into a position that allows him a chance to overtake me, let him do it."

"She doesn't have to let me." Antonio barks.

"Actually, yes she does," Rocco interjects, pinching his dark brows together like it hurts him to admit that. But hey, he admitted it. Progress, I guess.

"If you are good with that Billy, then fine. But." I raise a hand and point a finger at Antonio. "If you two get in some sort of dog fight and take each other out of this race, costing the team all the points, I'll be done with both of you."

I pivot on a heel and storm out of the room and head in search of that coffee I so desperately need. As I climb the metal staircase to the cafeteria, I feel eyes on me. Over my shoulder I glimpse Billy standing at the bottom of the stairs, staring up at me. Well, my ass. I pretend I don't notice, avoiding any eye contact at all costs, and continue up the stairs, making sure my ass sways enticingly the whole damn time.

He might not ever have me again, but that doesn't mean I want him thinking about it.

14

YOUR TIRES DIDN'T GET THE MEMO

FRANKIE

Lucia wins. I head to the garage to congratulate her and am shocked that Dad and Adelaide aren't there. Whatever words were exchanged when he followed her out of the hotel earlier today, they obviously made things worse instead of better. Dad has never not been in the garage, on the pit wall and by her side as soon as she finishes a race.

I slip past her engineers and mechanics and wrap her in my arms. She hugs me back. "You are on fire."

"I got lucky on turn four in the first lap and was almost overtaken in the fifteenth," Lucia is always her biggest critic. "And if it wasn't for that safety car being deployed after Hastings hit the wall, the results would have been different."

"You always focus on the bad," I reply and smile and hand her a soda from my newest sponsor. It's a vegan soda company. So far, the one flavor I can tolerate is black cherry, but I'm hoping my sister likes the other flavors.

She tips back the raspberry one and makes sure the label is visible for the photographers.

"Thanks," I whisper.

"You owe me," she whispers back when she finishes taking a sip. "This tastes like ass."

"So it's not just me." I sigh. "I didn't have time to taste all the flavors. I liked the black cherry one, so I just said yes. Fuck."

"Don't worry about it. Just promo the hell out of that one flavor," Lucia says and pretends to take another sip, but I can tell she isn't letting the offending liquid past her lips.

"Go, enjoy your victory," I take the bottle from her and give her another quick hug before she runs off to do the podium. I make my way to where her F2 crew is gathered at the bottom podium and stand with them as they play the French national anthem and give Lucia her trophy. The whole time, as I lean on the barricade, I make sure to hold the soda with the label facing out.

When the ceremony is over, I blow Lucia a kiss and make my way to a quiet corner of the garage. I ignore yet another call from Jennie, who is furious I've been neglecting my influencer contracts, and call my father immediately. "I get that you two are not on the same page right now, but you've never missed one of her races, Dad."

"She doesn't want me there," he huffs. "She told me flat out."

"Doubtful." Lucia and I made a pact after our mom died to never shut out our dad or each other. She wouldn't break that now over a baby. Even if we were kind of blindsided.

"Well, she might as well have said it. She doesn't support my marriage, Frankie, and I've had enough of it. From both of you, so know if you take her side, I will start pulling away from you too," Dad warns.

"This is how you make a problem worse, Dad," I explain through gritted teeth because I am furious. This is the vortex of hell that can come from second marriages and mixed families. It doesn't have to, but it can. "Look, we knew one day you might remarry. We wanted you to be happy and in love again. We just didn't get what we were expecting, and now there's a baby thrown in that we didn't hear about from you. So give us a minute, okay? Especially Louie. You know she doesn't handle change well. It like shorts out her brain or something. Don't escalate this hurt into something we can't mend."

"I'm giving Lucia some much needed breathing room." He hangs up before I can argue with him further.

I sigh and open up the alert that says I have fourteen text messages. They are all Jennie.

Hello? Can you tell me when your next break is so I can book you a flight to Amalfi so we can do that promo with the yacht company?

You made me Google the race schedule. Thanks for nothing. Booking you on a flight Monday. Ok?

Hellllloooooo?! OK? Please respond asap.

Fuck it. I booked you. If it's wrong YOU can rebook it.

The texts go on and increase in profanity because she's asking more questions about other promo stuff, and I am not responding, and then finally, they end on a positive note.

At least you remembered to promo the soda. Yay. NOW ANSWER ME.

I text her back while I take my position on the pit wall in the garage and wait for our race to begin. Rocco is in some deep conversation with Rhett, one of our other engineers. I put on my headphones and tune out the world as I answer the million personal business questions Jennie has not so patiently thrown at me in the last twenty-four hours. I feel horrible about blowing her off. I know she's just doing her job, and I know I've been shit at balancing my influencer stuff and the race team stuff, which I promised her wouldn't happen. I have a pile of new shoe designs to approve or reject sitting in an unopened envelope in my suitcase back at the hotel, too. I promise myself I will work on that while I fly to the Amalfi Coast for that yacht photo thing and then do more work on the flight to Mexico for the next race.

I'm deep in my own work-zone, still glued to my email, when there's a tap on my shoulder. "Are you the Team Principal today or not? Because I'll gladly step in if you aren't going to pay attention."

"What?" I blink and put my phone in the back pocket of my jeans.

"They're doing the formation lap. Are you in this or what?" Rocco demands, annoyed. I wish I could blame him, but I can't. I'm fucking up every which way today.

I ignore him but turn to the wall of screens and flip on my radio so I can hear the drivers, and they can hear me. "Okay, remember boys. Plan A unless I announce otherwise."

"Amended Plan A," Antonio says flatly.

Right. Plan A is soft tires until lap twenty one at the earliest. Then switch to mediums. Billy to pit first. Antonio to hold position and hopefully be in a spot to give Billy a lap of help or two before he's brought in.

Amended Plan A is same tires and lap count, but free-for-all when it comes to pit strategy and defense and overtaking. Great. I fight the urge to tell Antonio he's a little bitch and just say, "Amended A. Of course. *Bonne chance mes amis.*"

My father always said that to them when he was Principal, and I'm delighted when Billy answers back the way he would if it was my dad. "Don't need luck, but I'll slap it on like aftershave for the hell of it."

"Sounds good." I smile, and the radios go silent as the drivers line the cars up on the grid.

Lights out, and both of them get off to a brilliant start. Billy is forced wide by Luke Hannaford, an American driver who is always way more aggressive than I think is safe. He's a contender, I get it. He hasn't had his first championship, but he's always in the top five every year. He's hungry, but he lets that hunger make him dangerous. As Billy is almost pushed into the wall, Hannaford gains the lead.

"That was bullshit," Billy's voice booms over the radio.

"We know it," Dario says, and he immediately calls the stewards who tell him they're investigating.

"He should get to retake the lead," I tell them. "That's what we want."

Dario looks at me like, *duh*, and continues pleading our case on the phone. I grit my teeth and try to take solace in the fact that Antonio has moved into third. If Antonio wanted to be a team player, this news would sit better with me, but he won't do what I want, which is help Billy regain the lead. So now I have to manage my own drivers racing each other.

Antonio is within DRS of Billy, and they battle through the long straight. Antonio almost passes, but Billy manages to hold him off. There's a tense moment when it looks like they might touch, which would likely cause one or both of them to career off the track.

"Antonio…" I just say his name, warningly through a clenched jaw, into the radio. Rocco glances over at me. Dario actually shushes me. I ignore it.

"It's a race, Frankie, so I am racing," Antonio responds, and his jaw sounds clenched too, and I'm sure it has nothing to do with the stressfulness of the actual race.

I turn to Rocco and give him a WTF gesture with my hands because if I speak anything out loud, the cameras and mics will pick it up. Rocco stares back passively and shrugs before turning back to the monitors.

By the time we're almost halfway through the race, both Antonio and Billy have pitted once. We've moved them to soft tires, which won't last the whole race. We're on a two-pit strategy, which everyone knows now by the tire choice, but the key is when we pit them again. I scribble a note to Rocco that says Billy is the priority because he has managed to hold onto a very close second against Hannaford. The stewards did not, in fact, give him his position back, which Dario told them was not the right call, but as usual, they give zero shits what we think. Antonio had fallen to fourth but just overtook again to reclaim third. He's back to gunning to try and overtake Billy, which is putting unnecessary wear on his tires.

"Antonio, we need some good old fashioned restraint from you for the next few laps," I say over the radio.

"It's a race."

"I am aware, but perhaps your tires didn't get the memo." It's bitchy, and I want to regret it, but I don't. He's being an ass. Joaquin snickers beside me on the wall. Rocco shoots me a disapproving glare for a second, which I ignore. "We need these to last a little bit longer than your current strategy will allow."

"I need to concentrate," Antonio barks. "Please stop yapping."

The rage is instantaneous, like a firework discharging in the depths of my gut, and it spreads like wildfire through my body. That fucking asshole would not have said that to a man. I've heard him get frustrated before in a race, with Bash and with Rocco, and the condescending tone and a word like 'yapping' would never have left his mouth.

I rip off my headset and stand up. I close my eyes and take the deepest breath I can without choking and then I let it out as slowly as possible. I am firing him at the end of the season whether Lucia is ready or not, I think to myself. At least, I'm going to tell him that at the end of the race so he has ample warning. Maybe that's the reality check he needs to get the fuck on board.

And then, as my eyes open I watch everyone on the wall cringe simultaneously. My eyes fly to the screen. Another driver has crashed in the third turn. After spinning out, his back end plows into the barrier. He's already getting out of the car, so he's fine, thankfully, but there are car parts littered over the whole track as soon as the drivers come out of the turn.

I jump back in my seat and shove my headset on in time to hear the yellow flag announcement. Rocco covers his mic and turns to me. "Pit?"

I shake my head. "Give it a minute."

"But it's the perfect opportunity to get them fresh tires that will last the rest of the race," Rocco argues, and I shake my head firmly. He frowns. "You're gambling."

"I said give it a minute," I repeat.

"Box," Antonio says it. He doesn't ask it, which fuels my rage further.

"Please hold, Tony," Rocco grumbles back into the radio.

"Tires are struggling," Billy warns.

Hannaford has a good two seconds on Billy, and I know Billy can't pass him on a safety car. And I also know that if he stays on these tires for much longer, he won't have enough grip to overtake when they pull the safety car. So yeah, I'm gambling, but when Hannaford approaches the pit lane and pulls in, I get back on the radio in the calmest but sternest voice I have and say, "Do not pit."

"Are you sure?" Billy questions in an equally calm voice, but I know he's actually kind of panicking.

"Yes. Stay out there."

And then I tell Antonio the same thing as he nears the pit lane.

"What?" Antonio barks.

"Stay out."

"Rocco? Rocco! I need to pit," Antonio replies, ignoring me completely.

I curl my fists into balls and turn to Rocco. He looks at me with confusion and frustration on his rugged features, and then he stands up and folds his arms across his chest. "You heard your Principal."

I know it's killing him to back me up. I rip off my headset again and walk over to Rocco, he covers his mic and I whisper, "There's too much debris. They'll call a red flag. If we stay out, Billy keeps the lead."

Dario interjects from his seat next to Rocco. "I don't think it's enough debris."

"It is."

The duo frown.

"I've made the call," I say firmly and storm back over to my seat and put my earphones back on.

Then, two laps later, still under the safety car. I hear Billy's voice crackle over the radio. "It's getting harder. I don't think I can finish on these, Frankie."

"I know. You won't have to," I promise. "Trust me."

There's a long silence before I hear him say, "Okay."

And then Antonio fills my ears. "I can't. This is bullshit. Rocco, I'm losing a perfectly good opportunity."

"Pit. Pit." Rocco's voice startles me.

"No! Stay out!" I cut in tersely.

"Pitting," Antonio replies. "Thanks, Rocco."

Antonio pulls into the pit. I stare at the screen in disbelief. The pit crew is not ready and panic ensues. Panic for everyone except Rocco and Antonio. I pull off my headphones and walk over to Rocco. "Leave."

"Excuse me?" Rocco looks truly shocked. Like he thought I would just roll over and take it. He clearly has never paid an ounce of attention to me on any level, or he would have known better.

"Get the fuck out of my garage. Now."

"My job is to—"

"Get the fuck out now because if you think I won't call Nick and forcibly remove you, you are wrong," I reply, cutting him off and stepping even more into his space. "Just like you were wrong to conspire with that obstinate child in the driver's seat of 61 instead of listening to me. Now, one last time, get the fuck out of my garage."

Rocco's entire face fills with a look of disbelief, but a flicker of fear is more than apparent in those smoldering eyes of his. He knows he's made a fatal mistake. Fatal for his career. I turn to the corner of the garage, where Nick is standing. I wave him over. He starts stalking right towards us and almost looks gleeful at what is going to have to transpire.

Dario is staring at me with his mouth agape. Rocco hurls his headset across the garage and storms off, swearing loudly. Nick pauses and turns and walks back to his corner. I put on my head-phones again, and everyone around us tries to pretend that didn't just happen.

"What's going on? Where's Antonio?" Billy's voice fills my ears.

"Tony is in the pit," I reply calmly even though I have to ball my hands up to keep them from shaking. "You just stick with the plan and don't worry about it, Billy. I've got you."

"Okay."

He doesn't sound like that's the answer he wanted to give, but I appreciate he gave it anyway. And then, an instant later, as Antonio is finally making his way back on the track, now in sixth because of the pit stop, a red flag is announced. Too much debris on the track, and we're going to have a re-start. Billy will be able to change his tires and will be on pole now when the races begins again. Antonio will start in sixth instead of second where he would have been if he'd listened to me.

I want to roar like a fucking lion after a kill because I was right. I gambled, yes, but only because I know the sport. I know what the fuck I'm doing. Dario is stewing so hard I'm surprised there isn't steam coming off him. Joaquin and the rest of the pit are smiling and clapping at the coup I pulled off.

"Rocco, what the fuck is happening?" Antonio growls over the radio.

I don't even bother to respond.

Fuck that little bitch.

BILLY WINS THE RACE. Antonio finishes seventh. That's good overall points for Mirabella and great points for Billy. I walk over and congratulate him, and he hugs me, lifting me off my feet. It makes me blush, and so I walk away as soon as my feet hit the ground. He hugged my dad after every race he won when Dad was Team Principal too. You are not special, I tell myself, but… it felt special. Fucking oxytocin is getting reactivated every time he touches me. And I realize as I stand in front of the podium and watch him and Joaquin accept the team and driver trophies, and his eyes lock with mine while they play his national anthem, that the post-coital hormone floods my system when he just looks at me now.

I wish they made a pill I could take to suppress that. Jesus, how has that not been invented yet, I wonder as I make my way back to our paddock. Of course, I get stopped by media. Sky Sports wants to know where Rocco Conti disappeared to halfway through the race. "He had something to take care of."

I don't let them press me into any more of an answer, side-stepping any more questions about my disobedient Track Engineer. Then they ask me why there was confusion with Antonio's pit stop. "It seemed like the team wasn't expecting De Luca to pit under that yellow flag. Why did he pit and Billy stayed out?"

"They weren't ready because I had specifically told both drivers to stay out," I reply honestly. "Perhaps Tony was more panicked about his tires than I was or didn't trust my judgement that there would be a red flag shortly. I'm not clear on his motivation. You would have to ask him."

"So, you're having trust issues with your drivers? That must be making for a difficult season," the reporter prompts.

"I think a new Principal on any team will always have an adjustment period," I reply coolly and take a slow, long breath. "Billy trusted me, and he was rewarded with a win and points. There's a lesson here. I hope everyone learns it."

I make my way back to the paddock and am not surprised my father is waiting for me at the entrance doors. He looks concerned. Dario, standing behind him, looks like a bomb about to explode. "Frankie, you can't fire Rocco."

"I didn't fire him. I relieved him from his duties for the rest of this race," I clarify, refusing to look either man in the eye. I don't want to bear the brunt of their anger. I'm emotionally exhausted at this point. "He and Antonio defied my orders. I am the person in charge out there, and I'm done with their bullshit."

"My son deserves her job, Bash, and if you won't let him have it after all these years of loyalty to Mirabella, the least you can do is make sure she doesn't fuck up the position he does have," Dario snarls.

I spin toward him so fast I almost make myself dizzy. "Dario, he undermined my ability to do my job and he paid a price for that. I am not going to apologize. I am going to have a frank, professional discussion with Rocco, not you. Your position in this race team is not related to this dispute, and your input is not required."

I storm toward the staircase and stomp my way up them. Lucia is at the top of them. She's changed from her race gear into a pair of jeans and a Mirabella T-shirt. Her hair is still slicked back in a pony. She's beaming down at me with pride. Good, at least someone is happy with me.

15

LIFT OFF

BILLY

The first class lounge at the airport is blissfully empty. Just a couple people at the bar and one or two peppered around the different seating areas, most of them on their phones or laptops. I get recognized in airports more than anywhere, and despite the win last night, I'm not in the mood to take a million selfies and sign a million hats, jackets, cocktail napkins or whatever. Why? Because Frankie disappeared after the race. Just poof. She was nowhere.

Not at her hotel. Not at the track. Not at my hotel with her father. Not celebrating with the crew. She was nowhere.

I wanted to see her again—alone. I wanted to fuck her again too. But it wasn't *just* that. She made a brilliant call out there during the race. One I doubted but I stuck with her anyway. That loyalty and blind faith earned me a podium and points that now has me second in the title race. I wanted to thank her for that, to her face. And lastly, yeah, I wanted to fuck her again.

Both those first few reasons are why I'm wandering the airport lounge four hours before my flight to Mexico and without Clara. I did see Bash last night. He and Adelaide had dinner with

179

Mum and me. Not at all awkward pretending Mum wasn't hitting on Bash every five seconds, in front of his pregnant wife. Luckily Adelaide either didn't notice or didn't care. Probably the latter. Adelaide has never doubted Bash's love for her and my tipsy mum isn't going to sway that confidence. Anyway, Bash happened to mention that Frankie had some business in Positano on this bye-week and so of course when my mum asked if I could take her to the airport at the crack of dawn for her flight back to Australia, I said yes and told Clara I would meet her there for our flight later in the day. I went through security with mum and kissed her good-bye at her gate, and now here I am looking for Frankie.

There's always next week in Mexico. But waiting that long feels physically painful. I am about to sit at the bar when I notice a flutter of white out of the corner of my eye. I glance over my shoulder and there, by the juice bar across the room, wearing a flowing white cotton dress, is Frankie Castera. A smile overtakes my entire face. The kind of grin you feel in your chest. I make my way toward her.

She's about to take a sip of the frothy green juice in her hand when her eyes land on me and she freezes. She doesn't move a muscle until I'm right in front of her, and then she manages to finish that sip of juice. She doesn't speak to me. But when I extend my hand she puts hers in mine with nothing more than a quick glance around the room, to make sure no one is watching us. Then she lets me lead her to the farthest, least occupied corner of the lounge, near the private relaxation rooms and the shower rooms. There's an older guy who walks by us, exiting one of the relaxation rooms, who doesn't even glance at us as he passes. She subtly pulls her hand out of mine anyway.

"Hi," I say simply.

"Hi yourself." She sips her drink. And I know when her tongue slips out to wipe her bottom lip, it's extra slow on purpose. She knows how much I enjoy that tongue. "Heading home?"

"Nope. Straight to Mexico. Later," I reply. She raises an eyebrow so I explain. "Australia's a little too far of a trip for a small break."

"I thought you lived in Monaco now?" She snaps her mouth closed after she says that, like she wasn't supposed to let me know she has kept tabs on me. I don't allow myself to smile at that, even though it feels like a victory.

"I own a place there. And Biarritz. And Paris," I reply. "I usually spend the bulk of the down time in Paris when I can."

"Love Paris," she says with a contented sigh, and I watch her brush her hair back over her left shoulder. One obstinate lock stays forward, curling against her exposed neck, and I want to push it back for her with my face as I nuzzle and kiss that freckle on her collarbone. "But I'm surprised you do."

"Great city to get lost in. No one pays me much attention because Parisians would rather die than profess any fan-like adoration. Oh, and the architecture is spectacular."

"There's nothing like a sunset stroll through Montmartre." She sighs softly and gets a faraway look in her eyes.

"I'll have to add that to my to-do list next trip," I reply instead of saying 'Why don't you take me with you next time?' which is really what's on the tip of my tongue. This isn't going to still be something by the time I make it back to Paris. It can't be.

She nods. "Also, shopping in the second hand stores in Le Marais. And the salad at Les Philosphes. Damn. Now I'm hungry, and I'm on a juice cleanse until Wednesday."

I laugh and she does too. When it dies off, I change the subject so I'm not tempted to ask her to ditch Italy and join me in Paris this week instead. "How did you celebrate the win?"

"I worked," Frankie replies and takes another small sip of the juice. "I had some stuff to handle with my shoe line and planning out next month's sponsorships with Jennie, and then I did a deep dive into the Mexico track. We've underperformed there in the past."

"We have," I agree. "You know what you're doing, Frankie."

"Told ya," she says after a beat.

It's like someone turned a dial up suddenly on the chemistry between us. I feel my need for her in my bones. It's heavy and intoxicating and like nothing I've ever felt before. That's a lie. I felt it when I was with her at seventeen.

"Thank you for trusting my judgement," Frankie says softly.

"Trust has never been my issue. It's yours," I reply, and the honesty in that sentence seems to take her off guard. Her hazel eyes grow wide for a second, like she didn't think I had figured that out about her. "When will you start trusting me?"

"I'm working on it." She bites her lower lip and her eyes slide to the gold clock on the wall to our right and then to the hallway that leads to the showers and sleeping rooms. She tries to hide a smile, but I'm so hypersensitive to that perfect full, plump mouth of hers that I catch it. "I have forty minutes until I have to board. I was planning on drinking this smoothie while I lounged in one of the relaxation rooms. When does your flight leave?"

"I've got a lot longer than forty minutes until I lift off."

The smile breaks free. "I think you'll lift off much sooner if you join me in a relaxation room."

"That's the worse pun ever." I'm smiling anyway.

"My ability to make puns isn't why you're here right now, is it?" She takes one last sip of her drink as I shake my head because she's right. She could dump a truckload of bad puns and dad jokes on me, and I'd still want to be with her.

I watch as she places her drink on a side table by a leather couch and casually saunters her way down the hall. I follow behind her, not even the least bit concerned that I might appear like an eager puppy. I am one. And she's the treat I've been begging for all my damn life.

She heads to the farthest room. There's a privacy sign, much like the ones given at hotels, and it is flipped to the side with a cartoon sun. Frankie flips it to the other side which has a moon and "Zzzz" written on it. Then she pulls open the blackout curtain that divides it from the hallway and steps inside. I follow and pull the curtain closed behind us. I've been in one of these rooms before on layovers. They're in almost every first-class lounge. They're small, square rooms with a double-sized, flat chaise-type piece of furniture. This one is in a slate gray. There's a panel on the wall that controls the lighting, which throws beams in any color you choose at the ceiling. It can also be dimmed. I'm standing right next to the panel, and so when Frankie turns to adjust the settings, she's directly in front of me. Our eyes lock. My body is vibrating with the need to touch her.

Frankie dims the lights and sets it to rotate through the colors. It starts green… then slowly transitions to blue, then pink, then red… It keeps going to other colors, but I don't notice because Frankie's taken one tiny step closer to me, and I've finally given in to the urge to touch her. My left hand drops to cup her hip. "Is it time for that take off you promised?"

"Fasten your seatbelt," she whispers back a millisecond before she kisses me.

It's not timid or tame or unsure like her kisses have been in the past. She's bold and claims my mouth with a sweep of her tongue and god damn, it's fucking flame-throwing hot. I kiss her back the same way as a weird sense of relief also settles over me. I didn't realize how much it meant to me to have her give in, completely, fully, with more than just her body.

Rein it in, James. This is still just fun and frivolous. My brain is scolding me. In order to remind myself, I start walking her back toward the lounge-like bed, pushing her carry-on bag off her shoulder and dropping my own along with it.

"This can't be… more than what we're doing. Anyone can open that curtain."

"The sign is flipped to occupied."

"People are idiots," she reminds me, her voice shuddering as my hand cups her ass.

"Can't argue that," I say and holding her by her slender hips, I walk her backwards until her calves hit the back of the lounger. "But I also know the rewards far outweigh the risks between us when the clothes are off."

"I'm not getting naked in an airport lounge," she argues, but her tone is weak, and I bet if I pushed just a little bit, she would be bare and writhing under me. But, as always, I respect her boundaries.

"Luckily, this dress is big enough for the both of us." I smile and give her a tiny push so she sits on the edge of the lounger. "Take off your underwear."

She doesn't move until I kneel in front of her. Then, way too slowly, she slips her hands under her long, flowing dress. She lifts herself off the lounger just an inch or two and a pair of simple, white cotton bikini undies appear at her ankles. I reach down and unhook her feet from them, and then lift them to my face. They're damp. I grin.

"You're smiling like you were yesterday on the podium," she says, and her cheeks pink as I inhale deeply and press my mouth to the damp spot.

"Knowing the sight of me made your pussy wet is a bigger victory," I reply before tucking the underwear into my back pocket. "Now spread your legs and let me taste my victory."

"Oh my God you're—"

"Going to make you come so hard you might not be able to board your flight without assistance," I promise and slide my hands up her calves, lifting her dress with it, and dipping my head under it when it reaches her thighs.

Her legs finally fall open as I slide my tongue over her perfect little bundle of nerves between them. It takes less than five minutes to have her panting and squirming on that lounger and I'm almost depressed when she breaks over my tongue. Her whimpers are muffled, which, when I finally lift my head out from under her dress, I realize is because she's covering her mouth with her hands.

I crawl up beside her and gently tug on her wrists. She's still panting and her body is like overcooked spaghetti. My work here is done.

"You are dangerously good at that," she manages to mumble. I start to get off the lounger, but she wraps a hand around my bicep. "My turn."

"You've got a flight to catch."

"I've also got a dick to suck," she replies and reaches for my belt.

I let her get it mostly undone before I cover her mouth with my own and pull her hand away. "Another time."

"Now I owe you. Again," she pouts.

I walk backwards, staring at her flushed cheeks and glowing post-orgasm face. "Just the way I like it. Safe travels, love."

I slip past the curtain, making sure to close it fully and head straight into a bathroom, locking the door, and then I splash some cold water on my face and try to tame the erection in my pants into submission. When I hear the last call for her flight over the loudspeaker, I finally unlock the bathroom door and step back out into the lounge. I do a loop of the place before heading to the bar. She's gone, and I'm both disappointed and relieved. I swear this woman has made my brain into a short-circuiting ECU system in a race car. It's dangerous.

"Billy James?" The bartender says my name as he saunters over to take my order. "Great win yesterday."

"Thanks man. Can I get a…" I sit on the stool and it's uncomfortable because of a lump in the pack pocket of my jeans. I reach under my untucked shirt tail and realize what it is. I still have her underwear in my back pocket.

"A…" the bartender prompts because I'm sitting there with a stupid grin on my face saying nothing.

"Caesar. Spicy," I say, and as he turns I subtly pull the undies out of my back pocket and put them in my carry on. There's a glint from a tiny, sparkling rhinestone sewn into the middle of the front of them. I decide right then and there I am never ever giving them back.

I'm still smiling when I'm done with the drink, and Antonio and Rocco enter the lounge. They don't see me at first. They're walking side-by-side, their heads tipped toward each other and scowls on both their faces. The expressions and posture on both of them makes the hair on the back of my neck stand up.

Antonio spots me watching them first and frowns, which makes Rocco look up too. His expression is more welcoming as he strides over and shakes my hand. "Good job, James. I didn't get to say it yesterday."

"Yeah thanks. You were M.I.A after the race," I note and offer him the stool beside me. Antonio walks up just as Rocco declines the chair but orders two espressos from the bartender.

"I was kicked out of the garage," Rocco replies tersely, his dark brown eyes smoldering with anger even twenty-four hours later. When the bartender puts two espressos on the counter, they each take one and Rocco motions for me to join them as they make their way to a little alcove with three club chairs and a view of the runways.

We all sit down, and Antonio burns his lip as he sips his espresso and swears. I settle back in my chair and Rocco continues to explain. "Antonio wanted to come in on the safety car, and I'm the one who agreed with him, so Frankie lost it and kicked me out."

She failed to mention this to me, which shocks me, but I don't disagree with her decision. "Well, listening to her got me the win, so maybe next time we all go with that."

Antonio looks like he could spit nails at me. "How about next time you have my back instead of kissing her ass?"

Antonio's never been my favorite person, but we've managed a civil working relationship. Now… well that might not continue to be the case. Rocco glances around the room super skittishly, which has the hair on my neck lifting again. He rubs his hands together nervously. "Well, actually… off the record. I don't think that we'll have to deal with her much longer."

"What? Why?" I sit straighter in my chair.

Rocco and Antonio exchange glances and an argument seems to be happening inside that glance. Finally Antonio sighs. "I don't know if we can trust you."

"Antonio, I want what's best for Mirabella and both of us," I reply. "I've always been a team player, and I know you know that."

Antonio runs a hand through his black hair. "I don't think Frankie cares about what's best for the team or us. She cares about her brand and giving her sister the first female F1 seat. That's all. Then her sister will become this unique little brand just like Frankie. They're using the team for their own success."

I do not believe any of that, but telling him will only create a bigger rift between us than the one we have. And he definitely won't tell me whatever it is he and Rocco are planning. "The team is their birthright, and I guess we have to accept they can do whatever they want with it. If she drops me because she wants to give the spot to Lucia, I'll find another team. I've had a few reach out to tell me they'd be interested, as I'm sure you have. You won't end up without a team."

It's cold comfort, I'm sure. I mean, it feels that way for me anyway. I love Mirabella and don't want another team. Rocco looks at Antonio again and then turns back to me. "You're right about that. They technically can do whatever they want. So Antonio and I are going to let them."

"I'm not re-signing with them after this season," Antonio tells me.

"And I'm leaving too," Rocco adds before I can react. "And so is my father. And his money."

Boom!

That was one hell of a bomb they just dropped. I felt a second of relief when Antonio said he would be leaving because it essentially secured my spot on the team next year. I mean, I figured in the end Frankie and Bash would pick me over him based on my performance alone, but now it's a sure thing. But Rocco leaving—and Dario along with their financial contribution—that's a blow. I am slightly worried that might put Mirabella in a precarious position.

"You look worried," Rocco says and then smiles. "And you should be. Unless you decide to leave too and come join us."

"Join you where?" I ask.

"My father is working on starting a new team," Rocco explains. "I'd be Principal. Antonio would be one of our drivers."

"Oh."

"Oh?" Antonio lifts one of his bushy eyebrows. "I think you have a great or fantastic to add to the end of that sentence."

"Adding a new team isn't an easy feat. There's a lot of red tape and hoops to jump through," I warn. "But of course I'm not against the idea or anything."

"Well, we may also join forces with another existing team," Rocco explains. "As a last resort. Lord knows a couple of them wouldn't say no to the money that my father can inject. And taking his money would mean taking on both me and Antonio. And you, if you want."

I nod slowly as the idea settles in. I am so *not* interested, but I don't dare blurt that out. The fact is, I have never been a driver for pay, and I don't ever want to be one. There's two types of drivers in F1, those who earned their spots based solely on abilities and those who, although they have decent skills, are in their cars because they brought sponsors or plain old cash to the team.

I can't understand why Dario and Rocco are so hell bent on keeping Antonio with them. He's okay but, like Lucia, there are a lot of worthy contenders in F2 who a new team would be stupid not to scoop up. Of course I can't ask Rocco about that with Antonio right here so I just say, "I think it's definitely worth considering. And I very much appreciate the offer."

Antonio leans forward and puts his espresso cup on the small coffee table between us. His eyes lock with mine. "Look, I know Bash is like a father to you. I get it. And I know he's always said that the Mirabella is his baby. But if he really cared about us, he wouldn't have dumped us with his inexperienced, hot-headed bitch of a daughter."

"Whoa now," Rocco says before I can even object, which I intended to. "Frankie is headstrong and inexperienced, but she's not a bitch. She's been through a lot."

"She lived," Antonio barks back.

"I found her Tony, it was…" Rocco actually shudders and I feel cold inside.

Antonio then stands up. "I mean, fuck, can we stop talking about something that almost happened ten years ago? It was an accident."

He storms off, and I'm left sitting there with Rocco. He rubs the back of his neck like he does after a particularly shitty race. "When did he get so… angry?"

"I'm not sure," I reply and lean back in my chair. "But he's been off the rails since Bash retired. Something about Frankie triggers him irrationally but why is anyone's guess."

Rocco shakes his head. "To be honest, my father had to talk me into making him part of this plan. I wanted only you."

Oh wow.

Rocco sighs. Suddenly, he seems much older than me. Much more than the five years he's actually got on me. "Fuck man, I don't hate her, you know? I get that the whole overdose thing threw her off-track. I know if it hadn't happened, she'd have spent all her time working under her dad, for the team, and she'd be more than ready. But she didn't. And I did."

I swallow hard and take a deep breath. "What exactly happened that night? You were there, right? It was your boat."

"It was a yacht my dad was renting," Rocco explains, with green eyes staring at the tarmacs outside the lounge window but seeing some horrible memory in his head instead. "We were throwing a party in between races for my uncle who was spending the summer with us after a shitty divorce. There were a lot of parties that weekend because of my uncle and his mid-life crisis, which I thought was fun, you know? Anyway Frankie said she wasn't coming, but then, suddenly, she was there. I remember seeing her, even though I was drunk as a skunk and there were about a hundred people on the yacht."

"Why do you remember her?"

"Because she looked upset," Rocco replied and my chest tightens with guilt. "Later, Lucia told me she'd been stood up or something, and so she was angry, and they were going to party it off or some such shit. I don't know. Maybe Antonio can tell you more, he was there too and spent more time with her that night. Anyway, I was hammered but the next thing I remember, I walked into a bathroom off one of the bedrooms and there she was. Lying on her back in the bathtub, covered in vomit and barely breathing.

I… I fucking screamed like a little bitch until someone called an ambulance."

Clara has arrived and is walking toward us. Rocco sees her first and nods and smiles. "Hey."

"Hi," Clara says with a brief smile. Her hair is loose. "Flight boards in ten."

"Okay. Yeah." I stand up. I was beginning to feel gross talking about Frankie like this anyway. But I want to talk to her about that night on the yacht… when I can face her without looking as horror stricken as I feel.

16

PANDERING TO THE PATRIARCHY

FRANKIE

This week has been a total bitch. I have so many problems I lie awake at night ranking them in order of bad to worse. The easiest one to handle is probably Jennie. She's pissed I am not as available as she wants me to be, not just for the work she gets me but for her. She's my best friend, not just my manager, and I've been doing a shitty job at staying in touch. Then there's the brands themselves that are pissed. The bathing suit company I'm working with is happy with the posts and coverage I've been giving them, but the liquor company is pissed because I've had to skip two in-person events because of the race schedule. Jennie is putting out fires and I've promised to devote the two week break after the Mexico race to my work with her.

And a bigger problem is my shoe deal. I don't like some of the designs for the shoes, and they're pushing back. And I don't have the time to argue as effectively as I wish I did, so I've just been blowing it off. Now they're talking about pulling the deal completely, and demanding repayment of the fifteen thousand dollar advance they gave me for the partnership. That's not an issue, I can give them back the money. I just really want this shoe line to happen. I've had to wear flats my whole life because of my back problems, and let me tell you, the selection isn't always great. I wanted to make some really cool, beautiful designs for people like me.

And then there's the family feud. Lucia and Dad still haven't made up. Since mom died, this is the very first time we haven't worked through something in less than forty-eight hours. I've tried playing referee and therapist, but neither of them want to hear it. Lucia has stopped answering my calls altogether.

And then there's my biggest problem of them all. That I can't stop thinking about Billy James. Even with all this other stuff going on, he is constantly on my mind. Especially at night when I'm alone… in bed… then Billy is *all* I can think about.

So I'm stressed. And sleep deprived. And so horny I can barely stand it. I'm losing what little faith I have that this job will ever become enjoyable. Antonio and Rocco ignored me completely in the meeting after practice today. At least they aren't being outwardly hostile anymore. They both seem to be listening, but… that actually makes me a little bit more nervous. I feel like something is brewing. I just don't know what.

There's a gentle knock on my door. I roll over and lift my useless silk sleeping mask off my face. "I know. Nap's over. Time to get ready."

"You've got some time. Can I come in?" It's Adelaide, not Nick. That's beyond weird. I get out of bed, shove my feet into slippers, and grab the hotel robe. I cinch it as I make my way through the suite and swing open the door.

"Come on in," I say and motion with my hand not holding the door. "We've done fashion shows together. You've seen me naked so…"

Adelaide laughs. "Remember that show in Paris? The one where the designer wanted us to tape raw fish over our bits as we walked down the runway wearing his heels?"

"How can I forget that?" I ask and smile. "I said no way in hell."

"And I didn't and will never eat tuna again." Adelaide shudders lightly but she's still smiling. "I needed the cash. My parents' assets had been frozen."

Ah. For me, the public, that news came out in the tabloids about three weeks later. I guess I should have put two-and-two together. Adelaide's dad is still in prison serving out one more year of his embezzlement sentence. Her mother moved to Costa Rica with a guy named Manuel, who apparently owns a bamboo farm or some crap. She and Adelaide haven't talked since Adelaide announced her engagement to my dad.

"Speaking of which, have you told your family about the baby yet?" I ask. It's nosy but if she wants to be family I'm gonna be all up in her business. She slips a hand over her middle, caressing it lightly, and even though she's in an empire waist dress, the bump is detectible. I don't know how I missed it for this long. I'm an idiot.

Adelaide shakes her head softly, her hair rippling around her shoulders. "I wrote my dad. He appreciates getting snail mail. As for my mom, I don't even have a number for her."

When I first met Adelaide, about six months before the embezzlement news, she and her mom were very close. They were as close as me and my mom had been and the way I hoped we still would be if she hadn't died.

Adelaide lowers herself onto the settee in front of the bay window in my suite. "You know, when she found out I was dating Bash, she wasn't worried about the age gap or any of that crap. She was angry that I scooped him up because, and I quote, 'you should have given him to me. I'm the one who needs the money. You're young and can still make money off your looks and body. I can't.'"

I'm stunned by that revelation, but Adelaide just shrugs.

"Anyway, whatever. This baby will have the best big sisters in the world. What more will it need?"

"Well, I appreciate that, but right now, Lucia isn't exactly acting like a good sister," I reply. "And I'm sorry. I hope I can get her to come around before the little one pops out."

Adelaide cringes. "Can we not use pops out in reference to something coming out of my vagina, please?"

I snicker. "Pops out is better than claws its way out. Or would you prefer tears its way out?"

"Oh my God, shut up," Adelaide groans.

I laugh. "I'm sure it will just slide out gracefully, like Lucia and I did."

"Really?"

"No, my mom was in labor for forty-seven hours with me and I ended up breech with the cord around my neck, and she had to have an emergency c-section," I reply casually as Adelaide's eyes widen with every word. I smile again. "But the point is, my dad loved her more than ever. Even though I was ten pounds and left her with stretch marks like a road map that she never got rid of."

"This is helping, but not," Adelaide replies honestly and shakes her head. "Can we change the subject?"

"Sure." I walk over to my closet and flip through until I find the right outfit for today. It's qualifying day, so I'll be in Mirabella gear.

"Are you going to wear one of those low-cut shirts again?"

I lift an eyebrow. "Why?"

"Because it's hot and you should," Adelaide replies. "I liked that you stopped pandering to the patriarchy."

I smile. I officially do not hate this woman anymore. But I'm still not calling her step-mom, like ever. I pull out one of the custom shirts I had made when dad gave me the job. It's got a plunging V-neck and three quarter length sleeves made out of a clingy jersey material. It'll go perfect with the white jeans I intend to wear. Adelaide smiles in approval. "Billy will drive off the track."

I freeze, which just makes her giggle. "That was an educated guess. Nailed it, didn't I?"

"No. I mean he's my employee and the only person who seems to listen to me, but it's not…" I give up mid-sentence because it's clear from the look on her pretty little face she's not believing a word I say. "It's nothing. And it's over."

Adelaide squeals like a driver winning their first Grand Prix, but I ignore her and head into the bathroom, leaving the door open so we can continue this conversation but moving out of view to change. "I know you told me to never date a driver, and I heeded that advice, but I'm glad you broke your own rule."

"I didn't." I pause and shake my head. "We fucked, not dated. Oh my God, why am I talking about this with you?"

"Because I'm here and you need to talk to someone," Adelaide replies breezily. "And your father and sister are too busy fighting to notice what's happening with you."

"Nothing is happening with me."

"Your father loves Billy like a son. He'll be thrilled when this works out." Adelaide smiles brightly. "You have to let me plan the wedding. I love throwing a good party."

"Oh my God, you're insane." I emerge from the bathroom, changed into my Mirabella garb. "And you need to keep those crazy comments to yourself. If this thing with Billy, which is over, gets out to the media, I'll be labeled as the whore who took advantage of her driver, and he'll be the stud that banged his boss. That's the only narrative that people will grab onto, and I'll never get any respect no matter how long I'm in this job."

Adelaide rolls her eyes and tips her head back. "Oh my God, so dramatic. Here's the thing I've learned marrying your dad. Nobody else matters. You gotta live your life to please yourself and absolutely no one else."

"Easier said than done."

She stands up as I grab my tiny Mirabella knapsack, which is custom made and covered in sponsor patches of course, because it gets photographed a ton. Adelaide steps into the hall, where Nick is patiently waiting for me. "Definitely easier said than done, but eventually, giving a fuck takes more out of you than not, Frankie. Trust me."

She's like a gorgeous, little, British Buddha dropping wisdom bombs everywhere she goes. I can't help but smile back even if I know in my heart Billy and I are truly never going to be anything more than what we are—make that *were*. "Well, I've learned in my life to never say never but… I'd bet money against this being more than it was."

"I'll take that bet," Adelaide says as we walk with a silent Nick to the elevator.

"Are you and Dad coming to the qualifying?"

She shakes her head and rolls her eyes again. "Your father wants us to head to San Diego and have a romantic weekend alone. He says it's time you fly solo and he gets used to not being at every race. And yes this is him pouting over Lucia."

I feel a moment of panic. There was a level of comfort to knowing he was there, at the track, during a race that I didn't really understand I relied on until now. And even more disturbing is that he has never missed one of Lucia's races and if he isn't going to be here for the F1 race, then he's not here for the F2 race. My heart aches for my mom. She would never let Dad miss one of Lucia's races no matter what the fight was about. She could talk sense into him like no other. And she had a way of soothing Lucia's stubborn and obsessive ways.

I hug Adelaide good-bye when the elevator reaches her floor, and then Nick and I continue on to the lobby and out the doors to our awaiting car. The heat is heavy and thick today, which will affect the tires. I spend the whole drive to the track with my nose in my phone ignoring Jennie's texts and trying to do extra research on the tire options we have for today. When Nick parks, I shove on my sunglasses and step out onto the scorching pavement. We've taken about two steps when the ground shakes and a ball of fire and smoke erupts in the distance.

"Frankie."

Nick says my name in that tone he has and rarely uses that both rattles me and grounds me. I can't seem to take my eyes off the black cloud that's shooting into the sky. "Frankie."

I finally start to move, but my whole body feels disturbingly heavy and slow. I can't move fast enough. I feel like pieces of me are falling off and sticking to the sweltering pavement as I move. My heart, my lungs, my brain. I can't think or breathe.

"It may not be her," he says. That statement acts like a slap to the face, sobering me and pulling me from the terror-fog I was slipping into.

It's a crash. A race car. F2 qualifying.

"It's someone," I croak out. It may not be Lucia. But it may be her too.

And then we reach the security gates to the paddock area, and people on the other side are all running, and there's pure chaos. The guard lets us in, and I see Billy. And his eyes lock with mine as he runs towards me, and I know. It is my baby sister in the fiery ball of smoke.

17

THE GRAVITY OF IT

BILLY

You know going in that death is a very plausible outcome to any day you are in your car on a track. But it becomes one of those things you refuse to really process. You make it abstract, the odds of it all, because if you didn't, you would never get behind the wheel. I have become especially gifted at it because my dad died doing this in front of me, and I chose to do it anyway.

I've witnessed more than a few serious crashes since I started in Formula One, and sadly some fatalities. This… today… I realize as I hear Clara gasp and follow her gaze up to the television bolted to the wall of my dressing room, looks like another one. I've personally never witnessed so much smoke and fire. The flames are huge and everywhere and there is no one emerging from the car, which isn't even visible.

"Who?" I manage to choke out because I hadn't seen which team's car hurtled into the barrier, and right on through it.

Clara's voice is strangled when she says, "Lucia."

"No…" I argue stupidly.

The TV announcer's serious voice fills my ears. "There's no movement from Lucia Castera's car. Oh no… this is horrible.."

"They're putting the flames out fast, which is a good sign. We can only hope…" the second announcer's voice trails off ominously.

"No," I say again, louder, like if the universe hears me it'll somehow change the outcome of the catastrophic wreckage I'm staring at.

"Billy…" Clara's voice is soft and sad.

"I need to find Frankie," I bolt toward my door, but Clara calls my name again, more urgently. I turn and she points to the television.

I see Lucia emerge from the ball of smoke and fire, and a rescue crew guy runs toward her. She jumps from the car, through the flames and smoke and falls to the pavement in a lump. The crew sprays her with extinguishers even though she didn't appear to be on fire, and one of them rushes over and picks her up, I can see her legs are under her. She's conscious, walking, albeit with help and very unsteady. That's something. That's got to be something, right? I leave the room in a full-on run without looking back. Everyone in the hall is frozen like mannequins staring at the closest TV, tablet, or phone screen. We are about two football fields away from where this horror is unfolding, on the track, but no one dares to go there. They all know it's better to let the rescue crews do what needs to be done, and no one wants to be a looky-loo in this business.

I see Rocco standing like a stoic lamp post in the middle of the team paddocks. I grab his arm, and he looks at me with a mask of horror on his face I have never seen before and hope to never see again. "Bash… Frankie. I can't find them. I don't think they're here yet."

I look at my own phone for the time and then run to toward the parking lot entrance, calling back to him. "You find Bash. I'll find her."

Frankie usually gets here before the end of the F2 sessions at the latest, so she's either on her way to the track, or she's still in the parking lot. I run toward the parking lot, figuring I'll start by asking security if she got here. When I get to the entrance from the V.I.P. parking, there she is. She's walking in. Actually, it's almost more of a run. Nick is beside her. My eyes lock with hers.

I experience the torture of watching her expression change. It goes from strained to panicked to completely shattered. She's stopped moving just inside the gate and I come to a stop in front of her.

Frankie releases a small, pained sound followed by a deep shuddering breath and her left hand raises to her chest. "Lucia?"

I nod and I reach out for her. My hands land on her shoulders, which are so tense it's like clasping rock. "But she got out of the car. It took a minute. But she got out. On her own."

Nothing in her body relaxes. She knows, like I do, that adrenaline can hide a lot of stuff. The last person to die from a crash four years ago also climbed out of the car. But he died en route to the hospital from a brain bleed. "I don't know what to do."

Her confession is a hoarse whisper, and I want to hug her so badly, but as I step closer, she steps away, causing my hands to lose their grip on her shoulders and drop. "You can go to the hospital. Rocco can run qualifying… if we go ahead."

It will be delayed no doubt, but if Lucia is… it might be canceled and done tomorrow, after a memorial ceremony. Frankie doesn't move. She just stands there. Nick looks at me. "Call Bash."

"He's not here?" I ask, shocked as Nick shakes his head. "Fuck."

"He's flying to California. Someone needs to keep trying his phone," Frankie says, her voice sounding a little less fragile. I know what's happening. Her survival mode is kicking in. She just needs to get through this, and she knows it. "I'm going to the hospital. They'll bring her there. No matter what."

I want more than anything in the world to go with her. In this moment, I would skip qualifying, hell, I would skip the entire race and even walk out on my career if she asked me to be with her instead right now. I watched my mom go through this alone. I don't want Frankie to be alone. But she doesn't ask me for anything more.

Instead, Frankie takes one more shuddering breath and blinks back tears. Photographers have started to line the chain link fence that sections off the private parking from the general public. "You should go back," Frankie tells me. She turns and takes a few quick strides toward her car with Nick but then stops and turns back. "Billy."

"It will be okay," I promise. Nick frowns like I'm an asshole writing checks I can't cash, but in this moment, in my heart, I mean it. Because no matter what happens to Lucia, I will make sure Frankie will be okay. I swear on my own life.

She turns away again, and I run toward the gates as I hear her car start up and tires screech behind me.

Rocco is standing exactly where I last saw him when I get back, but other people are moving again, some frantically, some clearly in a daze. I approach him, and he looks up from his phone.

"Do you know anything?"

"Responsive and coherent in the ambulance," Rocco says, relief seeping into the edges of his stressed expression. But only the edges because we all know that isn't an all-clear. There was fire. Lots of it. She will have smoke inhalation and burns. We wear protective gear but…I reach for my phone.

"Bash isn't answering. His phone is off I think. Did you find Frankie?"

"She says you run the quali if we have it. And someone needs to keep trying to reach Bash," I say, and he nods tersely as I watch his father attempt to run towards us. He must have been in the garage when this happened because he's coming from that direction. It's clear that he's out of shape even before I can hear the huffing and puffing coming from his mouth.

"Rocco, you should take over today," Dario says.

"Frankie already gave him the go-ahead," I say.

Dario frowns a little. "Oh. Good. I was thinking she might still try to run the show, which is ridiculous because she can barely contain her emotions on a normal day."

"Are you fucking kidding me right now?" I bark, and Dario looks honestly confused by my angry reaction.

Rocco doesn't. "Let's all just shut the fuck up and get through this day so we can all go support the Castera family."

Dario and I both nod, thankfully, because if he'd opened his fat mouth to argue in any way, I swear I would have clocked him. Dario follows Rocco back to the garage. I head back to my dressing room.

Four long hours later, our qualifying is done. I manage to snag second and Antonio fifth. I wish I'd done better, for Lucia and for Frankie. She would have wanted Mirabella on pole, even with everything. I feel like I let her down. Now that it's all over, I have the torture of interviews. I give as few as I can get away with. Every single reporter asks about Lucia and my thoughts. I find out from a female reporter for a Canadian channel that Lucia is alive and stable, at least that's what her source at the hospital says. "Good. Great," I reply with a sigh. "Well, sounds like you know more than I do. Thanks for sharing."

I don't change, and Clara must anticipate my next move because she meets me in front of the Mirabella paddock with a bag full of my stuff and the car keys. "You should drive," I tell her as she falls in step beside me and we head towards the parking. "Because I'm not going to be able to drive the speed limit."

She just nods.

We get to the hospital and Clara lets me off at the front door.

"I'm going to park this in the visitor lot and Uber back to the hotel, okay? Give everyone my best."

I nod and rush inside. First I have to make my way through a cloud of reporters to get to the door. They all immediately start snapping my photo or filming me and yelling out questions. I ignore them and slip past the security who lets me in with a knowing nod.

After a brief stop at the first nurses' station I stumble across, I'm directed to the fourth floor. I jump into an elevator. I'd unzipped the top part of my race suit as I was walking back to the paddock, like I always do, so it was hanging at my waist. I play nervously with the cuffs of the arms until the elevator doors open. I didn't even think to ask more details about where I was going, so when I step off the elevator and see the sign that says Burn Ward, it's like getting slapped in the face.

My heart feels like it's turning to stone in my chest. I swallow down bile and turn left and start down the hall as the nurse directed. There's a small room tucked into the corner of the hallway with a marker on the front that says 'Waiting Room. Private.' The door is open though, and Nick and Lucia's body-guard Michael pace inside. Frankie is nowhere to be found.

"I came as soon as I could. I hope that's okay," I say.

Nick nods. "Bash isn't here yet. He was already in the air when it happened. The flight landed in California, and he got Frankie's message and a billion emails and texts, I'm sure. Anyway, he's on his way back."

I nod. "How is she?"

"Burned, but not severely," Michael explains. "Her left hand. Glove didn't protect her like it should have for some reason. But other than that, a mild concussion is all, miraculously."

"The halo worked," I say with relief, referring to the metal T-bar in front of our cars that has been mandatory for a few years.

"If it wasn't for that, she would have been decapitated instantly," Nick tells me, his voice gruff and choked. "Even the doctor said it."

We both stand there at opposite ends of the small room and stare at each other in silence, absorbing that hideous fact. "You can go in. I'm sure Lucia won't mind, and Frankie will be happy to see you."

"I don't know. I mean… I'm not… I just feel like…" I want nothing more than to walk in there and see them both, but on paper, I don't belong. I'm not family. I'm just a guy who races for their team. That's it. I should go back to the hotel like I'm sure Antonio did. And Rocco even.

"Look, Frankie is handling this like a boss. And I don't mean that figuratively," Nick explains, and I notice his hands clench and unclench repeatedly at his sides. "She has called her dad, released a statement, dealt with the doctors and hospital paper-work and team insurance. But she's not just a boss. She's a sister. A sister who has already lost one person in her small, close-knit family. She needs to be taken somewhere private with someone safe so she can react like a sister and have a good old fashion cry."

I nod. "I can wait here until Bash arrives if you need to take her back to her hotel. I promise I'll call if anything happens."

Nick shakes his head and the veins in his thick neck seem to pulse as his brow furrows. "I was actually going to ask if you could take her."

"Oh."

Nick's dark eyes lose a layer of polite denial they've been harboring, and I didn't even know it. "She won't let me take her from here, but she will let you, and we both know it. And besides, I want to stay with Lucia."

I nod, slowly. I could ask why he wants to be with Lucia over doing his job, which is taking care of Frankie, but I already know the answer. The same reason I'm here to check on Frankie. Nick is sleeping with Lucia, and judging by the look on his face, up until today he, like me, was fooling himself into thinking it was just sex.

"Okay, yeah. I'll try and get her to go back to the hotel with me." I nod. He nods and then points to the open lounge door.

"Room forty-seven," he says. "End of the hall on your left. Can't miss it. There's a security guard outside."

I nod and leave without another word. The door to Lucia's room is closed. I explain to the guard who I am. He nods like he knows but then says, "I have to check with Ms. Castera."

He slips inside the room, closing the door behind him, but before I can take a full breath, he's back holding the door open for me to enter. When I walk in, he walks out, and I close the door tightly behind him. Lucia is in her hospital bed, her left hand completely bandaged in white gauze to just past her wrist. Other than that, and some messed up hair and a hospital gown, she looks completely normal. She even smiles at me. "Billy, no flowers?"

"Sorry I… didn't stop at the gift store on my way in."

"You should have stolen some from outside the Mirabella paddock," Lucia jokes, and I smile. "Or at least taken a second to change into something more fancy."

She winks so I know she's joking. "I'm here to see if…" I pause and watch Lucia's eyebrows raise with the corners of her mouth. She knows I'm not entirely here for her, and she's good with it. "If either of you needed anything."

"I'm good," Lucia says. "Got a drip for the pain. Not sure what drug is in here, but I give it five stars."

Lucia lifts the cord and button she's holding in her good hand.

"Dilaudid, I asked," Frankie murmurs.

Lucia motions towards her sister. "This one here could probably do with a rest."

"I'm fine," Frankie replies, and I finally look at her.

She looks absurdly normal. Calm and chill standing beside her sister's hospital bed, glancing down at her phone. That's the only giveaway she is less than okay. She won't look me in the eye.

"If you want to do me a favor, Billy, you could drag her back to the hotel and force her to get some rest. Or, you know, de-stress somehow."

Another doped up wink from Lucia followed by a giggle.

"I'm not leaving you here alone," Frankie replies sternly, like this isn't the first time they've had this conversation and she's a bit sick of it.

"Nick volunteered to stay," I tell them, and now Frankie looks up but at Lucia, not me.

"Power of the pussy," Lucia announces.

"Louie!" Frankie scolds, but she's biting back a bit of a smile.

"Those really are some good drugs," I mutter.

"Not as strong as the pussy power," Lucia says and giggles again.

"Oh my God, stop before Dad gets here please," Frankie groans.

"So, you want to honor your sister's wishes?" I ask Frankie. "Or is the power of my dick not strong enough to make you?"

Lucia laughs so loud I swear she almost shatters my eardrum. Frankie finally looks at me, hazel eyes wide and fighting to appear indignant, but she wants to laugh. She can't though, because a laugh might become a cry. I watched it happen to my mum. So many times as she reminisced about my dad after he died, before she found out about Clara and started hating him, she'd bring up a funny memory and laugh until she hiccupped, and then that hiccup would turn into a sob..

So instead of laughing, she shakes her head and tips it down to stare at her phone again. "I want to be here when my father finally arrives. And I have to give something to the press outside. Another quick statement."

"You can do that on our way out. And then you can FaceTime

Bash in the car," I tell her calmly but firmly, which earns me a grateful, doped-up smile from Lucia. I reach for Frankie but barely get to touch her arm before she pulls back.

"Frankie, seriously. I'm okay. Dad and I will work it out, I promise," Lucia replies. "But right now, I just want to sleep. Alone. Not with an audience. I've been told I snore."

Frankie looks like she's about to argue, but the door to the room flies open, and Bash is there. His eyes are red-rimmed, and his cheeks are flushed. Or maybe it's just that his skin seems so desperately pale any color is jarring. Bash's coloring is always sun-kissed but right now, he's downright ghost-like. He stops short at the foot of Lucia's hospital bed, where he seems to quake. His eyes fill with tears as he stares at his youngest.

"I'm okay, Dad," Lucia says, but her voice is soft and as shaky as Bash himself. "But I need a hug."

Bash is suddenly at her side, leaning over the bed and clutching her to his chest. He's whispering words in French that I don't try to catch. This is a very private moment. I find myself stepping closer to the door, but then Frankie reaches out and catches my hand. It's a brief grasp and squeeze, and then she lets go but the message is clear. Stay.

When Bash finally lets go of his youngest, gently, he turns to Frankie. "*Ma Louloutte*"

He pulls her into a hug. It's just as tight and loving as his hug to Lucia, but Frankie just pats him lightly on the back. "You just concentrate on Lucia. I've got everything else covered."

He lets her go, but it's reluctant. Lucia is wiping at her eyes with her good hand now. "Frankie, please go get some rest now."

"Fine," she replies but it's hesitant.

Bash looks at me. "Can you make sure she actually does, son?"

I nod and follow Frankie as she heads to the door. She glances over her shoulder one last time to watch as her dad sits on the edge of Lucia's bed, holding her good hand as Lucia says, "Where's Adelaide? If she's here, she should come in."

Frankie continues out into the hallway, walking robotically, and turns toward the private waiting room, but I hook her arm and lead her to the elevator where I punch the button. "You can message Nick and update him. I'm taking you home."

"Billy, I have work to do too. I can't just leave," she says, her eyes hard and her beautiful face stern. Like I'm suggesting she play hooky or something.

"I'm taking you back to the hotel," I say quietly as the elevator pings and the doors slide open.

I tug her into it with me and punch the ground floor. She says nothing and stares straight ahead the whole way down. "I didn't get pole for tomorrow," I tell her because the silence is suffocating.

"I know," she replies, her voice suddenly robotic. "I've debriefed with Rocco too. He said there's nothing more you or Antonio could have done, and I believe that. I managed to watch the highlights while they bandaged her up. Our cars just aren't as strong on the warmer tracks. Mercedes does better. We'll work on it for next year. You have a good shot at taking the lead from Samuels. Especially if he takes that first corner wide like he tends to. Stay tight on that turn and you could grab him early and then never look back."

It's surreal. She's so... businesslike. I understand it completely though. It's a coping mechanism. She's tuned out the emotion of the day, the gravity of it. But that only lasts so long. She will break, and to be honest, the sooner the better. I know. I watched my mother carry too much emotionally after my dad died. She didn't want to bury me, but then we found out about Clara, and she snapped, and I drown in her emotional baggage. Hell, I'm still treading water in all the trauma if I'm honest.

She heads straight to the front doors of the hospital so quickly

I have to jog for a second to catch up. I didn't expect her to take off right out of the elevator like that. There's a smattering of media still milling about the parking lot. When they see her emerge, they cluster together around her, and it seems crushing. I want to step in but hold myself back. I'm just a driver to them. They probably wonder why I'm even here. I don't need to give them anything to gossip about.

Frankie gives a brief summary of Lucia's injuries and assures everyone she will be fine. She answers some questions, most of them completely invasive and kind of crude. Stuff like 'is she disfigured?' and 'how close was she to death?' Frankie answers all of them as cool as a cucumber to the untrained eye. But I know her. I know her body now, and I see the truth. Her posture is too stiff. Her eyes focus slightly above the journalists, not at them. The fingers on her left hand, clutching her phone by her hip, are bone white from the pressure of her grip. And then there's the way she keeps shifting from one foot to the other. It's subtle, but I notice.

"Okay, as per her family's request, I'm going to sweep her away," I interrupt suddenly after a stupid ass asks me if Lucia is going to retire now. "No, she won't retire. I wouldn't either if it was me."

They start yelling questions at me, and I ignore them and the fact that Frankie is trying to shake off my grip on her hip as I guide her out away from the media to the cab stand because I realize that although Clara left the car, I didn't grab the keys. All I managed to remember to grab was my room key and cell. I open the back of the first car in line, gently push her inside, and climb in after her, giving the guy the address the hotel. "Drop us off in the alley behind it, please."

Frankie says nothing. She either stares out the window or at her phone, typing furiously to someone about something. I send a quick message to my concierge to arrange things. The driver does what I've asked, and I pull her out of the cab with me after paying him with a hefty tip on top. The back door, the one staff use and the kitchen uses for large deliveries, opens immediately. My personal concierge is there with a smile, until she sees Frankie, and then the smile drops. "Welcome back Mr. James. Ms. Castera."

I can tell she is struggling to figure out whether or not to say something. All of the hotel must be buzzing about what happened. Hell, all of Mexico probably is. I hold her eye and nod. She clears her throat and leads us through the kitchen. "Let me know what you need."

"Extra bathrobe, and can you have room service send up a club sandwich and fries?" I say. "Not right away but in an hour or so, please."

"I need to get back to *my* room," Frankie argues, but she's letting me lead her through the staff hallways to the service elevator.

"You will. Eventually," I tell her. The concierge lets us in the service elevator, swipes her pass card, and punches my floor before stepping out again.

As the elevator chugs upward, Frankie unleashes on me. It's a high level of anger and completely uncalled for, but I just stand there and take it because I know it has nothing to do with me. "I am not a child, Billy. Jesus Christ I'm your boss, and I don't need a babysitter of any kind, least of all *you*. I just want to go back to my room and watch the qualifying so I can dissect it and figure out how we can improve before the race tomorrow. Then I have to send out another official statement from Mirabella and call our social media manager and yell at her for not updating the team's official Instagram with something more positive than that horrific crash picture. I mean holy fuck, I get it, everyone is using it, but we can do better. Lucia is more than click bait. So I need my hotel room. Not yours. If you think that this is the time for a quickie, it's not."

She keeps rambling and ranting as I take her hand and drag her down the hall to my room. I swipe my key card and push her inside. Frankie spins on me as soon as the door is closed and repeats herself. "I don't want to be here. I have work to do."

"Yeah. I know. So do it here."

"No."

"Frankie. She's fine."

"I know she's fine. I was there with her in the hospital. I talked to her doctors." She sighs angrily and turns back to stomp across the room, toward the bathroom. I follow her.

"She's okay."

"I know!" Frankie bellows at me, glaring daggers at me through the mirror she's facing. She turns on the water and sticks her hands underneath. She bends over and splashes water on her face. "Fuck off Billy. You're not my boyfriend."

She yanks a towel off the rack and pats her face, then throws it on the floor and curses.

I speak with a level voice. Slow and calm. "Let it sink in. Really. Let it. Lucia is going to be just fine."

She swallows so hard I can see it in the mirror. And then she blinks, trying to hold back the tears and her next breath is a shudder. "She… could have…"

"I know. She could have. But she didn't." I walk closer, and as Frankie's head dips, and her shoulders sag, and she lets out her first sob, I turn her toward me.

It feels like every bone in Frankie's body melts as she collapses onto my chest. My arms around her back are the only thing holding her up, and I'm okay with that. I'm more than okay with that. I hate that she's gone through this trauma, but I am here for it. For her. I will give her everything, anything she needs right now. I won't be whole until she is whole again. That's a feeling

I've never experienced before, and if it wasn't so all-consuming, I would be having my own panic attack right now.

Instead though, I hold her in my arms and kiss the top of her head and whisper words of encouragement to her. And when she lifts her tear-streaked face to press her lips against mine, I kiss her back.

18

———————

WE'VE GONE TOO FAR

FRANKIE

I don't know if it's stress or pent-up fear releasing or just some form of PTSD leftover from my mom's death, but suddenly, I am in love with Billy James. At least it feels that way, and I'm drowning too hard and fast to fight it. I've been fighting for control all fucking day, when all I wanted to do was cry and scream, so now... I give into my feelings. Including the ones for him.

I kiss him hard and deep, and he kisses me right back. I know this is truly a form of self-sabotage. We aren't on the same page. He doesn't like me like *that*. Hell, he doesn't like anyone like that. I am not just playing with fire as I slip my hands under his shirt, I am dancing in the middle of an inferno. I sniff back the last of my tears, his warm skin and hard muscle under my fingertips, calming me. "I just can't believe she survived that. I thought... when I felt the ground shake and saw that fire..."

"I know. I thought she was gone too and my heart was breaking for you," he whispers as his lips move from mine, and he pulls me tighter to him. Smoothing my hair and cupping the back of my head with one of his big, strong hands. "But the car

214

and most of the protective gear did their jobs, and she's okay. You'll be okay too, love."

"I'm not so sure about that…" I confess and tilt my head up. His eyes are clear and sure. Billy James is so damn sure of everything. And I'm only sure of one thing right now… I need him. My hands slide down his bare back to his ass.

"Tell me what you need," he whispers, his voice like sandpaper, gritty and raw.

"You, Billy. I need you," I admit and kiss the column of his neck, savoring the feeling of his skin against my lips, across my tongue, and his scent all around me.

"You said no quickies," Billy murmurs.

"I don't want quick," I confess and look up at his beautiful face. "I need you to make love to me."

The words are… a lot. Too much. I know this. I crossed a line. But he doesn't stop or correct me. Instead, as I hold tighter to his firm butt, he dips his head to find my lips again and starts to unbutton my white jeans.

I push thoughts of boundaries and right and wrong out of my head and start undressing him too. Before long, my bare ass is resting on the edge of the thick marble vanity and he's between my legs, naked, driving into me in long, slow strokes. We're holding each other tightly, desperately, our mouths are colliding, and our tongues are dancing, and we're making noises that are raw and uninhibited. He's gentle with his mouth but rough with his hands as he buries them in my hair and tugs, and it's got all my nerve endings on fire.

"I want to give you everything, Frankie," he pants against my neck, and that's all it takes to for my orgasm to rip through me.

He comes at some point, but I'm already too gone to really notice. I hope it was as good for him as it was for me. I think it was judging by the way he collapses on me, breathing heavy, as he curls his head into my neck. We stay like that until there's a knock on the door and then he reluctantly peels away from me, pausing to hold my face gently in his hands and press his lips to my forehead before grabbing a towel off the rack and covering himself. "I'm going to answer the door, and I want you to take a long, relaxing steam shower okay?"

I can't find a reason to argue, so I do what he says. A couple minutes later, Billy joins me in the cavernous, marble shower and washes my hair and my back, and then I push him back on the bench and ride him. We don't have a discussion about the fact he's condom-less but we aren't being reckless. I have an IUD, and I know he's clean and safe. The company does complete physicals on him every three months, and I get those now. But the moment goes unspoken, twice now. That deepens the trust between us, which further deepens the connection we don't admit we have.

I feel drunk by the time I get out of the shower. It's all the stress, trauma releasing, and giving myself to a man, in every emotional and physical way, for the first time. Billy wraps me in the extra bathrobe that must have been delivered with the meal he ordered. We sit at the bottom of the bed crossed legged, facing each other, and eat the club sandwich and drink the fizzy water he also had delivered. I'm famished, and I realize I haven't eaten a thing today. I have no idea what time it is, but the sun is long gone. Billy watches me eat with a smirk. "You should put this on the 'Gram."

"Only douches call it the 'Gram. And no one wants to see me devouring a sandwich," I say after I swallow down another big bite. "I've never promoted a diet or meal supplement company. I don't promote anything that makes money off a negative self-image. I won't even promote shape wear. Turned down a huge deal."

"I know. I just meant that you look cute ripping into that thing like a wild animal," Billy replies. I laugh and try not to choke on the fizzy water I just sipped.

"I haven't eaten all day," I admit. "I've been too…"

"Busy avoiding an emotional crash landing?" Billy says bluntly but in the softest possible way. I nod, and his smirk slips into something softer and more compassionate but just as sexy. "I've been there, remember? I was in the paddock when my father died. I watched the crash right in front of me with his team while they screamed and gasped around me. His Team Principal kept trying to pull me away from the monitors, like averting my eyes would erase the memory of what I already saw. What I knew. I knew he was dead in my heart before any doctor or hospital declared it."

I remember his father's deadly crash. I wasn't there, but I have watched the footage on internet clips. His dad's front tire blew out unexpectedly, and he spun into the barriers. That likely did not kill him, but another driver hit the debris from the crash and spun out too. He careened into Tommy James' car, flipping over it and landing on top of him. There were no halo bars back then to protect the driver's head space, and despite the helmet, Tommy James suffered life-ending head trauma and a snapped spinal cord.

"I can't imagine having that memory." I reach across the small space between us and take his hand in mine.

He squeezes. "I think you can imagine what it felt like now."

I nod slowly with the sick realization and try to fight the tears that want to flood my eyes. "Lucia would have been dead six different ways if she'd had that same crash just five years ago …"

He squeezes my hand again and cups my face with his other one. "Hey. Do not dwell on what might have happened because it didn't. She's here, and she's great and will race again."

"Yeah." That realization is cold comfort. "Right now, all that means to me is that it could happen again."

Billy's face flickers with something dark. Hard. I instantly regret saying that even if it's the truth. He doesn't give me a chance to mull over that odd expression of his because suddenly the trademark casual grin is back. "You need rest. It's been a day."

"I need to handle business," I sigh and swallow the last of my fizzy water to wash down the end of my half of the sandwich. "I have to touch base with Rocco and watch the qualifying footage. And I should probably touch base with my dad."

I yawn, long and hard. He moves the room service cart across the room as I stand up to get changed back into my street clothes. I hate that this is ending, this bubble I'm in with him right now. I know when I walk out that door, it's over. All of this. It has to be right? We've gone too far as it is.

I walk toward the bathroom where my clothes are still in a heap next to his race gear. My drunken, euphoric feeling is wearing off big-time, and I'm into the beginning of an emotional hangover. Billy circles my waist from behind. His lips brush the side of my neck and I shiver. "Billy…"

"Reality will be there waiting for you in the morning," he whispers. "You don't need to rush off and find it."

He's right but he's also wrong. Just like this thing between us. I am so drained, emotionally and otherwise, so I give in. I let him turn me in his arms and start to untie my robe, and I let his kiss take me away to a land where all that matters is this. Him. Us.

I know I'll regret it later, but I don't care.

19

—————

FOR LUCK

BILLY

When I wake up the next morning, she's gone. I lie there a second and try to pretend I hallucinated the whole fucking thing. But the scent of her perfume along with the deliciously achy feeling in my body of a night well spent under and on top of her makes that impossible. Also the feeling in my chest she caused last night. That warm, deep, satisfying ache. I was her person last night. Her partner. And in those moments, taking care of her needs in every way possible, a revelation occurred. I've always wanted to be that. I saw with blinding clarity that I was never just in this for sex and was always in it for the emotional connection. The way she makes me feel: happy, whole, bonded. I have been fooling myself.

But then she said Lucia racing again was a cold comfort and that warm feeling she always gives me turned sour like day old milk. Because I can't be with someone when there's a very real threat I will leave them destroyed like my mom was. Like Frankie almost was yesterday. I don't want to be the next person to put that shattered look on her beautiful face. So this thing with her can't continue. I can't fall in love with anyone. Not until this life, my career, is in the rearview. And I'm not close to giving it up.

When we talked of Lucia's crash as we ate and I saw the look of anguish on her face, I realized what I've known all along. I can't be the reason someone looks like that. If I let her in and then I have a crash like Lucia's or worse…

I pull myself out of bed. That ache from a sex-a-thon that usually makes me smile, makes me frown. It's just another reminder of all I've got to give up. I get ready, and as I'm throwing on my clothes, there's a tentative knock at the door. I open it and find Clara, right on time. Her deep brown eyes dart around the room as she takes a hesitant step inside. Her eyes land on the rumpled bed. "Are you alone?"

"I am… now," I admit because there's no point hiding it from her anymore. I wasn't doing a good job, and it's over now anyway. "Frankie disappeared a few hours ago."

Clara nods slowly. "How is she?"

"Better. I think. I mean it was rough," I say, but my brain is filling with not just the visuals of last night, how warm and tight and welcoming her pussy was, but also the desperate, vulnerable look in her eyes when I kissed her. The expression of love I saw reflected back in my own face in the bathroom mirror as I hugged her after we came.

"You look freaked out," Clara observes flatly. "What are you not telling me? Is Lucia really okay?"

"Yes. I mean, she'll need help with her hand. It's burned. Somehow, the fire-resistant glove failed. But she's good," I reply and hold her gaze for a second.

"So it's Frankie that has you looking like a bear in a trap who needs to gnaw off his own leg to survive?" Clara drops her bag onto the floor and drops onto the chaise by the window in my room. She gives me a small, superior smile, like she knows something I don't. "You realized you love her." I twist my face up like

I just smelled a fart, which makes her laugh. "I knew this would happen one day. I just didn't know it would happen with Frankie."

"What would happen?"

Clara lies back and laces her fingers behind her head. "Someone would get you by your heart, not just your…stick shift."

"Please stop." I shudder at her veiled reference to my penis.

"So the question is, what are you going to do about it, Billy?" Clara wants to know.

"I have to focus on the rest of the season, and she has to focus on her part of the season too."

"Uh-huh." Clara nods, but now, as I come out of the bathroom, she's looking at her phone. She pauses and types something quickly before looking back up at me. "So you two stop knocking boots and focus on the season. And when the season is over? Then what?"

"I go back to…" Where was I going to go again? Paris? And watch sunsets in Montmartre without her? That sounds depressing as fuck. The longer I remain silent, the bigger Clara's smile gets, and I'm about to tell her to fuck off when she glances at her phone again and she shakes her head, her smile dropping. "Who are you texting with?"

"No one," she mutters.

"Clara."

She puts her phone down and looks up at me and sighs. "I went out last night. I needed to blow off steam after I found out Lucia was alright. Basically drink and dance away the thoughts about dad and stuff that a crash always brings up. Anyway, I ran into Lady Ava What's-her-face. Remember her?"

"Lady Ava Markham. Twenty-seventh in line to the throne. I've seen her naked, so yes I remember her." It was last season, when she was a VIP guest at the London GP. I won and after flirting all night at an after-party, she made it clear she wanted to give me her own little victory party, no strings attached, in her words. And so who am I to turn down royalty?

"Anyway, now she's pestering me for a pass for today."

"So give her one."

Clara's eyebrows shoot up. "Really? But like… won't it be awkward?"

I shrug. "It was a year ago. A good time was had by all. She hasn't been weird about it since. I mean she hasn't called or texted or anything, so let her come to the race. I don't care. She's got connections, so if we don't give her a pass she'll get one anyway."

"Okay…" Clara seems to think it's a bad idea, judging by her tone and her face, but whatever. A couple minutes later as we head down the hall to leave the hotel for the track, Clara finally shoves her phone in the pocket of her track suit. "I put Lady A on the pass list and let her know. She told me to tell you she can't wait to celebrate another win with you."

"Oh." A bowling ball of dread has been dumped into my gut.

"Yeah. I saw that coming a mile away." Clara steps into the elevator and I step in beside her. "I don't know how you can be so successful at driving a car when you're clearly blind."

"Ha. Ha."

"And also, for the record, since you can't see this clearly either," Clara tells me pointedly. "When you click with a woman in and out of the sheets, that means she's girlfriend material."

"Yeah, Frankie is girlfriend material, but I can't handle a girlfriend," I reply. I can't. I really can't have a girlfriend. I swear.

"Okay. So this off-season when she goes off and finds herself someone that can manage a career and a girlfriend…" Clara pauses and her dark brown eyes narrow. "You'll be fine with that?"

No. No I will not. In fact, just thinking about that makes me want to puke.

"Who says she wants a boyfriend? She's got two all-consuming jobs and trust issues," I argue.

"Yeah, and she let you in, so she'll eventually let someone else in too," Clara says to me and shakes her head at my level of stupidity again.

"Shut up. I need to focus," I say and dig my headphones out of my hoodie pocket.

"You mean you have to distract yourself from the cold hard truth," Clara mutters.

"Shut up."

WHEN WE GET to the track, we go through the usual procedures in unusual silence. I'm not mad at Clara. I'm annoyed she's right and knows she's right. We run through some coordination drills and neck stretches and then she heads to the cafeteria to get me my favorite green juice, and I change. I'm on my way to meet her when I run into Lady Ava Markham of… some fucking British place. She's as beautiful as ever with her long, perfectly posh blonde hair and bright, inquisitive blue eyes accented in subtle make-up … all of which still pale in comparison to every single thing about Frankie Castera. Ava smiles so brightly I almost squint.

"William, honey!" She opens her arms and leans forward, and before I know it, her lips are on my cheek and her arms are around my shoulders. Antonio walks by with Rocco, and they both smile. Antonio even gives me a thumbs up. I want to groan in protest but manage to simply pat her back and untangle myself. "Hi Ava. Should I curtesy or bow or something?"

"You asked me that the first time we met." Ava giggles and leans a little closer again. "And I told you, you can do either as long as you're naked."

Oh right. Fuck.

"I hope you enjoy the race today," I say with a friendly but hopefully dismissive smile as I start to climb the stairs. "I have a schedule to follow right now. I'm sure you understand."

"Yes. Of course," Ava says but she starts to climb the stairs right next to me. Fucking great. "I wouldn't want to pull you out of your routine. I just wanted to thank you for the pass and say that I hope to see you after the race."

"Hopefully," I reply vaguely. We're on the landing now, directly in front of the large opening that leads to the cafeteria, where it seems almost everyone who works at Mirabella is gathered at this current moment. Including Frankie. I can see her, standing about five feet away, listening to Joaquin as he points at something on a tablet. I glance at Ava. "It's going to be a bit of a weird race, with what happened to Lucia Castera yesterday. So I mean, I'll probably spend a lot of time with media regardless of whether I podium or not."

"I understand," she replies, and damnit, she's walking alongside me again. I like her. She's nice and means well, but ugh. I don't need this on top of everything else. "I saw footage of you at the hospital yesterday. It was so kind of you to go and check on Lucia."

"She's part of our team," I say honestly because I would have checked on Lucia with or without my feelings for Frankie. I mean, maybe just by phone if I wasn't in love with her sister, but still. I would have checked. "And her dad is like a father to me."

"You were the only driver to go, you know," Ava tells me. Her eyes soften a little and she looks suddenly embarrassed as we join Clara in front of the juice bar. "I thought maybe it was about more than being a teammate."

"Me and Lucia?" I sound completely flabbergasted because I am. I can't remember one minute of time where I was alone with

Lucia, anywhere for any reason. Why would Ava think I was dating her?

And then I hear it. A snicker. My eyes dart to the left and I see Frankie, who has stepped into line behind us. And she's covering the smile on her mouth with her hand and pretending to read the juice list on the wall.

"I mean, I wasn't sure. It's not my business anyway, I just..." Ava's usual cool, collected British decorum is failing her suddenly. Her cheeks are pinking. If Frankie is watching this at the very least, it's easy to tell Ava has a crush. But Frankie is astute and probably reads more into this. Because there was more once. "Anyway, I'll let you get back to your pre-race routine. But since you're single, I just wanted to give you this for luck."

And then she kisses me. On. The. Mouth.

It's quick, a peck really, but *fuck*. It's a kiss. It's in front of Frankie and everyone, and it's not okay. Clara steps in. "Ava why don't I show you the view of the track from the balcony?"

Without waiting for Ava to answer, Clara takes her arm and pulls her away. I turn to Frankie. Her eyes are glued to that Juice of the Day board like it's the only thing in the room. But I know she saw what happened. "Frankie... I didn't know she was going to do that."

"But somehow it didn't look like a first time thing," Frankie comments, eyes still on the board.

"No. It wasn't," I admit and then, I see it in my mind. The door is open. The door to having the conversation that will end this. I just have to step through it. "But it's not something that has happened recently. Or frequently."

"Not my business," Frankie says. It's not biting or sharp, though, which I was expecting. And finally, those hazel eyes leave the menu board, and she turns to me. "We've both had pasts, right?"

"Yeah, of course. And I mean, you said yourself last night I'm not your boyfriend," I say, knowing it isn't the right thing to say, and I hate myself instantly for it, but I keep going. Because I have to. "We're just casual. Like I was with Ava."

Oh my God, I fucking hate myself. Frankie's face is passive. She's an expert at maintaining a game face in a public situation. But I can see the hurt in her eyes. I feel fucking horrible. "Frankie, I didn't mean—"

"Green Smash?" The guys calls out the order. "Where's the lady that ordered the Green Smash?"

"It's for me, thank you," I say and reach out to grab the drink Clara had ordered for me before I waltzed in here to blow up my life. I turn back, and the hurt in Frankie's eyes is gone and has been replaced by a cold, blank stare.

"Melon Madness please. With a shot of wheat grass," Frankie tells the server. He nods, and then she turns back to me. "You should go get ready."

"I just don't—"

"James, there's nothing more to discuss." Frankie interrupts. "Not here."

"Right. Okay." I sulk off like the miserable idiot I am. I want to say this day can't get worse, but it can. So I need to refocus and try and get my head in the right place so I can win this fucking race. Frankie hates me, and I deserve it, but maybe I can apologize by getting her team, our team, some points.

And I do. I drive like it's my whole world, because it is. It has to be. Unfortunately, I also channel all my anger and frustration into my race, and I get dinged by the stewards for an over-aggressive overtake of Samuels. Later, he gets too aggressive himself and spins out in the gravel, hitting the barrier in a way that damages the car but not him. And even with the time penalty, I manage to win. Antonio is fourth, missing the podium after his own penalty for not slowing down under a yellow flag.

The victory doesn't feel the same as any of my others. It's

hollow. Frankie didn't come on the radio once, it was all Rocco, which isn't totally abnormal… but it felt it. And she isn't there to congratulate me with the rest of the team. I don't see her as I scan the crowd from the podium as my national anthem plays.

I dedicate my entire race to Lucia, making a point to say it in every interview. It's not bullshit P.R., I truly want this win to be for her and the Casteras. The Sky Sports guy, my last interview of the day, confirms what I already knew in the back of my head. "With this win, you are now officially in the lead for the World Championship. And Mirabella is tied in points for the Constructors' Championship."

"That's amazing news," I say.

"You must be excited, so close to matching your dad's total for Championships," he says and points the microphone at me.

I run a hand through my hair and let my emotions get the better of me for the last time. "Actually, I think I'm more excited about Mirabella potentially winning. Frankie Castera and the whole Mirabella team has been instrumental in every win I've had since she came onboard. She deserves the Constructors' Championship. If my win helps her, *them*, that's what makes me happiest."

I walk away, but there is no missing the look of shock on the reporter's face. I am the king of cocky. I've always been respectful and grateful to my team when asked about any of my wins, but I've also always made it clear that there is no chicken-versus-egg debate here. My success comes first, Mirabella's second. Only now, I just said the opposite. And I meant it, because I'm in love with my Team Principal. Since I'm going to have to leave her, I am going to try like hell in every race left this season to leave her on top.

20

IN DESPERATE NEED OF A GOOD SHAG

BILLY

I don't see Frankie at the impromptu victory party at the bar next to the hotel. I'm not at all surprised. Rocco mentioned she went straight to the hospital as soon as the race ended. Didn't even stay for the podium ceremony. He said she told him to tell me congrats.

I sigh and swirl the rocks in my gin and tonic, wishing I could drown in it like the lemon wedge is currently doing. Clara decided not to come to the party, but Lady Ava did. She's currently a few feet away at the bar talking to Antonio. I'm hoping that it's more than just small talk. I don't want to have to turn her down later and make things awkward between us. I sip my drink and contemplate abandoning it and just heading back to my room when Rocco drops into the vacant chair at my table. "Where's your trainer?"

"I don't know," I say and feel dread. "Don't tell me you're one of those people that think I'm involved with her. I'm not. Never have been. Never will be."

"Yeah, I know," he says easily. Too easily? It's weird. "She usually comes out after a race. Especially one where you win."

"Yeah," I say. Is this just weird because Rocco is making an effort to make small talk, which he never ever does, or is it something else? I'm too exhausted and depressed to figure it out. "She decided to stay in tonight. I think it's just… been a weird weekend for all of us, you know?"

"Oh yeah. I know," Rocco takes a long swig from his glass of amber-colored liquid. He blinks slowly as he swallows and turns to me. "Given any more thought to our conversation at the airport?"

"About the possible changes next year?" I make sure no one is in earshot before I say that. I put my half empty glass down on the dark wood table.

"I heard your interview today, so I guess you've made up your mind," Rocco says and frowns. "You don't know how to say no to me is the issue, right?"

"I probably should change teams," I admit, without giving him the reason. "But I won't. I love Bash."

"This isn't Bash's team anymore," Rocco reminds me.

"She isn't doing a horrible job, Rocco. Admit it," I say, and the creases deepen around his eyes as he frowns harder than I think I've ever seen him frown before.

"I've earned a chance to run my own team."

"Okay. But is this an ego thing? Because you have more actual power on the engineering," I remind him.

He takes another swig of his drink until nothing is left but the ice, and he puts the glass down next to mine. "I can be whatever the fuck I want at my own team. At Mirabella, it's all up to her, and I'm not waiting around for her to decide my fate."

He stands and glances down at me one more time. "I'm gonna miss working with you, James."

"Yeah. I'll miss you too," I say, but he's already stalked off toward the bar.

A second later, Ava has taken over Rocco's empty seat. My

God, this day just won't get better. I give her a tight smile. "Did you enjoy the race?"

"Of course! Thank you so much for the pass," Ava says and flips her silky blonde hair over her shoulder. "I should be in bed already. I'm exhausted. I've been partying in Mexico for two weeks already."

I nod, it's the most interest I can bother to show. If she realizes how disinterested I am, she doesn't show it. She sips the cocktail in her hand and smiles at me again. "I extended a couple days because I wanted to go to the Grand Prix, but now I have to get home. Have an early flight out tomorrow."

"Well, I guess you should get a good night's sleep," I say politely, and she blinks. She's not offended, just surprised by the brush-off. I decide to vaguely tell her the truth to avoid this getting more complicated than it already is. "So listen, I wasn't involved with Lucia like you thought. But I have been involved with someone. It was… as serious as I get."

"So not serious at all?" Ava lifts a perfectly shaped brow and then smiles and pats my forearm resting on the tabletop. "I'm just throwing in some humor. Sorry."

"You're not wrong. I don't do serious, but this was… complicated." I sigh and scrub my jaw. "Anyway, I think it's over now. I just… I think it's just best if I take a breather from hook-ups for a bit."

"Yeah. That's fine, William. Honestly, don't look so wrecked about it. I'm a big girl, and I can handle it." Ava winks at me and takes another sip from her glass.

I feel like a weight has been pulled off my shoulders. "You know there's other drivers that are single. And they'll consider it an honor to curtsey for you naked."

She laughs. "I think I'll pass, but thanks for trying to stroke my ego."

"I'm serious, Ava," I tell her.

"Look, I'm not in desperate need of a good shag," she tells me and pats my forearm. "I just thought since you were here and I was here, it might be fun. But contrary to what I might have led you to assume, I'm actually pretty particular about who I let into my chambers… and I've seen the dark side of running with this crowd. Look at what happened to Frankie Castera."

"What happened to Frankie Castera?" I blurt out.

The way Ava says that is ominous and turns the gin in my stomach acidic. Ava is shocked by my reaction, and I realize that I sound gruff and almost angry. She blinks a minute and then leans closer. "There's been a few girls… through the years that have fallen ill at parties with race crews."

"What?" I feel sicker with every word she says.

"I mean, not a lot. It's not some epidemic or anything but…" Ava glances around at the people milling around the small, dark club with the jazz music pumping. My eyes do the same. Ninety percent of the people in here are from a race team.

"I just know a couple of girls who…" she leans close, going so far as to cup her hand by my ear, like we're in second grade playing a game of broken telephone. "Think they may have been drugged at a race party."

"What?" That comes out full volume. Two pit crews who are chatting near our table turn and look over. She covers my hand with hers, patting me gently as if that will calm me down.

"You Aussies really are hot-tempered." Ava laughs but quickly stops when she sees my scowl. "It was ages ago. I don't know any new stories, so I'm sure whoever it was doing it, if someone was doing it, has left the scene. It's all rumor really anyway."

"You said Frankie had something to do with this," I say in a whisper because I definitely don't want people to hear me bring her up. I would never normally gossip about her, but I've always known there is something she dances around with me. A truth she won't tell and a reason why she distrusts racing crews.

"I have no evidence of anything, William," Ava whispers, her hand gracefully moving from mine. She heard what I said about not wanting a repeat, and she isn't pushing my boundaries one bit. "I just know that she was not a drug user at the time she had that overdose."

"Okay…" I wait for more words to daintily drop from her mouth and put these puzzle pieces in order for me.

"I might have dabbled in the snowy stuff at boarding school. I was a minor, lashing out. Testing boundaries. Being an idiot," she whispers, cupping my ear again because her posh British life would be blown up by the tabloids if that fact got out. "Nothing too intense but you know… anyway I partied with Frankie a lot back in the day. I mean, enough that I offered to share with her and her friends on multiple occasions, and she always declined. Always."

I don't know what drug was found in Frankie's system that night. I never asked, and no one in her family mentions that night, ever. Ava finishes the last of her drink and smiles at me. "I know nothing. Honestly. But that whole thing was the exact same season two other girls ended up blacked out. After one drink. I found one passed out in the washroom of a club the teams were partying at in Tokyo and another girl, a model friend, was taken to the hospital after being found unconscious in an alley outside a club in London. She'd spent the night partying with race teams. That's the last thing she remembered. And when they tested her blood, they found GHB."

I feel like I'm in some sort of alternative universe or nightmare and I can't wake up. This is not what I've ever seen or experienced in the race world. But then I think of that douche guy I punched who was being aggressive with Frankie. That was the night before she allegedly overdosed. That guy was a race fan. I'd seen him at a few after parties throughout the season…

"This is horrible," I whisper and she nods and then pats my hand again.

"Like I said, it's been years," Ava replies. "And it's all conjecture. But ask Frankie. She's your boss. I'm sure you two get along great. Who can resist your charm, Billy?"

She stands, leans over, and kisses my cheek gently without anything other than friendship. And as if to prove it, she then ruffles my hair like I'm a precocious toddler. When she's gone, I stand up and head to a quiet corner of the room and text Clara.

Did you ever hear of any girl having their drink drugged at a race party?

I wait, watching the bubbles come and go as she crafts a response.

No. What's going on?

I sigh and pace back and forth as I give her the short version of what Ava told me.

Fuck, that's gross.

"Yeah it is," I say out loud, then realize she can't hear me and type the same words to her. Then I slip my phone into my pocket and head back toward the bar, where I politely ask to pay my tab so I can get the hell out of there. As I wait for the bartender to run my card, I notice Ava is sitting with a girlfriend at another table. Antonio saunters over and sits down beside her.

I sign for the drink I had, leave a hefty cash tip, and turn to leave. One last glance in Ava's direction makes my heart pound heavier in my chest. Antonio is leaning in, gesturing with his hands as he smiles, telling some big story of his, and Ava is leaning back… her hand covering the top of her glass in the most uncasual, casual way I've ever seen.

She's making sure nothing gets dropped in her drink.

21

THIS DOESN'T FEEL REAL

FRANKIE

Jennie is jumping up and down as soon as our feet hit the Parisian sidewalk. When I don't join her she gets confused. "It's done. Your shoe line will be on shelves in two short months! How are you not as excited as I am? You've been talking about doing this for years and it's finally happening!"

"I am happy. I swear." I smile. It feels uncomfortable because I haven't done it in a while.

Jennie and I start down the street, in no particular direction. Nick falls in step behind us. I've only been in Paris forty-eight hours. I left straight from the hospital with Lucia, who they discharged after the race. She is now at a new hospital and rehab facility in Paris where they say she'll be for at least a month while they work on healing the burns on her hand. Dad and Adelaide are settling into the George V hotel for the break so they can be close to Lucia. I opted to stay with Jennie in her Paris apartment so we can get more work done. Rocco is in Rome with his dad for the short break, according to his Instagram photos. Antonio is there too, according to his wife's TikTok videos and Billy... I have no idea where Billy is. I broke down last night and sent him a text asking to talk. He saw it but didn't respond, which is the worst response I could have asked for, really.

"Okay, let's grab take away and head back to my place where I intend to ply you with wine until you tell me the reason you're such a sad panda," Jennie announces.

Panda. My heart aches.

"Frankie, seriously. What is going on?" Jennie stops me and pulls me to the edge of the sidewalk away from the rest of the people bustling by. I take a deep breath and tell her everything.

I blindside her, I know. I haven't mentioned any feelings for Billy James since that night he met us both. But she takes the news like a champ. "Shit. So you had time for an affair with your driver but not your promotion deals I lined up? Thanks a lot, Frankie."

I know she's kidding so I smile, but again it feels off. Jennie hugs me. "Why did he go from being your rock to being a dick the next morning? What triggered him?"

"I have my guesses but I really wish he would be man enough to tell me himself," I sigh. The sun is getting lower. It's a warm breezy day and I realize the last thing I want to do is hunker down in Jennie's apartment and talk about this more. "I'm going to go for a walk. I need to clear my head. Nick, you can go. I'll be fine, I promise."

"I need you to text me later so I know you made it back to Jennie's," he says and I nod. He turns and walks away, and I bet he's heading to see my sister.

"Okay." She hugs me again. "Come home anytime. I'll be there. And remember tomorrow we have more meetings and some photoshoot stuff to do."

I nod and wave and start walking. I know exactly where I want to go and when I get there, I'm not disappointed. I reach the steps to Sacre Coeur just as the sun starts to paint the sky in color. I doubt this is where Billy watches his Montmartre sunsets. The steps are a tourist trap. There's already probably over fifty people scattered across them, but I don't care. I just want to be here, seeing what he loves. Because I love him.

I find a spot midway up the steps and sit. It takes some time but eventually the sky is a brilliant orange color, streaked with pink, the Eiffel Tower glinting off in the distance. I glance around and am not surprised to see just about everyone capturing the moment with their cells. Everyone but me… and a man at the other side of the steps, one down from me. He's not even looking at the sunset. He's looking at me. Because he's Billy James.

I'm frozen in shock but he isn't and as I stare at him, he gets up and walks over. "Hi."

"Hi?"

He quirks his lip. "That sounds like a question."

"Because this doesn't feel real."

I stand up. I'm a step higher so we're basically, finally, eye-to-eye. "I told you I love sunsets in this district."

"Yeah, you also told me you'd do anything for me," I blurt out softly. "It's the words you said the last time we had sex so it's probably not fair to hurl them at you now. Or to take them seriously but stupid me, I did. I thought…"

"That I meant them?" Billy finished for me. "Of course I did, Frankie."

Why doesn't that make my heart stop hurting? Why do I still feel like he's rejecting me? Billy looks over his shoulder at the sky and back at me. His expression is pained. "You're more beautiful than that you know?"

"Than the sunset?" I ask incredulously.

"Yeah, love. To me you are." I want to kiss him but I know with everything in me, he won't let it happen. "And we weren't having sex that night. We were making love. You asked for it and I had it to give. For you."

"This isn't a reconciliation is it?" I croak.

"No," he admits and his blue eyes water but he blinks it away. "Frankie, I'm never going to date someone while I'm driving. It's just not going to happen. How do we even function like that? It would be bad enough if you were just some woman, but you're a Team Principal. Mine. You think we can separate our feelings from our track life?"

"I've done fine so far. I haven't given you preferential treatment."

"And I haven't had a severe crash but what if I do?" My breath disappears at the thought. Billy nods like I've said something he agrees with. "Exactly. You'd be shattered. I can't put you in that position. I can't have that in my head when I'm out there."

"So don't think about it," I counter. I'm fighting for this. I'm fighting to make my life and his more complicated, because the fact is the alternative feels worse. "You don't think of your dad every day or you wouldn't race."

"Bash quit because your mom died and he didn't want to have something happen on the track that orphaned you and Lucia," Billy says and frowns. "When he told me that, you could see it still pained him. It remains to this day one of the most amazing sacrifices for love I've ever known personally. And it's not one I'm making."

"I'm not your kid, Billy. I'm an adult who will accept the risks," I argue. "But you aren't brave enough to make them, are you?"

"It's not about being brave."

"Yeah it is. Or else it's that you don't love me enough."

He blinks. He opens his mouth. But he says absolutely nothing.

Someone taps his shoulder. "Billy James?"

"Yeah mate. *Oui.*" He nods and tried to turn back to me but of course they ask for a photo. With a clenched jaw he nods and gives them what they want and I turn and leave.

Billy catches up to me around the corner from Sacre Coeur, halfway down a winding cobblestone street. "Did someone drug you?"

Oh my God. How does he know about that. "I don't talk about that."

His eyes widen. "Frankie… why? My God, if it was someone on the team…"

"What Billy? What can be done about it?" I ask, angrily and hurt. "I have no idea who did it, or even what they used. Telling my dad would have just made things worse. I wasn't assaulted, I had them check at the hospital. I was just drugged. I think. It's my word against a hundred party guests. And my dad, he was struggling so hard to be a good single parent and he would have taken it like a personal failure. And he would have ripped apart his own race team until he found out who did it. And I don't even know if it was someone involved in racing."

He shakes his head, like he doesn't approve, and rage spikes inside me. "You don't get to judge me for keeping secrets. You have your own, remember?" I feel one tear slide down my cheek. "And besides, you're not brave enough to let yourself love me so don't judge me for being a coward about this."

I keep walking. Billy doesn't follow.

THE REST of the two weeks between the race in Mexico and the race in Japan feel like the longest of my life. It makes no sense because I'm so damn busy. I barely have time to brush my teeth or get six solid hours at night, but somehow, I'm sad. Lonely. I stare out the living room window of Jennie's Paris apartment from the sofa where I'm curled up with a cup of mint tea. The day outside is as dreary as my mood. Gray skies and wet pavement from a rain shower that just finished. Not a great day for the photoshoot we did earlier, with the prototypes of my shoe line, but it matches my mood perfectly.

"You really need your own place here already," Jennie surmises as she walks back in from the kitchen. "I worked hard with my designer on re-doing this entire place last spring, and your depression is clashing with the design esthetic."

"I should laugh at that. It's funny."

"But you can't because you're heartbroken," Jennie replies and plops down on the navy-hued leather wingchair in the corner.

"No. I'm over-worked and exhausted," I argue, but it only makes her laugh.

She points to her own face. "Oh sorry, that was pure sarcasm escaping. I'm sorry."

I ignore her and check my messages on my phone. I need to be at the airport by nine tonight to catch the private jet Dad and Dario rented for the trip to Japan. I'm dreading it so much I spent half of last night trying to find a commercial alternative so I wouldn't have to spend eleven hours hurtling through the sky in a small confined space with Billy James. But there was nothing that worked time-wise.

I swear I would have sat in a center row, middle seat in economy on any commercial airline if I could avoid this. "Lucia is doing well," I murmur as I read my sister's latest message. "She's going stir-crazy and she's excited Dad is going to Japan for the race because he's been suffocating her with love."

"And the thing with Nick," Jennie asks.

I shrug with heavy shoulders. "I think she ended it, which is why he took vacation. Mick, Lucia's bodyguard, is meeting me in Tokyo."

"Fucking men," Jennie sighs.

"I think that I have to give up one of my jobs," I confess, changing the subject to something even shittier than my dumpster fire of a love life. It's the first time I've said it out loud, but

I've been thinking it for a while now. It started as a little nagging thought and became a full-fledge worry. I am running on empty.

"If you keep working for Mirabella, you definitely need to start scaling back the influencer stuff," Jennie says after a long pause where my words seem to sit between us on the herringbone patterned floor. "And you also won't need a manager anymore."

"I didn't say I was keeping the Mirabella job," I counter.

Jennie smiles softly and smooths back her hair, which has grown longer since the last time I saw her, and she's added some lighter highlights. "Honey, we both know no matter how hard it seems, the job you were born for is Mirabella."

"I can't work with him every day for the rest of my life," I say, and I'm fighting tears. "Because I won't be able to move on."

Jennie shrugs. "So fire him."

I almost smile at that. "Even if I did get rid of arguably the best driver in the sport right now, he would still be in Formula One. I'd still see him at every race."

"Honey these are bigger problems than we need to solve today." Jennie stands up and takes my mug and puts it down on the table. Then she basically proceeds to tackle hug me until we're both toppled over on her couch and giggling. "Just know whatever you decide, I'm here for you. Always. Even if you fire my ass."

"I love you," I tell her.

"I love you too."

～

I FEEL SLIGHTLY BETTER, but still full of dread, as I make my way across the tarmac to the chartered plane. The rain has come back, almost as hard as earlier today, and the wind has picked up significantly. This is a rare and volatile summer storm for Paris and I'm almost certain it's going to delay our take-off. Which means more time in the plane with Billy. Great.

As soon as I get on board, he's the first person I see. The plane has two long, sleek leather couches against the walls as you step onboard. He's sitting on one of them, across from Rocco and Dario. I didn't know the exact passenger list, but I assumed it would include both of them along with Clara, Antonio, and Joaquin. And of course my Dad and Adelaide.

I nod at both of them, making sure not to show any emotion at all, and bustle by them. Behind the two couches are a series of single pod seats, also plush two-toned leather like the couches. But they recline fully into beds and have little curtains that drop from the ceiling for privacy. I pick the one at the very back just to get away from everyone. The wall behind me has a door at the end of the aisle that leads to a small hall with two restrooms, one on each side of the plane, and the staff area and kitchen past that. I fight the urge to ask the female flight attendant walking toward me if I can sit back there with her the whole flight.

She smiles at me as she passes and asks me if I need anything. I shake my head and go about settling into my seat. And then I smell him and see the tips of his shoes in my vision as my head is tipped downward and I try to dig out my ear pods from my carry-on. "James."

"Frankie, I need to talk to you," he says. His voice sounds different. Maybe I just don't remember it right.

"Talk then."

"Privately."

"It's a private plane," I quip, still digging around in my bag even though I feel the ear pods against my fingertips as they sweep the left pocket of the Tumi bag. "So consider that as private as the conversation will get."

He doesn't respond, but he doesn't go away either. Fuck. Antonio wanders by and doesn't even acknowledge my existence, which for some reason right now, I find hard to take. Everything is hard when your heart aches this much.

"Please Billy…don't make this public now that it's nothing," I whisper and finally raise my eyes to his. There are tears threatening to push their way out of my eyes, and I know he can see that. He looks shocked.

"We're delayed!" My dad's voice fills the plane cabin as he and Adelaide make their way onto the plane. He's carrying both her purse and his leather carryon satchel. I have to admit it's adorable as he holds her hand and makes sure she is comfortable in one of the seats. "But I've been promised it's not long enough to disembark, so everyone hold tight. I've asked for some tapas and juices to be brought out to make this more bearable."

He finds me with his eyes and he winks. *"Ca va ma louloutte?"*

"Oui papa." I wave at Adelaide, who waves back. And then I look at Billy. "I have nothing more to say to you. It was fun. And thank you for your help grounding me that night Lucia crashed. You're a good guy, Billy."

"I am," he says, following me down the aisle as I start to walk over to my father and Adelaide. "But I'm also an idiot and a pompous panda that needs to stop being a coward. At least that's what my sister told me last night when she caught me sulking for yet another night."

The length of this plane suddenly seems to double as my gait slows. I'm barely walking now. Luckily, Adelaide and my dad are busy settling in and haven't noticed, but Rocco is watching me with curious eyes. Clara too. She's now sitting across from him on the couch Billy vacated.

I turn slowly in the aisle, trying not to make any sudden movements, because I definitely don't want more people paying attention to this conversation. "What are you doing?"

He's so close, and all I want to do is touch him.

"Everything okay kids?" My dad asks.

"Yeah," Billy says as I bend to hug Adelaide. "Except that I'm in love with your daughter, and I think someone on this plane hurt her, and I want to kill them."

Oh my God. What the hell....

22

WELL, THAT'S A LONG STORY

BILLY

I've never been the quiet type. The one who does things subtly or with patience and a gentle touch. When I was six, I was sick of the slow, tentative pace of my swimming lessons, so I left the group, telling my instructor I had to wee, and then, when no one was looking, I hurled myself into the deep end. And that's pretty much been an example of how I've done everything in my life. And that now includes love. Because this is the first time I've been in love, and well, I just threw myself in the deep end.

Bash is staring at me, eyes wider than I have ever seen them and mouth agape. Rocco and his dad are glued to me like I'm doing some performance art piece in front of the Louvre or something. Antonio is watching from the other side of the plane, near the flight attendants area. He looks pale.

"Son… what did you just say?" Bash finds his voice. It's a low rumble, like he's beyond pissed off, but at least he still called me son.

"I said I love your daughter. This one." I point like a true fucking idiot. "In case you're confused. Some people get confused. Anyway I love her and I think she still loves me. She used to anyway but I've been a bit of a pompous panda."

"You do *not* love me," Frankie's whisper is filled with disbelief. She's standing now and facing me. I missed that. I was too glued to Bash, but anyway, she's looking right at me. Her eyes are wider than her dad's and her face is red. Like Ferrari red. Not my favorite color since they're rivals.

I try and muster a smile. My survival instincts to keep things light that I adopted through years of trauma with my own family are hard to kick completely. "Love, you know I do. I'm just fucking terrified of it. Or at least I was until I realized denying it was more painful. My feelings for you just wouldn't go away or turn off. And also, when Ava told me what she thought happened to you that night I stood you up I realized I wouldn't ever let that go so why in the hell was I trying to let you go."

"What the hell happened to you?" Bash says. His voice raises with every word, getting rougher and heavier. "Frankie, are you okay?"

"I'm fine Dad. I promise. He's talking years ago," Frankie whispers. She lifts her hands and puts them to her forehead. "Oh my God, what are you doing, Billy?"

"That night on the yacht. She didn't overdose," I say flatly.

"What the fuck, James?" Dario's voice booms. He sounds irate. Like, over-the-top furious. Why? I turn to him. He doesn't look confused. He looks panicked. "I don't know what the hell you think you're doing here. You weren't there that night. You don't know what you're talking about."

"It was your boat, wasn't it?" I say, and he doesn't answer me. "Did you do it?"

"What the hell are you talking about?" Rocco stands up. "Do what? Give her drugs? Tell her to take pills or snort whatever the hell she snorted? Who the hell do you think my father is? And in case you forgot, he owns the team you're on."

"He co-owns it," I correct and glare at Rocco. "For now, right? Because you guys are going to leave anyway. And it was his boat the night Frankie was drugged, but it was your party, so did you do it?"

"Drugged?" Bash repeats the word like it's foreign to him. "*Ma louloutte*, did someone *drug* you?"

"I didn't… this isn't how I wanted to tell you," Frankie says. Her voice is small, and I hate that because she isn't the one who should feel shame here. Not an ounce of it.

I walk toward her. It's a small space, so it takes half a foot. She shakes her head to stop me as I reach out to touch her. "I'm sorry Frankie. For everything. For not calling you or reaching out after I missed our date. For pretending I didn't want you this entire ten years because I think we both know now that was a lie."

"Billy…" She almost smiles. Almost.

Bash is like a wild animal though. The look on his face is almost too pained to look at. His caramel-colored eyes glint with rage as they bore into every single face on this plane. They come to a rest on Dario. "Did you do this? Did you know about this?"

"I didn't drug your daughter, Bash," Dario barks back, but something in his tone feels false.

"Well, do you know who did?" I interject.

Silence.

Dario looks at Antonio.

"You're the last person I saw her with that night," Rocco points at Antonio.

"I don't drug women!"

"You son of a bitch!" Bash hisses and lunges toward Antonio, which causes Adelaide to scream and Frankie to grab her dad by the shoulders and hold him back.

"I didn't drug her!" Antonio yells. His skin is green, his eyes wild. "I wouldn't do that to anyone. I just put her in the bathroom, like Dario told me to. He said she would sleep it off."

"Holy shit," Frankie gasps.

"I didn't know she would vomit. I didn't know she would choke!" Dario yells.

And then Bash charges Dario, and no one gets there in time, and they're a pile of elbows and left hooks on the floor of the plane. A flight attendant screams and drops a plate of tapas on the floor. Rocco and I dive in and get the two of them separated after a struggle. Then Rocco punches his dad himself, and we all gasp. Dario stumbles backward, holding his split lip.

"You fucking drug women? Who the fuck are you?" Rocco spits out.

"I didn't drug her!" Dario insists. "Markus! Markus did it."

"Markus?" I repeat as my brain scrambles to figure out who the fuck that is.

"Uncle Markus?" Rocco's scowl deepens.

"Yes," Dario confesses and yanks his pocket square out of the pocket of his blazer to mop up the blood leaking from his lip. "He spent that summer with us. It was right after his divorce, and he was full of money and lord knows we needed it. Bash, you were wining and dining him and begging him to invest. You would have given him the world at that point. Mirabella needed the cash."

"I wouldn't have given him my daughter," Bash barks.

"And I wouldn't either!" Dario replies heatedly. He heaves a deep breath. "I didn't know he was drugging anyone until I found him trying to drag a barely conscious Frankie into one of the bedrooms on the yacht. I kicked him off the boat immediately."

I glance at Frankie, and I can see this is all news to her just like the rest of us. I've spent the last two weeks trying to research the hell out of the GHB – gamma-hydroxy acid - and exactly what can happen when you're slipped it. Frankie could have been just conscious enough to walk and maybe even mumble some words, but she wouldn't necessarily remember a thing when it wore off.

Frustrated, Dario throws his bloody pocket square he's been moping his bloody face with onto the floor. "I saved her. I didn't hurt her. I told Antonio to put her in a bathroom to sleep it off so it didn't ruin the party."

"Are you fucking kidding me?"

"Rocco," Dario addresses his son like he just had an outburst about something as trivial as a curfew, instead of his father covering up an attempted rape. "Do you think Mirabella or our family would have survived a drug scandal at that point? It was our boat, our party, and my fucking brother. We had to keep the police out of it. And she would have been fine if that idiot hadn't left her on her back."

"Because I fucking know what do to in that situation?" Antonio is on the verge of tears now. "I was barely fucking twenty-one. I was drunk. I had no clue what to do."

"You call the fucking cops yourself asshole," Rocco yells at him. "Is this why my father loves you so damn much even though you barely perform out there?"

"Fuck you!"

"It is, isn't it?" Rocco looks horrified. "You gave him a spot on the team for his silence."

Dario doesn't deny it. Frankie takes a breath that makes her shudder. "I need air."

She starts for the door, which is still open since we're delayed. Bash moves to follow, but Adelaide grabs his arm. "Let Billy."

I rush off the plane after her.

The rain is coming down sideways in thick sheets. Neither of us have any protection, and we're both soaked in seconds. But I don't care and neither does she. I reach her and pull her into a hug. She clings to me. "How the hell did you know?"

"That I loved you? Well, that's a long story," I tell her, raising my voice to be heard over the storm.

"That's not what I meant," she replies sternly but when she

lifts her head she's smiling ever so slightly at me. "What happened to me."

I explained everything Ava told me. "Where is this Markus asshole now?" I want to know. "Can we have him arrested?"

"He died about six years ago now," Frankie tells me and she frowns and shakes her head. "Aneurysm. I went to the funeral with my dad and everything. I should have spit on his grave."

"We can add that to our to-do list when the season ends," I reply and kiss her forehead. It feels like a bold move. Because I've laid my heart out there, but she hasn't done the same.

She hugs me tighter though. "So, Nick picked a hell of a week to take vacation."

I let out a whoop of laughter.

Then suddenly Dario and Antonio are storming by us, toward the airport. Clara yells our name from the stairs, waving us back to the plane as her umbrella flips inside out in the wind. Frankie breaks our hug but takes my hand in hers as we run back to the plane.

Inside, the flight attendants are cleaning up the spilled tapas. Rocco is pacing. Clara has opened up my carryon and is pulling out a change of clothes for me. Adelaide is holding Bash's face in her hands, whispering something to him, but she lets go as we enter.

Bash turns to his daughter and pulls her into his arms, ignoring the fact she's dripping wet. "*Ma louloutte*, I have so much to say and so much I need to know."

"We'll talk," Frankie promises. "But know I'm okay. I'm really okay."

Rocco clears his throat. "I'll go too. I just wanted to tell you I am so sorry. About everything. About more than you even know. I had no idea about any of this, but I still feel like I should officially resign because of it so—"

"Do you want to go?" Frankie asks him. "Because you can't work with me?"

"No. I don't want to go. Not anymore," Rocco says and wrings his hands a moment. "I was a fool."

"Yeah, well, you're also an incredible engineer with great instincts," Frankie replies. "And now we need a sporting director because your dad is so fired. So stick around. I think we can accomplish great things together."

Rocco is stunned, but he nods.

"Antonio, obviously, will not be racing for us next year. Lucia will," Frankie explains. "Along with Billy, if he'll stay."

"I'm not going anywhere," I promise.

She smiles. "Good. Because I love you too."

My heart beats harder, thumping against my sternum like I've never felt before. Up until this moment, I thought the biggest adrenaline rush in the world was taking a turn on a racetrack at three hundred and seventy-three kilometers an hour. Now I know it's having the woman you love tell you she loves you back.

EPILOGUE
INSTAGRAM OFFICIAL

BILLY (*THREE MONTHS LATER*)

I can see it. I can fucking see it. Through the rain, there it is. The checkered flag. And even though Samuels is right next to me, his front tires almost at the midway point of my car. It's not going to be enough. I zip by the flag and the crowd roars.

"Billy James you pompous panda you are the world champion!" Frankie's elated scream fills my ears through the radio.

I let out of bunch of sounds. Expletives, and a bunch of other words that make no sense until it all jumbles up into a victory scream. I blink back the tears and slow the car. "Thank you Mirabella team. Thank you fans. Thank you all of you. Especially you, Francesca."

"You're welcome, Billy. And thank you."

Rocco yells his congratulations into the radio and I can hear the pit crew bellowing behind him in the garage. This season started and ended very differently. I have no words, but I know I have to find them for the interviews. But right now, I just scream again.

I pull into that spot in front of the number one marker and pull myself out of the car, standing on top of it, arms in the air. The crowd is loud and the crew is crushing when I leap into their arms. Clara and Mum are also jumping all over me. I am floating so I must be hard to reach. The accolades are wonderful but I only want to celebrate with one person. My person.

We haven't told anyone we're dating. I mean, people at Mirabella know. It's probably been obvious for longer than we both even realize but we don't talk about it. We maintain a professional distance in public. Thankfully every night is spent in one hotel room together, even though we have two. I want people to know and so does she, but we decided to wait until the season was over.

"Son!" Bash bellows and I rush over to him, leaving Clara and Mum who immediately distance themselves from each other. He wraps me in a bear hug and lifts me off my feet, bouncing me so hard my helmet drops to the pavement. I hug him back, laughing. "So proud of you!"

"I'm sorry Mirabella didn't snag the Constructors' Championship," I say, and he is already shaking his head.

"We got you boy. And once we drop the dead weight, we'll get that trophy too," Bash declares. He's talking about Antonio who finished the season with us, but did us no favors. He raced liked shit, costing us points. Dario was immediately terminated. Well, the official release said he retired but he didn't. Rocco is now our Sporting Director.

"Where is she?"

"Giving you your moment," Bash says and smiles. "She'll be there when the trophy is presented."

It's not enough. I want her now. But it doesn't dim my celebration. Lucia tackle hugs me, almost knocking us over. "Good job bro!"

She's started calling me that and I can't say I hate it. When asked about the nickname, because she's used it in interviews, she says it's because we're going to be teammates – racing brothers. People believe it. Her hand is no longer in bandages. The skin is bright red and puffy but it's healing well. Jennie hugs me too. She's got a pass for the day.

"I want your sister," I complain to Lucia.

"You have her, dummy," Lucia laughs.

I'm whisked into interviews before I can argue. Finally, I'm on the podium and Frankie is walking out too, to collect the trophy the team of the first place driver gets every race. She's holding an Australian flag for me. I jump off the podium and walk over to hug her, picking her up and twirling her off her feet. She's giggling in my ear. "Good job, baby! I can't wait to sleep with a reigning world champion."

"I can't wait to let you," I whisper back before running back to the podium with the flag around my shoulders.

When it's time for the champagne we spray each other – exclusively. Fuck the other two drivers, this is all about us. We sip from our bottles and I pull her into another hug. "Ready to make this official?" she ask, surprising me.

I pull back and catch her eye. She's serious. She points down to the Mirabella crew gathered below us. Jennie is there holding up her phone, poised to take a photo.

"Instagram official?" I ask with a cocked eyebrow.

"Is there any other kind?" she replies.

I put down my champagne and my flag and I grab her waist and dip her, right there in front of everyone. And then I kiss her with all the love and passion she's filled me with over the last few months. The cheers from below, for the victory, turn to whistles for the unexpected make-out session. The second and third place drivers shower their remaining champagne on us.

When the kiss breaks and she's back on two feet, she hugs me again. "I love you."

"I love you."

"I've never had a better victory," I tell her. "And I'm not talking about the race."

And then I kiss her again.

ACKNOWLEDGMENTS

First and foremost I have to thank my husband, Jack, who is the one that convinced me to watch *Drive to Survive* on Netflix. I'm a sucker for all things docu-drama, but racing? I never thought I would like anything to do with racing. Boy, was I wrong. Thanks to our good friend and neighbor, DJ Conrank (using his stage name because you should check out his music), for introducing Jack to the world of F1 so he could introduce it to me.

Just like hockey, my obsession with the sport gave birth to plot bunnies and there's a long list of people who helped me turn the first plot bunny into The Chase. Thanks to my agent Kimberly Brower for her constant support. Big love to Mignon Mikel at Oh So Novel Designs for creating a custom cover I am in love with. And thanks to Katie Kenyhercz for her editing skills, Brandi at Notes in My Margins for her meticulous proof job, and Claudia Fosca Stahl for her eagle-eyed beta reading. Also big thanks to my other beta readers on this one, Jenn Dall, Serena Macdonald and my favorite Fryman bestie Sarah Jillain for their candid thoughts and feelings.

To readers, bloggers and everyone who gave Billy and Frankie's story a chance, I am forever grateful.

MORE FROM VICTORIA DENAULT

The Ocean Pines series

Blindsided, Moo U

The San Francisco Thunder series

The Hometown Players series

www.ingramcontent.com/pod-product-compliance
Lightning Source LLC
Chambersburg PA
CBHW021311190726
48288CB00003B/795